ECHOES IN THE MIND

DOCTOR WISE BOOK 9

ARJAY LEWIS

MIND
BENDER
PRESS

Echos In The Mind—Doctor Wise Book 9
Copyright ©2020 Robert J. Lewis Updated November 2025

Cover Design: Marianne Nowicki, PremadeEbookCoverShop.com
Editing: Brandi Aquino; www.editingdonewrite.com
Editing: Libby Broadbent

ISBN-13: 978-1734229127
ISBN-10: 1734229128

Published by:
Mindbender Press
474 South Main Street
Phillipsburg NJ 08865
www.mindbenderpress.com

Prologue...1

1. Random Reverberations 7

2. Riotous Remnant 23

3. Conceding Counterpart 36

4. Rendezvous Repeated 45

5. Dead Ringer..57

6. Rat's Tale 66

7. Fallen Facsimile 81

8. Resounding Realizations.................................94

9. Answer Back...113

10. Ricocheting Rebukes 128

11. Mirror Image..146

12. Bounce Back 162

13. Reflections..183

14. Splitting Image 195

15. Answered Attempt....................................211

16. Holiday Hints 226

17. Double Danger 243

18. Tunnel Effect..265

Epilogue..277

Infection In The Mind 287

Author's Note..293

About the Author 295

Also By Arjay Lewis......................................296

DEDICATION

To my father
John B. Lewis
A writer himself,
He taught me the practice.
Love you, Dad.

"Empathy is about finding echoes of another person in yourself."

—*Mohsin Hamid*

"The person who tries to live alone will not succeed as a human being. His heart withers if it does not answer another heart. His mind shrinks away if he hears only the echoes of his own thoughts and finds no other inspiration."

—*Pearl S. Buck*

PROLOGUE

Brett Morgan jolted awake, an icy grip of fear tightening around his chest, the instinctual certainty that he was not alone clawing at his mind.

He was a man who cherished solitude, with rigidly maintained sleeping arrangements. He even relegated intimate encounters to his dates' apartments or carefully chosen hotels. His bedroom was his sanctuary, a space where he was the sole occupant of his world.

Yet now, as shadows danced in the corners of the dimly lit room, he was painfully aware of the violation of that sacred space.

Why had he awakened?

He struggled to sift through the remnants of sleep, and the prickling urge to flee.

What had disrupted his night? With a furtive glance around, he slipped from the covers, the fine silk of his scarlet pajamas clinging to his skin, creating an unsettling sensation of being unprotected.

Grabbing a plush robe, he padded barefoot through the darkened expanse of his house, turning on a few lights along the way—a cautious beacon against the encroaching darkness.

He reached the alarm panel and turned off the alarm. The last thing he needed was an embarrassing visit from the authorities on account of a sleepless night.

But something deep inside him urged caution; after disarming the system, he scanned the blank screens of the security feed, unnerved by the reality that something felt deeply wrong.

He adjusted the thermostat—though his home usually held a steady warmth, the chill in the air crawled over him, wrapping him in a shroud of unease.

Brett...

His name, whispered in the shadows, ignited a primal fear. This wasn't a figment of his imagination; he was sure of it. A voice —distinct yet shadowed, layered as if two spoke at once—echoed from the depths of the upper floor.

"Who's there?" His voice trembled, frustration mingling with fear as he called into the silent expanse, tiny and distant against the emptiness.

You know where I am...

The words slithered through the air, taunting, originating from the armory.

With a hesitant determination, he continued to the end of the hallway. There stood the formidable door of his collection—the armory. It wasn't an actual armory, but it held an elaborate collection of ancient and unique weapons from around the world.

He had studied, purchased, and curated the items from locations that would make powerful men squeamish. Ancient civilizations had used the specific knives and swords in ritual sacrifice, but that did not stop him from acquiring each item.

He often found beauty in their craftsmanship, despite their grotesque purposes in history.

He retrieved the emergency flashlight stowed in a hidden nook of the richly paneled wall, his pulse quickening as he navigated the darkness.

The keypad lit as he punched in the code, the soft beeps mocking his growing trepidation. The door clicked open, and for a moment, he expected—the lights to blaze to life with their comforting glow, but when he crossed the threshold, only deafening darkness met him.

Stepping into the room cautiously, he left the heavy door open behind him.

"Hello?" he called again, the word now tinged with a sense of dread. The temperature in the room was freezing, an oppressive cold that gnawed at him. He saw his breath, ghostly tendrils swirling in the flashlight's beam as he tightened his robe.

The glass cases that lined the walls beckoned him deeper into the chamber. Shadows cast by the flashlight flickered over the sleek blades of Japanese katanas and European swords, weapons of lore and bloodshed. The air was heavy with history, and the chill intensified, pressing down upon his chest like a burden he couldn't shake.

You know what I want…

The voices, now clearer, drifted through the room, reverberating off the glass and ricocheting through his bones—a relentless echo that nudged his heart into overdrive.

He glanced at the secondary panel of the alarm system here in the display room. All he had to do was press a button to summon the police, but his eye went to the thermostat connected to the unit instead.

The device showed the temperature in the room had dropped below thirty-two degrees Fahrenheit. He gasped, a frozen cloud of breath, stunned by how cold the room had become.

He gripped the flashlight tightly, warily skimming its beam through the displays, searching for the source of the unseen voice.

His eyes went to the case containing one of his most prized artifacts: an ancient Kris blade. It was bright silver with a handle made of ancient gold. The blade was wavy, which allowed for a quicker, rougher cut. Whoever had forged this devastating weapon did so for only one purpose—human sacrifice.

It lay next to its scabbard, which was also silver with green jade inlaid into the metal. When he purchased it from the Korowai clan in an isolated part of New Guinea, he could not track down its entire bloody history, although he was sure they used this blade for unholy rituals for centuries.

A burglar had stolen it from him the previous year, and he had been lucky that the police had recovered and returned it.

Through a haze of fascination and fear, Brett felt a dark urge compelling him to free the blade from its storage case. His mind screamed to resist, but his fingers tightened around the door, opening the glass. With his free hand, he grasped the Kris. The coolness of its metal sent chills racing up his spine, but its shimmer captivated him.

The whispers echoed louder now, imbued with urgency.

Very good, that is the one...

The voices were right behind him, and Brett spun on his heel, the knife raised.

The flashlight revealed only empty space—nothing tangible, only the oppressive silence of his sanctuary. Yet the fear clawed at him, raw and real, despite his martial arts training.

Panic stirred within him, sweat beading on his forehead despite the frigid temperature.

"Who is it? Who's there?" The tremor in his voice betrayed his bravado as he moved closer to the panic button, the only thread left to grasp at sanity amidst the gathering storm.

A pity we never met, considering you caused my death…

Brett's rage ignited, chasing away some of his fear. "What are you talking about?"

He had harmed no one—this must be the work of an intruder, a burglar orchestrating this twisted scenario in his carefully guarded life.

"Show yourself," he screamed, his voice rising in defiance, desperation clawing at him.

I will…

Suddenly, the knife quivered in his grip, his own hand now betraying him. The knife moved as if on its own. Brett watched his hand, not believing what his eyes showed him and completely unable to stop what was happening. His right arm slowly, deliberately, turned the blade until it pointed at his chest.

"What the—" With a sudden, violent thrust, he felt the blade pierce flesh and sinew, an unbearable agony blossoming through him as excruciating pain unfurled from the wound like a dark flower.

He dropped the flashlight, its beam spiraling wildly across the room, illuminating the display cases as darkness seeped into his vision. Breathing became a desperate struggle as he fought against the blade buried deep within him. His hands clawed at the handle to withdraw the knife, but it only cleaved deeper.

Screams erupted from his lungs, a raw panic as he collapsed against the stark, chill wall, fingers fumbling blindly for the panic button—a final desperate call for help in the void of despair. The alarm blared to life, flooding the house with a cacophony of red lights and sirens.

As the world spun around him, Brett fell to his knees, despair overtaking him, his body crumpling like a discarded afterthought.

I think we took care of you…

His breath was a mere whisper of life left as he gasped, "Who are you?"

I am an echo of what was…

Wracked with agony, he croaked out, "Why?" His vision blurred, and the final pulse of life flickered within him.

Because I can…

The room exploded in a blaze of light, temperature lifting from the freeze.

The lights in the room came on suddenly, and the temperature rose. Police sirens wailed over the beeping of his own alarms as Brett's heart stuttered and with one last sigh, stopped beating.

1. RANDOM REVERBERATIONS

When I woke up, my head felt like wet sand filled it, every ounce dense and unmoving. My mouth felt parched, cracked as if I had chewed on desert dust all night. At least I'd slept.

The previous evening's holiday party at Garden State University, where I teach, played back in my mind like a blurred, half-forgotten film. There had been eggnog—laced generously with alcohol. I'd taken a glass, desperate for a respite from the ceaseless cacophony inside my mind.

That's because I'm not like most people. A psychic gift, so potent, blessed or maybe cursed me: the moment I step into a room, everyone's unguarded thoughts jostle and batter my consciousness. Their hopes, fears, ambitions, regrets—they don't just whisper; they scream in vivid images and disjointed words.

To survive, I have to build mental walls, enormous and exhausting fortresses, just to keep the noise from crushing me.

Unless I have a drink.

One sip of wine, beer, or spirits—whatever the magical ingredient—slams those voices shut like a steel door. Suddenly the world is quiet, and I can breathe. The endless complaining, the gossip, the tangled webs of desire all mute into silence.

So, I indulged—one drink, then two, then three more. Blithely unaware of the consequences, I was grateful for the Uber that carried me safely home. Back then, I was feeling no pain. Free for a few hours.

Now, it was all back—and worse. And add to that, my head throbbed relentlessly, a dull, pulsing assault behind my eyes. My paralyzed right leg ached with a deep, unyielding throb. I lay in my bed, cloaked in loneliness, the memory of the woman I loved —and lost—still gripping my heart like a vise.

Can anyone truly blame me for needing a drink?

Apart from the fact that I am an alcoholic.

I reached out to the nightstand and gripped my cobra-headed cane. Its familiar weight steadied me as I maneuvered onto the edge of the mattress, then pushed upward and into a shuffle.

Each movement brought a fresh sting of pain, but I forced myself forward to the bathroom. I opened the medicine cabinet and put a pair of aspirin in my mouth, followed by a stiff swallow of water.

Stripping off my clothes, I stepped into the hot shower. Steam enveloped me, momentarily dulling the pounding in my skull and the ache in my limbs.

Today was Monday—the first free Monday since the semester had ended on Friday. With the fall term behind me, the long holiday break stretched ahead, silent and empty except for one task: recording a lecture that my students could watch on their own time.

A small obligation, but one I couldn't shirk.

Clean and shaven, I dressed slowly and made my way to the kitchen, drawn by the promise of coffee. There, waiting like a comforting reminder of normalcy, was Mrs. Higgins—my landlady and housemate—with her perpetually warm Irish brogue.

"Hulloo Doctor," she greeted me softly.

I forced a smile as I shuffled to the coffeepot.

"How was the party?" she asked, her tone light but with an undercurrent of genuine interest.

I sighed, the weight of last night pressing down again. "A bunch of academics trying to outwit each other with half-baked cleverness. Mostly proving they're neither witty nor urbane."

Mrs. Higgins raised an eyebrow. "Did you meet anyone?"

Her question felt loaded. She was acutely aware of what had happened last September—that horrifying night when my world unraveled. When Jyanette Emery, the love of my life, who'd been carrying our child, lost the baby and nearly her own life.

Afterward she left New Jersey—and abandoned me—leaving a wound so deep I thought I might bleed out.

Mrs. Higgins, ever hopeful, probably asked because she wanted to see me move on. To find someone new, to live again. I couldn't blame her; I could barely stand the person I'd become—a ghost wandering through my life.

I tried to be patient, though the ache in my chest made it difficult. "Mrs. Higgins, it was just the usual crowd—people I work with, their spouses. Most of them I wouldn't talk to if we didn't share a paycheck. No, I didn't meet anyone."

She handed me the container of light cream. I added it to my coffee and took a grateful sip.

"I'm joost concerned," she said, returning the cream to the fridge with a soft click. "Ye're a young man. Ye need to get out and meet people. When ye hide away, ye stay in yer room—"

"Mrs. Higgins," I interrupted gently but firmly, "you're a dear for worrying, but I already have a mother, and she's enough."

Her expression tightened. "Well, excuse me, Doctor, for carin' about yer happiness."

Why was it that both my mother and Mrs. Higgins could make me feel guilty just for existing?

I sighed, weariness dragging me down. "I need to record the lecture," I said, turning toward the door. My winter coat waited just inside; it was time to shield myself from the cold and the memories.

"Ye should eat," she called after me.

Mrs. Higgins had been generous, renting me the 'mother' half of her mother/daughter home in Mountainview, New Jersey, for a fraction of the cost most could afford.

Still, I wished she'd leave my life alone sometimes.

I stepped outside; the December cold bit through my coat. This cold snap was unusual for us, arriving before Christmas when usually the pale, brittle breath of autumn lingered. Snow would come soon enough, but for now the chill was relentless.

Sliding into my minivan, the specially designed front seat rotated automatically, easing me inside. Hand controls took the place of foot pedals—as my paralyzed right leg was useless to operate them without a knee joint.

Coffee in the cupholder, I pulled out of the driveway, breath visible in the frigid air before the heater could warm the cabin. Mrs. Higgins' words echoed in my mind. I needed to eat. So I grabbed a bagel from a nearby drive-thru, warmth and sustenance for the coming hours.

Arriving at the university, I parked in my reserved spot behind Williams Hall. My leather bag sat on the passenger seat—laptop inside, ready.

In the lecture room, I set up the camera and recording gear. Just as I was testing the sound, my phone buzzed. A message from Lieutenant Bill McGee flickered across the screen.

Got something weird.

Can you spare me time this afternoon?

I hadn't heard from McGee in weeks, the end of the semester keeping me buried in exams and grading. I quickly texted back that I was available, waiting on his address.

Whatever weird thing he'd found, I knew my day was about to take an unexpected turn.

Around noon, I pulled up to the Mountainview Police Department, the sun hanging high and casting sharp shadows across the street.

Recording the lecture had gone smoothly, almost too smoothly, but I'd crafted a lighthearted, engaging presentation to wrap up the class. I'd clipped together a montage of scenes from the various Ghostbusters movies, then juxtaposed their cinematic ghost-busting antics with the real-world tools and protocols paranormal investigators actually use.

I'd meant it to be a playful, humorous finale—something to make my students laugh while sneaking in a little learning.

I glanced up at the Public Safety Building, its austere tan brick facade sitting solid atop a granite foundation, the entire structure rising only two stories but feeling grounded and unyielding.

The pair of smooth pillars guarding the entrance gave it a vaguely classical air, but the sheer curved tower scaling the uphill side felt incongruous—a stubborn reminder the building had once been the municipal offices before the city offices relocated themselves.

Now, the first floor rang with the ongoing bustle and tension of the police department while the fire department operated out of the second.

I swiped my magnetic ID card through the back entrance from the parking lot; the door clicked open and led me past the rows of lockers and bunk rooms where officers rested between shifts.

A dull hum of activity drifted in the air as I headed toward Bill's office.

Stepping into the command area, I passed his door and saw CeeCee Carter at the dispatch center. She was a solidly built woman in her forties with an unshakable charm and a permanent twinkle of flirtation in her eyes. She was engaged in a heated call, headset glued to her ear, fingers flying across the console.

I decided not to interrupt, knowing well the chaos on the other end of those lines.

I stepped back and knocked on Bill's door. His booming voice came instantly. "Come in!"

Inside, the office was a controlled chaos of papers and folders strewn about like a hurricane had passed through. Bill sat at the center, an open dossier in one hand, his other hand idly hovering over a cluttered desk that seemed indecipherable to anyone but him.

"Hey, Len," he said without looking up. "Haven't seen you at meetings lately."

Bill wasn't just my police contact; he was my Alcoholics Anonymous sponsor, a steady rock in my stormy life.

"I've been busy, grading exams, prepping for the semester end," I said, my tone lacking conviction.

His piercing steel-blue eyes locked onto mine. "You know those meetings aren't optional. The program only works if you work the program."

Heat rushed to my face, anger surging beneath the surface. I fought to keep the edge from my voice. "Bill, I don't need a guilt trip right now. I just had Mrs. Higgins nag me this morning… because I'm not dating."

There was more temper in my voice than I intended. I was tired—so tired—of living up to everyone's endless expectations.

Bill's lips pressed into a tight line. After a heavy nod, he softened. "Sorry. You're my friend. I worry… especially after the breakup with Jyanette—"

"I'm fine," I snapped too sharply.

That name hit like a wound. Jyanette. She'd left town months ago, gone back to her parents in Virginia after telling me she'd always love me. That was after she said she never wanted to see me again.

Last September's events had shattered us both, and maybe she thought running away was safest. Still, hearing her name reopened scars I wasn't ready to revisit.

I forced myself to breathe out the bitterness and returned to business. "What's this you texted me about?"

"Got a scene for you," Bill said, pulling a file free from the chaos of his desk. "Thought you could offer some insight."

"What happened?"

"Apparent suicide," he said, flipping open the file. "But something's off. And you knew the victim."

I raised my eyebrows. "Who?"

Bill's voice dropped. "Brett Morgan."

My mind snapped into focus. "Wait—the guy with the sacrificial knife you and I found last March?"

"That's him. The rich collector guy—armory full of weapons, remember?"

"Yes, sure," I said, and felt shocked. He'd been so upbeat, so full of life. "What happened?"

"He stabbed himself with that same ritual knife."

My mouth fell open. "The one Claude used to kill Constance Newhouse?"

That previous spring, a madman named Claude Vandersteen had ritually sacrificed a young teen and was planning to do the same to another young woman in a ritual to empower a demon. Vandersteen created a drug that gave him psychic powers, and I'd almost ended up stabbed by that very knife. We stopped him and saved the second girl, but at a cost.

Bill nodded grimly. "I need you to tell me what the forensics can't."

An icy shiver ran down my spine remembering the gleam of that shining blade Vandersteen tried to plunge into my chest. "Let's go."

"Can you follow me?" he asked. "Might have to bail if another case comes in."

"I'm on vacation for a few weeks," I said. "You've got me, no matter what."

We headed out to the parking lot, and he climbed into his unmarked car. I followed in my van as we drove toward the upscale part of town.

Brett's mansion was a sprawling white-brick Victorian crowned with green copper domes and a view of the distant New York skyline. The estate was a moneyed fortress, sprawling and imposing.

There was a police cruiser and one of Doug Millbank's forensic vans parked out front. If the county forensic chief himself wasn't here, he'd surely sent his best.

Bill pulled up the driveway, but I pulled my van to the side to keep the way clear.

I joined Bill to walk to the house as he recounted, "He triggered his home security panic alarm. Officers arrived fast, but by the time they forced down that reinforced door and found him in the weapons room—he'd already bled out."

I looked up at the grand manor. Searching this place must have been like finding a needle in a haystack.

"It's a shame. I met him once. He seemed decent enough."

Bill steered us toward the front door. "How's the book coming?"

"The publisher bought it," I said, a flicker of pride beneath the exhaustion. "An advance check should come before Christmas. Not much, but enough for presents at least."

I'd written a novelization of our first case together. Getting an agent and a deal was a triumph, but the endless slow drip of the publishing world was brutal. The book wouldn't be out for months, but the prospect of recording the audiobook the next month kept me going.

Bill raised an eyebrow. "First time behind the mic?"

"Yeah, but I've been practicing voices," I said, smiling.

"Give my part a deep, resonant voice."

"Absolutely," I grinned.

The police had mangled the door at the frame to get in. It hung crooked—no doubt the result of using a battering ram.

We stepped into the grand foyer. McGee caught my eye. "You getting one of those 'buzzes'?"

Bill used my personal code word for a sudden psychic flash or an intuitive insight. Bill's knew my quirks, as well as my names for them.

"Nothing yet."

We passed through a decorated front room, moved down a hallway, and climbed the broad staircase. Blond, blue-eyed Officer Ben Galland waited, crisp and composed as we walked down the upstairs hall.

I smiled. "Good to see you, Galland."

"You too, Doc. Doug's new guy is on the scene," Galland reported.

Bill acknowledged him. "Thanks, Galland."

We entered the arsenal room—glass cases towering to the ceiling, packed with blades from around the world. Japanese katanas, Scottish claymores, even a pristine Roman gladius, centuries old, gleamed under the lights.

Each weapon bore a label with its name and history, a curious blend of fascination and menace.

A figure clad in worn jeans and a dark-blue jacket stood hunched over one of the display cases. Bold, tall white letters spelled out "FORENSICS" across the jacket's back.

"You must be the new guy," I said, breaking the heavy silence.

The person rose from the floor. A blonde ponytail tumbled into view as she kept rising… until she was almost as tall as me.

The woman facing me was striking, her Nordic features crisp and sharp. Her pale skin gleamed with a subtle rosy glow, framed by the loose jacket and pants she wore, which deliberately concealed any hint of femininity.

Protective plastic glasses shielded her prescription lenses, magnifying the large hazel eyes that sparkled with something unreadable—a mix of amusement and challenge. Her lips curled into a faint, knowing smile.

"Yeah, I'm the 'new guy,'" she replied, her voice husky yet steady, as I struggled to catch my breath.

Bill, standing beside me, shifted uneasily. "I thought Forensics cleared the scene."

"The ME took the body, and the recovery team finished their sweep hours ago," she said matter-of-factly. "I'm just following up. You're the LT for Mountainview, right? I was told you'd be here."

"Lieutenant Bill McGee," he said, extending his hand.

She glanced at her gloved hand and gave a sharp shake of her head. "Better not. I don't want to pick up any trace from you." Then, her gaze shifted to me. "And who's this? One of your detectives?" Her eyes flicked to my walking stick. "Oh—you brought me the cane!"

Before I could react, she snatched the cane from my grip with one swift motion, forcing me to adjust my stance to keep balance. I let her take it, both surprised and somewhat intimidated by this statuesque woman.

"Who are you?" I finally managed.

"Sorry. I'm April Simpson," she said, flipping over the cane in her large gloved hands. Without hesitation, she pressed a discreet catch and a polished sword slid free from the hidden sheath.

My mentor, Doctor Fritz Kohl, gave me this cobra-headed cane, which concealed a two-foot-long steel blade, razor-sharp and well-polished. A weapon like that was illegal to carry openly here in New Jersey, so only a select few knew of its existence.

"Hey, what are you doing?" I hissed, eyes wide.

April frowned. Even her frown was beautiful—arched brows framing those sparkling hazel eyes. "I'm examining the evidence," she said coolly. "I asked about this when I found those papers. Didn't you bring it for me to look at?"

"Actually, it's mine," I said, not reaching to reclaim it. "I kind of need it."

Her gaze locked on my leg, then back to the cane. She snapped the sword back into place, the click sharp in the tense air, and held it out.

"You're the owner?" she asked, watching me steady myself on the stick. "Is that why the LT brought you?"

Bill chuckled, amused by the exchange. "Actually, this is Doctor Leonard Wise. He's our civilian consultant."

April's eyes scanned me again—no makeup, no pretense, her flawless skin and natural beauty almost startling. Quietly she spoke: "This cane matches notes and photos I found in the deceased's office."

"I was here last March," I said, steadying my voice. "Mr. Morgan showed interest in my cane. Said he wanted to research its history."

"Oh? Well, he apparently did." April nodded. "There's a complete document about your stick."

I gave her a dumb, sheepish smile.

"What can you tell us about the victim?" McGee asked.

"I was here for tagging and bagging. Doctor Millbank is handling the autopsy. I took photos," April replied, emotion stripped from her tone. "A pretty brutal suicide. The victim used an unusual knife to impale himself. Preliminary findings suggest he sliced open his own stomach, then turned the blade upward, ensuring a fatal wound. The angle, the method—it resembles the Japanese rite of seppuku. Our office will email you digital photos shortly."

Bill looked at me. "Should I have my consultant glove up?"

Her eyes narrowed thoughtfully. "If he's going to touch anything, gloves are a must."

She unzipped her jacket, revealing a fitted turtleneck that clung to a slender waist and accentuated a full bosom. From an inner pocket, she pulled out nitrile gloves and held them out to me.

I put them on as she turned her gaze to McGee. "Do you need gloves?"

"No, I'm good. But I want to clear the room while Doctor Wise works," he said.

April's eyes swept over me once more. "What exactly do you do? No tools, no evidence bags. What do you have?"

Bill smiled knowingly. "He has what he needs. Trust me."

With a nod, he gestured toward the door, and April led the way out, McGee following. I heard the door click shut behind them.

Alone, I surveyed the room carefully. It had changed little since my visit last March. The glass cases gleamed under the flickering fluorescents, each placard precisely placed. The air was heavy with the ghosts of moments long past.

I deliberately skirted the large bloodstain where Brett Morgan had met his end. I read energy, and touching blood can overwhelm my senses with the memories of the victim's last moments. Memories too raw to dwell on.

Even experienced as I was, immersing myself in the victim's death was a perilous risk.

Instead, I moved toward a display case beside the bloodstain. One shelf held an empty space beside an ornate sheath—polished silver etched with jade patterns so intricate they seemed alive. I recognized the scabbard instantly.

Silver ceremonial Kris blade.

Origin unknown.

Discovered among the Korowai clans.

Someone stole the twisted, jagged blade that belonged there months ago—and used it to murder a young woman and even threaten my life.

Now, Brett Morgan had used that same blade to kill himself.

Why?

I assumed that the police and the ME had taken the knife into evidence, but the blade and its sheath remained linked on a subtle energetic level. Inhaling deeply, I fought the distracting haze left from the previous night's drinking. I forced my thoughts into an alpha state—calm, open, focused.

Closing my eyes, I unlatch the case and slipped on the nitrile gloves before reaching in to grasp the cold metal of the sheath. The jade inlays were icy against my fingertips, but gradually they warmed with my touch, even through the gloves.

When I opened my eyes, the room had faded into sepia tones —like an old film flickering into life. The twisted Kris blade rested on the shelf beside the sheath now held in my hand.

I was witnessing a moment frozen in time—a residual energy trapped in this place. My mind interpreted it as a vision.

Suddenly, the chill of the past seeped in. The door beeped softly as Brett entered barefoot, clad in pajamas and a robe. His flashlight beam swept the floor as he stepped in.

"Hello?" he called out, his voice tentative.

The light passed through my form as if I were a ghost. This wasn't the present.

His short, muscular frame tensed as he surveyed the room. A fitness fanatic, no doubt capable of defending himself.

He stopped midway, glancing upward, as if hearing something others could not. I followed his gaze, flicking to an alarm panel on the wall.

After a moment, he moved towards the display and retrieved the Kris—selecting it almost with reverence. He held it up; the flashlight illuminating the sharp curves of the steel.

A sudden flicker of tension seized him. Without warning, he turned and slashed the air behind him; the blade cutting nothing but silence. Confused, he glanced around, unsure of himself.

He returned to the alarm panel, his glare fixed on the ceiling as if issuing a challenge. "Who is it? Who's there?"

His voice echoed, but the shadows held no answer. No sign of another presence stirred the stillness.

"Show yourself!" Brett demanded. Then, something inside him twisted. His arm, still grasping the ancient blade, moved against his will. His eyes widened, astonished at his own betrayal.

In a brutal, sudden motion, he plunged the Kris into his own abdomen.

I gasped aloud at the raw agony in his scream. Clutching the blade, he dragged it slowly across the wound, turning it upward with grim finality.

He stumbled, holding the wall for support, blood spilling onto the floor. His trembling hand pressed a button on the panel— alarms erupted, shrill and insistent throughout the house.

Falling to his side, he lay motionless, eyes dull yet searching. "Who are you?" he whispered, his voice ragged.

Then came another voice. Familiar. Haunting.

I am merely an echo of what was...

The vision shattered. The room snapped back into focus. Brett was gone, the knife vanished, and I was alone, clutching the ornate sheath.

A cold shiver crawled up my spine as the weight of that final, terrible moment lingered in the air.

And the sheer terror that the voice I'd heard was familiar.

2. RIOTOUS REMNANT

"And that was it." I shrugged, finishing my hurried recount to Bill about the vision.

He stood there quietly for a moment, then disappeared out the door. He returned promptly, handing me a bottle of water he'd retrieved from his car. I took a long drink, the cool liquid a minor relief against the dry tension swirling from my experience.

He questioned me about specifics and I ran through the details again—the so-called suicide of Brett Morgan. I still had no explanation for the inexplicable behavior preceding his death, and, most importantly, the voice I'd heard afterwards.

Bill listened intently, his face unreadable. When I finished, his head shook slowly in disbelief. "You think... what? A ghost made him kill himself?"

I met his gaze, dead serious. "What happened to Brett wasn't normal and it had something to do with that knife. If I could do a reading on it—really focus—I might uncover more. I need to understand what we're dealing with."

Bill rubbed his chin, the weight of the situation pressing down on him. "You realize what you're suggesting isn't just weird—it's dangerous. If there's some entity out there powerful enough to make people kill themselves…"

"I know," I cut in, the gravity settling hard inside me. "But we've faced similar phenomena before. Remember the Stoller case? People hypnotized into believing invisible forces tormented them."

A flicker of recognition crossed Bill's expression. "Yeah. Do you think this is the same thing?"

I swallowed hard. "I don't know yet. But if I can get near that knife, do a proper reading, I might get answers. I need time and a quiet space."

He nodded slowly. "Alright. First, I will check with the coroner, get the autopsy report firsthand, then I will ask them to release the knife. I've also called in Kate."

At the mention of Doctor Katherine Yearling, an FBI profiler and hypnotherapist who'd helped us before, my stomach clenched. Months earlier, a demon-possessed man had savaged her—scalped her alive, a nightmare she had survived against all odds.

She hid beneath wigs and scarves now, covering the scars from skin grafts that marked her survival.

I frowned, doubts creeping in. "Is she well enough?"

Bill offered a faint smile. "I saw her last week. It's nothing short of a miracle. She insists she's ready to dive back in, says she misses the field."

That comment hung between us as Bill headed toward the door. "She'll be here soon. You sure you can drive after what happened upstairs?"

I nodded firmly despite the lingering nausea. "No problem. I'll call or text if I get any new insights."

"I'll let you know when you can examine the knife."

Bill stepped out into the dim hallway, Galland falling in step right behind him. They disappeared down the stairs and I lingered a moment before heading back into the armory. The room smelled faintly of stale air and old wood, the shadows deepening. My mind was a jumble, but I forced myself to focus.

A voice said, "Doctor? I still have work to do."

I turned to see Simpson in the door.

"Officer Simpson!" I said. "I'm sorry, do you need me to leave?"

"No you're fine. I just want to take photos of the prints I found on the alarm button." She came back into the room and glanced back at me with a raised brow. "And it's CSI Simpson, not officer."

I flushed—always awkward around women, especially ones as confident and striking as this one. "Sorry. I was wondering about the paperwork you found... about my cane?"

Her eyes flicked over my face, weighing me. Then she stepped out into the quiet hallway, checking that we were alone—Galland and McGee long gone. "What happened to the uniformed officer?" she asked casually.

"He left with the lieutenant," I said, managing a weak smile.

She stepped closer, her voice dropping to a teasing murmur. "Am I safe being alone with you?"

My chest tightened. "What—?"

Her throaty chuckle was intoxicating. "Just messing with you, Doc. Papers are in the next room. Follow me."

I couldn't help but notice the sway of her hips as she strode ahead. I'd follow her anywhere, though I kept that thought buried deep. I was very thankful she wasn't the psychic.

Inside the small office, the space felt both sterile and lived-in—an oak desk dominated the room, filing cabinets hugged the walls, and a small table sat near the window. She moved to the desk and gathered the papers and several 8x10 photographs, handing them over.

I flipped through the images—shots Brett had taken of my cane during my last visit.

April cocked her head, eyes sharp as she leaned against the corner of the desk. "So, how do you consult exactly?"

I wasn't sure why she was watching me so closely. "Bill—the lieutenant—calls me when they need a fresh perspective."

She smiled knowingly. "You're the psychic, aren't you?"

My head snapped up. "What?"

This delighted her to no end. "The CSI crew's been gossiping. They say Mountainview's got its own pet psychic. Told me you've saved the MPD twice from blowing up."

I exhaled, trying to maintain composure. "You shouldn't believe rumors."

She raised an eyebrow. "You didn't answer the question."

I hesitated. Keeping the truth quiet was vital. If word got out about my genuine talents, people would mock me. Worse, it might hamper my ability to help.

But April's gaze held something different—intensity, maybe curiosity. Or was it something more?

"I am... technically... a parapsychologist," I admitted cautiously.

Her grin broadened. "Still not a straight answer."

"It's complicated. Let's just say, I've developed abilities to read energy, to pick up on things others can't."

"So, basically, you're the police psychic."

I sighed. "I'm a consultant who donates my time to help solve cases."

She laughed softly. "I get paid for it, but yeah. I like to think I find the clues that catch killers."

"My work has helped save lives. But mostly, good police work leads the way. I just sometimes point them in the right direction."

She nodded approvingly. "You didn't have to be so defensive. I'm a believer."

I frowned. "Really?"

Her eyes lit up. "You should see me with tarot cards. It'd blow your mind. But I have to get back to work—just got a call for another scene."

"Do you go from crime scene to crime scene?" I asked, intrigued.

"Pretty much." She shrugged. "Been on the job a couple months. I also do lab analysis."

I gathered some courage. "I'd... love to tell you more about my work sometime."

She raised an eyebrow, that mocking smile returning. "Would you now?"

I stumbled over my words, suddenly tongue-tied. "If you want to... and you're not married." I could feel my face burning like fire, embarrassed as I could be.

"No, I'm single," she said with a sly smile. "And I'm free tonight."

"That... would be... swell," I managed, heart pounding faster than ever.

She let out that deep, throaty chuckle again—one that always caught me off guard. "Swell? Where on earth did you dig up that word? The nineteenth century?" Her eyes sparkled with teasing as she held out her hand. "Come on, give me your phone."

I nearly tore the device from my pocket, fumbling to unlock it before handing it over.

Without missing a beat, she tapped open my digital notepad and swiftly typed in her name and number.

"Can't do anything before 7:30, but if you're up for a late dinner, I like sushi," she said casually.

I tried to steady myself, still reeling a bit from the interaction. "Great. I like sushi too."

She handed the phone back; the screen showing her perfectly typed contact details. "You don't date much, do you?" Her voice was soft but teasing, like a challenge.

I couldn't help but laugh dryly. "Is it that obvious?"

"Well, you're anything but smooth."

I shrugged, feeling the sting of her words more than I cared to admit. "Sorry. I'm... not great at this."

"Some of us prefer men who aren't smooth," she said with a glint in her eye, "as long as they're tall enough."

With an exaggerated sway of her hips, she turned and walked toward the door. Stopping just short, she glanced over her shoulder, seeing me standing dumbfounded in her wake.

"See you later, Doctor," she called out with a mischievous smile.

I leaned against the desk, heart hammering in my chest, struggling to slow my racing thoughts. She was right—I was the exact opposite of smooth.

Over years spent buried in research with Doctor Kohl, relationships had slipped through my fingers. Since returning to

New Jersey a year and a half ago, I'd had two: one one-night stand, and Jyanette—a relationship that ended painfully months ago.

In the interim, I had a brief affair with a researcher from California who'd had a crush on me years ago. But when push came to shove, she'd been more interested in a colleague than me.

Was I foolish to ask April out, knowing how often terrible things happen to people around me? Maybe a simple sushi dinner would not invite danger—unless the fish was bad.

Not in the mood to sift through Brett Morgan's dense report on my cane, I spread out the pages and methodically scanned each with my phone, creating PDFs I could review later on my laptop.

Ah, the wonders of twenty-first-century technology.

I gathered the papers, returned them to their folder and left it all on the desk. Casting one last glance toward the armory, I spotted April finishing up, carefully taping the panic alarm button to preserve the fingerprint.

"I'll text you a time and place, okay?"

She offered that dazzling smile again. "You can walk me out."

I twisted around so fast I nearly stumbled over my own feet.

"Totally not smooth," she murmured, attaching the taped fingerprint into a cardboard holder before slipping it into what looked like a hefty tool bag. Hoisting it onto her shoulder, she stood upright and removed the protective plastic goggles she wore over her glasses.

"Need a hand?" I asked, my hand out for her bag in an attempt to be gallant.

"I've got this," she said firmly, striding toward the stairs.

She descended swiftly, a stark contrast to my cautious, measured steps—my right leg insists that I take my time.

At the bottom, she waited for me, arms crossed with a mock-impatient scowl. "Come on, slowpoke."

I grinned, wincing as I steadied myself. "Going as fast as I can. Stairs aren't my thing."

She tilted her head. "You just need more aerobic exercise."

"Know any good techniques?" I teased.

With a playful glance back at me, she said, "Several wonderful ones, low impact, works all the best muscles."

Heat rushed to my face as we stepped out the front door.

The forensics van sat on the driveway, its twin rear doors swung wide open. April's expression darkened instantly.

"What the hell?" she muttered, breaking into a run toward the vehicle.

I peered down the street, frowning as a battered red pickup sped away, its driver clearly in a hurry.

I limped after April, who moved with an urgency I couldn't match.

Raised voices hit my ears as I neared.

"You have no business here," April snapped.

"Look, girly, I'm FBI. I don't need some newbie CSI telling me where I can look," shot back a familiar voice.

Kate Yearling.

Rounding the corner, I saw April towering over Kate. At six feet tall, April used her frame to intimidate the shorter FBI profiler, who stood at five-foot-eight.

What struck me most was how different Kate looked from the last time we'd crossed paths in September. Then, she was thin to the point of brittleness, pale with sunken cheeks and haunted eyes. Now, though her face remained sharp—too sharp—her body seemed recalibrated, solid and fuller under a heavy coat. Her vibrant emerald eyes gleamed, her skin was clear, and the flames of red hair, though obviously a wig, made her presence impossible to ignore.

Kate caught my eye and grinned. "Len Wise! Care to introduce me properly?"

I hesitated, wanting to avoid sitting at the crossroads between my colleague and my date.

"CSI Simpson , this is Dr. Kate Yearling. She's an FBI profiler."

April's eyes narrowed, arms folding tightly. "What's the FBI doing on my crime scene?"

Kate's tone was crisp; her glare unwavering. "The weapon suspected of killing Mr. Morgan was part of an FBI investigation months ago. Lieutenant McGee alerted me. I came to investigate the scene." She jabbed a finger at April. "That's what the 'I' stands for in FBI, in case you forgot."

The tension thickened.

A fire ignited in April's eyes. "That doesn't give you the right to rummage through the back of the van."

Kate raised gloved hands defensively. "The doors were open, and I put on gloves."

"Still," April snapped, rifling through evidence containers collected from various crime scenes, "I'm on probation. You want me fired?"

With a sigh, Kate stepped back. "I contaminated nothing."

"I sure hope not," April hissed, scanning the van. "Where's the weapon?"

"What weapon?" Kate frowned.

"The big knife. I bagged it and set it on top of that case, over there."

Kate's gaze drifted around the inside. "Didn't see it."

"It was here," April insisted, slamming the doors shut. "I'll call Newark to check if the ME received the body. If my boss thinks I lost evidence, I'm done for."

Kate shrugged, unnervingly casual. "Relax. It'll turn up."

Her ease shocked me—this wasn't the Kate I knew.

"Easy for you to say," April sneered, casting me a pointed look before heading to the driver's seat of the van.

I stepped aside and pulled Kate away from the vehicle as April started the engine, carefully backing down the driveway.

Kate spat under her breath, "What a bitch."

"You weren't exactly a help either," I admitted. "She's new. Pushing her around won't smooth things over."

"You think that punk kid was right? How can you stand her talking to me like that?"

I sighed, glancing at her. "Actually, we have a date tonight."

Kate shook her head in disbelief. "Len Wise, always thinking with the wrong head."

"Hey!"

Without missing a beat, she turned toward the house. "Show me the crime scene. Bring me up to speed."

I followed, heart still racing with the tension of the afternoon and a glimmer of hope that—maybe—her mood might improve.

An hour later, I cruised through the quiet streets, driving Kate back to her office in Morris Plains.

I had walked her through the chaotic crime scene, sharing my vision and how it had haunted me. She had said very little, only listening—intensely, almost anxiously—to every word I uttered.

Kate had always been skeptical of my readings, treating them more like a parlor trick than anything credible. But over time, she had shifted—from outright dismissal to reluctant respect.

Still, I wouldn't call her a believer yet. That distance remained, an invisible barrier between her doubt and acceptance.

Breaking the suffocating silence that filled the van, I smiled and said, "By the way, you look great. Really great."

That earned me the first genuine smile of the day. "Thanks," she breathed. "You like the new wig?"

"It's very nice," I said. I knew the scars on her scalp made regrowing her hair impossible. But the wig, the exact shade of her original hair color, made her look like herself again.

It was astonishing—considering six months ago doctors didn't think she'd survive, or worse, that she'd permanently have a brain injury. Three months ago, she'd been nothing but a frail wisp of a woman, a ghost of her old self.

"Kate, it's astounding to see you like this."

She shrugged modestly. "Thanks. I guess all those hours in therapy and the gym are paying off."

"You look just like you used to…" I began.

She held up a hand, stopping me. "We never say that in my group. We say: trauma creates change you don't choose. Healing is about creating change you *choose*."

"Your group?"

"Survivors of trauma," she said quietly. "It's helped. A lot. And, when you last saw me in September, I was still under Anika Vanya's influence. That was the real barrier to healing. Breaking free changed everything."

I nodded, happy to see the spark in her eyes. "It's incredible to see you so alive."

She smirked, a mischievous glint in her gaze. "So, you're going on a date with Miss Piece-of-Fluff, huh?"

I groaned, shaking my head. "Let it go, Kate. She's new. She didn't know Bill called you in."

"Fair," she said, then leaned back.

"By the way—how did you get to the scene?"

"A friend drove me. I can't wait to drive again myself," she said with a sigh. "Man, all of my salary is going to Uber these days. This van is fancy, Len."

"Thanks," I said. "When do you think you'll be driving again?"

"Soon. I just need to get my reaction time back, but I'm close."

"Glad to hear it."

She groaned, her frustration surfacing. "But I'm bored! I'm a field agent, a good one. Now all I do is shuffle papers. I want to get back out there—to interrogate suspects, kick some ass."

"Damn right," I said, smiling.

"I feel like a china doll everyone's afraid to break. I wish they'd stop treating me like an invalid and let me do my job."

"I get it, Kate," I said gently. "Doctors weren't sure you'd ever wake up. Even the optimists didn't think you'd walk again."

She rolled her eyes. "Well, I'm over it. I want to work—really work—not watch everyone else do it while I babysit files. And December sucks. Everyone wants time off for family."

Kate hadn't chosen New Jersey; the FBI had assigned her to the Morris Plains office to keep her close to the doctors who saved her life. I thought about how alone she must feel—no family nearby, few friends.

"Can you see if you can work up a profile on this case for me?"

She nodded, frowning. "I think so, but something is weird—"

"Gee, a case I'm involved with gets weird. What are the odds?"

"No, I'm serious. That entire scene was… familiar."

"Could it have been last March, after the burglar stole the knife?"

"No, I was in Washington then. And they didn't bring me up here for that. The other strange thing was I looked up the guy on the internet on the way here. He showed up in a lot of pictures."

"Yeah, he attended a lot of social events."

"Exactly! And I swear I've seen him before."

"Maybe you reviewed the case files?"

"Maybe. But then, when you described the victim's death… I could see it all vividly. Like I was actually there. Like a dream."

"Last night, by chance?"

Kate's eyes locked on mine, serious and unwavering. "Actually, yes. I think that's when. Like in a dream or something."

An icy shiver crept down my spine. "Are you sure?"

She nodded firmly. "If I'm going to make sense of any of this, I have to stay involved."

I turned my attention back to the road, but her confession lingered in the air, heavy and unsettling. Something about this case was deeper, darker—and I wasn't sure we were ready for what awaited.

3. CONCEDING COUNTERPART

I dropped Kate off at the train station in Morris Plains, the familiar building glaring like a fortress across from her FBI offices.

She nodded firmly, her eyes serious. "I'll get started on the profile right away," she assured me.

I mustered a tight smile and nodded.

Driving toward Garden State University, my mind weighed down with unfinished tasks. I had a simple plan: I would lock my office tightly and grade student papers before the holiday.

I wouldn't be back until the new year, and the thought of working from home—or a nearby coffee shop—offered a welcome escape from the cramped, claustrophobic office with its gargantuan desk that swallowed most of the space.

After parking, the wind off Alumni Green stung sharply as I headed for the administration building. The campus felt deserted. Just last Friday, throngs of students packed the walkways, dragging oversized backpacks or wheeling suitcases, eager to leave for home.

Today, though, only a handful of stragglers crossed the chill stone paths—mostly those caught in the grind of makeup classes or scraping together grade-earning hours as teaching assistants.

I pushed open the massive oak door of College Hall. The grandeur inside never ceased to amaze me—gleaming marble floors and glossy, warm wood paneling. The building's history whispered from every corner.

Originally the mansion of an estate known as Shadowvale, it had burned to ash back in 1920. Then, in the Jazz Age, Julian Tutelage, a renowned African-American architect, reimagined the place. He blended the rugged hand-hewn stone fragments left behind with sleek, modern lines.

The result was a striking fusion of the old world and the new.

There was also the matter of Tutelage's second project: designing the stables and servant quarters. Despite his interest in the project, the architect vanished mysteriously before the workmen completed the buildings.

Now, the old stables had been renovated into a theater named in his honor—the perfect nod to his legacy, shadowed by his disappearance.

I made my way to the office of my oldest friend and supervisor, Jon Baines, associate dean of the university. His assistant, Trisha Heywood, sat rigidly at her desk. Anyone hoping to see Jon first had to get past her—she was strict about visitors.

I flashed a smile. Trisha looked up, returning it warmly. She was thin, dressed festively in a deep red jacket and a frilly white blouse. Her matching red skirt and high boots gave her an air of holiday cheer, but the sharp gray streaks at her temples and her glasses told of unwavering discipline and intellect.

"Happy Holidays, Len," she said warmly, rising to envelope me in a quick hug. "Doing anything special during your time off?"

I shrugged. "Planning to stay off campus until the new year. Thought it'd be nice to work somewhere other than the cave I call my office."

She sighed. "Jon and I won't be off until Christmas Eve. We'll be busy—sending out hand-signed cards to all our benefactors, begging for more money."

I raised an eyebrow. "Even during the holidays?"

"Especially during the holidays," she said ruefully. "Our endowment isn't endless. December is when people will give."

I reached into my pocket, pulling out a small, carefully wrapped package. "I got you something—a little token of my respect."

Her surprise softened into a grateful smile as she peeled away the paper to reveal a velvet-covered jewelry box. Inside were an elegant pair of black-tone Victorian teardrop earrings, faceted stones set in intricate vintage filigree.

"I noticed your fondness for Victorian designs," I said. "Thought you'd like these."

Trisha's eyes brightened. "Perfect. You did well, Len. Thank you."

"I'll be off-duty until the new year," I added. "Had to get it to you now."

She nodded. "Well, Jon and I will be here if you get bored. Need to see him?"

"No, just you. I'll catch Jon and Jen on New Year's Eve."

Her glance flickered with concern. "When does Chanukah start for you?"

"Friday," I said, "I'll be with my family, along with my brother and sister."

"Thanks for taking the time, Len."

"Merry Christmas, Trisha."

With a nod, I stepped back into the hall and headed to my office. I hoped I could catch my teaching assistant before he left.

Teddy Santos was my go-to TA, and I figured he'd be gone the following day, heading to his parents' home in Dover. They'd bought a sprawling old house, and his father was meticulously renovating it—one room at a time. That meant Teddy would likely spend his time off battling drywall and spackle.

I found him in the faculty-only computer room, his usual refuge. Here, Teddy could access resources without fighting the student mobs at the IT station. Plus, it was free; the student computers charged hourly.

I wished I could afford a good laptop for him—he deserved one.

"Hey, Teddy," I greeted as I stepped in.

He glanced up from the dizzying cascade of HTML code on his screen, thick glasses framing intense eyes. "Hey, Doc," he mumbled, already returning to his work.

The cascading computer language looked like some cryptic enchantment unearthed from a lost civilization. I wondered what archaeologists millennia from now would make of it.

"What are you building?"

"An app for computer science extra credit," he said, eyes never leaving the screen.

"Even with finals looming?"

"Pretty much." He typed with feverish urgency. "I have to do it here—the computer at home can't handle anything this heavy."

"Old machine?"

"Windows '95, I think." He grunted. "My parents just need email and web browsing."

I pulled a small package from my pocket and slid it across the desk. "Got something for you."

Teddy's face lit up as he ripped it open. Inside was a plastic card embossed with the logos of his favorite fast-food joints.

"No way! Where'd you get this?"

I smiled. "Figured you'd like to eat out once in a while—now you can."

"Thanks, Doc! Seriously, that's awesome."

"Thanks for all your help. Will you have the lecture I recorded posted before you leave?"

"Already done." He slipped the card into his wallet. "By the way, Doc, have you thought about next fall?"

"Next fall? What about it?"

"I'm a senior next semester. I'm leaving in the spring."

I paused, acknowledging the reality. He'd transferred to GSU as a sophomore, so this was his final stretch.

"I... I thought maybe you'd go for your master's or something."

"Doc, I want to get out there. I've been in school my whole life."

Given my long road through premed, med school, psychiatry, and finally parapsychology, I understood all too well that restless feeling.

"Well, I have some time," I said. "I mean, I think about a new TA in the new year."

"Just so you know, Doc." He looked up, earnest. "I don't want to leave you hanging."

"Enjoy your time with your family. Merry Christmas and Happy New Year, Teddy."

He waved, eyes back on the screen. "You too, Doc."

I went down the hall to my office, closing the door behind me. Flicking on the light, I sat at my desk and gathered the papers I would need for the next few days.

I pulled up the address of my favorite sushi spot, Subarashī, and quickly shot a text to April with the address and a simple message:

It's Len Wise. 7:30?

My phone buzzed with her reply just as I locked up:

See you there.

Preparing for a first date was a torment I loathed. My nerves gnawed at me relentlessly. I'd already showered once that morning, but here I was, stripping down and stepping into the hot spray again, hoping to wash away the jittery tension clinging to me.

Afterward, I shaved—twice now—and stood in front of the closet fretting over what to wear.

Jeans weren't my style, especially not those worn and artfully torn ones that seemed to be a uniform for most GSU professors who fancied themselves cool. I didn't care about looking hip. I wanted to look like a man who had his life together.

Something grown-up: tailored slacks, a crisp shirt, and one of my Harris Tweed jackets that carried the weight of tradition and confidence. December had turned frigid, and the layers were a practical necessity, but I hoped they wouldn't make me seem too formal or stiff for a casual date.

Would I come across as trying too hard? Or worse, as someone who didn't care enough? The uncertainty twisted in my gut.

When I'd told Mrs. Higgins about the date, she'd nearly fallen to her knees, praising the saints and heaven.

Now, as I walked down the long hall toward the front door, she appeared from the kitchen, a mischievous glint in her eyes. "Come here, I want a wee look at ye," she said.

I braced myself for criticism—"Is that the shirt ye'll be wearin'?" or "Ye're far too dressed up, ye should relax."

But she simply watched as I approached, hands drying on a flour-dusted dish towel.

Then she nodded approvingly. "Ye look foine, Doctor. This should impress yer young lady."

Her words made me suddenly self-conscious. "You really think so?"

"If not," she said firmly, "she's a damn fool and not worth yer effort."

I chuckled, the tension easing a bit. "Honestly, after Jyanette, I hadn't wanted to date again."

Her expression sharpened, somber now. "We all loved Jyanette. I know her leavin' hurt you deep, but ye canna be a monk neither." Then, breaking into a sly grin, she added, "Plus, yer poor mother's desperate for more gran'children, and if ye don't get out there, it'll never happen."

I shook my head in mock defeat. "Glad to know where your loyalties lie."

"There's been no doubt," she laughed. "Now go—ye don't want to be late."

The van's heater struggled against the frigid December air as I drove through the neighborhood, the festive spirit clear in every glowing window. Houses gleamed with strings of colorful lights; some yards boasted inflatable Santas and reindeer bobbing absurdly in the wind. It was cheesy, sure, but it brought a strange comfort.

Gliding into downtown Mountainview, the scene was magical. Tiny bulbs twinkled in the branches of sidewalk trees, blinking in playful rhythm. Old-fashioned black lampposts split into twin glass globes, glowing warmly like gas lamps from a bygone era.

Also, each one had an oversized snowflake, sculpted entirely in white lights, that transformed the street into a winter wonderland.

I passed the large Christmas tree in the park across from the police station—a towering spectacle of ornaments and ribbons standing proud in an empty lot.

Subarashī appeared ahead, housed in a white stucco building that would have looked more at home as an office than a restaurant. Large picture windows reflected the street's festive glow, and a blue awning stretched over the entrance. The illuminated sign above, shaped like a fish, flickered to life in the dusk.

I parked, checked my side mirror, and stepped out of the van, pulling my jacket tighter around me.

As the door clicked shut, a sudden, piercing buzz went through my mind, sharp and insistent, slicing through my thoughts with a single, terrifying word:

DANGER…

My heart slammed against my ribs as I flattened myself against the van, breath catching in my throat.

Out of nowhere, a red pickup truck roared down the street, tires skimming dangerously close as it barreled past at a reckless speed wholly inappropriate for quiet Mountainview. It missed me by inches yet kept racing, oblivious to the disaster it had nearly caused.

I gasped, trying desperately to steady my pounding heart when a voice, cold and chillingly familiar, echoed inside my mind—like the one I'd heard earlier that day in Brett Morgan's armory.

I am coming for you...

4. RENDEZVOUS REPEATED

I sat across from April, the two of us quietly picking at our maki rolls in the dim glow of the restaurant's paper lanterns.

It had taken every bite just to steady my breathing, to wrap my scattered thoughts into something manageable.

When I'd first walked in, April looked at me with sharp concern—she'd seen the damn truck nearly sideswipe me on the street, and even told me she wished she could've jotted down the license plate number, but it had sped away too fast.

But it wasn't the near-accident that gnawed at my nerves. It was the message—a cold, foreign voice, yet familiar. It had flashed straight into my mind.

Long-range telepathy; a thing I knew was rare even among psychics like me. Picking up stray thoughts from people in the same room was one thing; pressing into someone's psyche by locking eyes up close was another—but *receiving* a message across a distance, uninvited?

That was different, and dangerous.

I closed my eyes momentarily, getting my thoughts together. That was no everyday stray thought I'd received; it was targeted for me.

I'd had a couple of rare instances before—Anna Sokolov, kidnapped by criminals who trafficked young girls. She'd touched my mind in desperation, and that link helped us—McGee, the FBI, and me—to track her down. But trauma had pushed Anna out of her normal psychic limits.

The other was Claude Vandersteen, a cult leader, mad and drug-fueled, no longer alive after our last confrontation.

Now, someone else was worming their way into my mind, and I needed to stop it. There was only one way I knew to shut off the psychic static in my head—alcohol.

April, sensing the tension I was trying to mask, had ordered sake for the both of us, and a server placed a small porcelain carafe and delicate cups on the table. She poured the warm, clear liquid into my cup with practiced ease. I stared at it hesitantly.

"Don't you want it?" April asked, her voice soft yet insistent.

I shook my head but took a tentative sip, feeling the heat spread through me. Slowly, the edges of the psychic noise dulled, my special senses powering down like a machine sliding into sleep. Whoever was trying to reach me mentally would now find the line closed.

April popped the last piece of kappa-maki into her mouth, savoring it after a dip in tamari and wasabi. She hummed—a small, content sound that made my otherwise restless mind wander uncomfortably to what she might sound like in moments far more intimate.

"You still haven't told me anything about yourself," she said, topping off my cup with a gentle hand.

I forced a laugh, leaning back. "I'm much more interested in you. You said you were a gymnast as a kid, then studied martial arts, and now you're a forensic scientist?"

Her eyebrows lifted, one hand absently adjusting her glasses. "Wow, you remembered. Honestly, a few times I thought you weren't paying attention."

"Almost getting hit by a truck is a bit distracting," I muttered, rubbing my temple.

Her eyes narrowed slightly, measuring me. "I guess I can forgive it... since you recall the highlights."

I nodded, grasping at the thread. "You said you grew up in South Dakota?"

"Brookings," she confirmed as she refilled her own cup before topping mine again. "Now your turn—where did you grow up?"

"Copeland, New Jersey, about an hour from here. I'm Jewish..."

"That I knew," she said with a half-smile.

I exhaled, the weight of my history pressing in. "I grew up with an interest in medicine and was on track to be a doctor like my father. I graduated Summa Cum Laude from Johns Hopkins Medical School. Then my fiancée died in the car crash that took my right knee. It... shifted everything."

April frowned subtly. "You make it sound clinical, like you're delivering a report."

A sigh escaped me. "That's because a lot of it is dark. It's easier to keep it at a distance. Frankly, I'd rather hear you talk about gymnastics, or how you got into martial arts... or your bachelor's degree. You have a BS, right? You look too young for a master's."

Her cheeks flushed slightly. "Yes, I have a BS—and I'm working on my master's, thank you very much. And I'm twenty-six, for the record."

I raised my hands in mock surrender. "No offense intended. So... where are you studying?"

"Garden State University."

I chuckled before I could stop myself. "That's where I teach."

Her mouth dropped open. "You're kidding. I've never seen you on campus."

"My lecture room is in Williams Hall. You probably stick to the Life Sciences Building. I went there for my premed courses."

Her eyes lit up. "You have the silver minivan! The one always in the handicapped spot behind Williams!"

I let out a dry laugh. "The same."

"I thought it looked familiar."

The waitress appeared then, gliding over with a polite, practiced smile. "Anything else, or are you ready for the check?"

I took the moment to take control. "Just the check," I said.

April shook her head. "I can cover my half."

I smiled faintly. "Thanks, but I'm no longer a struggling student. Besides, I've got a royalty check arriving soon."

Her eyebrows knitted as curiosity edged into her expression. "Royalty check? You write, too?"

"Not quite. I'm a teacher, but I have... unusual hobbies."

"Like going to crime scenes and doing psychic readings," she said knowingly. "What did you pick up at the house today?"

"If you want to know, you'll have to go out with me again." I said as the server placed the billfold in front of me.

She propped herself on her hands, locking her gaze onto me with a sly grin. "I see how this works. You've got me doing all the talking so you can stay quiet and mysterious. Plant that seed of curiosity, make me want to see you again. Sneaky."

I smiled, a little amused. "Old guys need a few tricks."

Her laugh was low and throaty, the kind that made the surrounding air suddenly warmer. "Well, I'm working and on call the next few days," she said, the playful edge fading to something more real. "Remember, I'm the new guy."

"You have my number from that text I sent. Just let me know when you're free. I'll put it in your hands. That way, if you don't want to see me again, no pressure."

She chuckled again, more softly now. "Oh, I want to see you again. Especially if you're buying dinner."

I chuckled along. "Lucky you. I was a college student juggling a job and studying. I got lucky when my mentor made me his TA."

"Well, the semester's over. For a few weeks, life slows down, and my life has a little less chaos," she said, a shadow crossing her features. "Just work and getting presents."

"Are you going home for Christmas? South Dakota?"

She grimaced. "The new guy doesn't get holidays off. I'm stuck here."

We both rose. I steadied myself with my cane, grabbed her coat off the chair, and helped her slide into it.

"By the way," April said, watching me carefully as I pulled on my coat. "Did you read the report about your cane?"

I shook my head as I stepped toward the door. "I skimmed the pages, but didn't dive into it."

"It's really fascinating. That cane's older than you think."

I glanced down at the simple stick in my hand. "It keeps me upright. That's what is important to me."

Outside, the street glowed with the pulse of colored lights from shops, casting flickering shadows.

"Well," she said, pointing at the small white car outside the restaurant, "I'm right over there."

"I'll wait to hear from you," I said.

"It won't be long." She moved closer, the space between us shrinking.

Our lips met easily, the awkwardness that often comes with height difference replaced by surprising ease. April stood nearly six feet tall, matching me almost step for step. Her glasses didn't even get in the way.

Her lips were soft, warm, and I fought the urge to pull her closer. This was a first kiss, delicate and full of promise—not a seduction.

We parted, breathless. Her hazel eyes were bright. "That was nice," she whispered—and without hesitation, she leaned in again.

As our lips touched, the image of a blindfolded Jyanette flashed in my mind, tied to a chair with ropes on her arm. It was in one of the old rooms in the state asylum, Blackshale. A man stepped away from her with a scalpel in his hand, aiming it towards me—

We both pulled back as if shocked, gasping.

"What was that?" April's voice trembled.

I blinked, trying to catch up. "What—?"

"I saw a black woman tied to a chair. In an old, moldy room," she said rapidly. "And that man... was he holding a scalpel?"

My breath hitched. How could she see that? Even if I had wanted to touch her mind, I'd been drinking. There was no way I'd sent that vision to her.

Her eyes searched mine. "Did you do that?"

I stammered, "No. I mean, I didn't..."

She studied me a moment, then seemed to accept the weak excuse. "Warn a girl next time, okay?"

I just nodded—my mind reeling from the vivid, unwelcome memory we'd shared.

She walked to her car, slipped in, and waved before driving off.

I stood rooted, stunned, trying to unravel what had happened.

That image hadn't been a hallucination. It was an actual event the previous June—and I had not been there. The only people in that room besides the man were Kate and Jyanette.

So how had I, with April, just shared that vision? Even drinking couldn't explain this psychic overlap.

Lost, I crossed the street carefully, checking for cars that might not see me.

The drive home was quiet, the night growing colder with every mile. I parked the van in the circular driveway, mindful not to block Mrs. Higgins' compact car in the single parking slot she'd carved out.

Stepping inside, the warmth of the living room fire hit me—the flames flickering just ahead. On the mantel, a flat-screen showed a black-and-white movie: *It's A Wonderful Life*, one of the classic stations.

Mrs. Higgins peeked over the back of the sofa. "Oh, Doctor, ye're home early."

"Just dinner," I said, "First date and all."

She switched off the TV, and I eased myself onto the arm of the sofa, careful where my stiff leg went.

"So, who is she? What's she like?"

"She's a forensic scientist," I answered.

"On crime scenes?"

"Exactly. I met her at a scene with McGee today. Her name is April, and she's a new hire. She's close to six feet tall."

"Like Jyanette?" Mrs. Higgins asked, then covered her mouth quickly. "Oh, I'm sorry, Doctor, I shouldn't bring her up."

"It's okay," I sighed. "Do you remember that ritual knife we had that trouble with last March?"

"Oh yes, that madman out on Staten Island. Did it have something to do with all that?"

"It was the home of the owner of the knife. He killed himself with it, but I'm not convinced it was his choice."

Her eyebrows rose. "Really?"

"But something strange happened after dinner."

"Strange?"

"I kissed her good night—"

"That's nice."

"But then I had a flash… like a memory of Jyanette being held prisoner in Blackshale by that madman."

Mrs. Higgins folded her hands, attempting a knowing look. "Well, it's a recent breakup. I'm sure you're still feeling it."

"That's the weird part. April saw it too. And it wasn't a memory of mine, yet she described exactly what I'd seen."

A frown knitted her brow. "But it wasn't your memory?"

"Exactly. The only person who could have seen those events was Kate Yearling."

"Could ye have sent it into April's head, without meaning to?"

"I couldn't have, Mrs. Higgins."

"Why not?"

I hesitated, not wanting to tell her I'd been drinking. Mrs. Higgins knew I'd quit over two years ago. I couldn't disappoint her.

"I know how my abilities work," I said carefully. "It would take deliberate effort to project an image into someone else's mind."

"Aye," she nodded. "Unless this young lady has some abilities too."

I paused, considering. Earlier today I sensed nothing unusual about her. She seemed as surprised as I was to have received that vision. If she had gifts, she must at least be aware of it.

"I doubt it," I said, considering it. "She'd had rice wine with dinner. If she had any gifts, that would've dulled them."

"Just because that happens to ye," Mrs. Higgins said with a knowing look, "doesn't mean everyone's the same."

I nodded, the weight of the moment settling heavy on my shoulders. "If I get any other flashes like that—"

Mrs. Higgins cut me off, her eyes sparkling with curiosity. "But—ye kissed her?"

A smile tugged at the corners of my mouth despite the knot in my gut. "Yeah. I did. And… I'm going to see her again."

Her face lit up with a broad smile, a warmth I hadn't seen in days. "Well then, that's good news."

"Very good, Mrs. Higgins," I replied, more to convince myself than her.

I drifted out of the living room, the murmur of the television flickering back on behind me as I left. My steps were slow, almost numb, as I made my way down the hall to my end of the house.

With a sigh, I shrugged off my jacket and sank into the solitude of my desk chair.

I carefully arranged my space with a larger sitting room that doubled as my office, accessible through a private entrance I hardly used, a bathroom bridging the sitting room and my bedroom. The bedroom itself overlooked a screened porch at the back, and I always felt at peace there.

But the chaos inside me was anything but peaceful.

Opening my laptop, I downloaded my emails; the screen glowed cold and impersonal in the dim room. I stared at the blank inbox, the silence pressing in.

Making sure I'd shut the hallway door, I glanced furtively and reached into the bottom drawer of my desk to pull out the pint of brandy waiting patiently. It was a bottle I told myself I only relied on occasionally, to keep the incessant psychic noise at bay.

As I deleted trivial emails and read a few that piqued my interest, I took two measured swigs from the bottle, the burn steadying my nerves, blurring the edges of my restless mind. I told myself the alcohol was for protection—an insurance policy against unwanted intrusions during sleep.

At least that's what I hoped.

Back in college, I'd tried to drown out the psychic storm in my mind with drink. It almost consumed me. I was deep in the throes of alcoholism before I found my way to Alcoholics Anonymous. The struggle to stay sober was brutal, with only a few slips over the last two years.

But when Jyanette left me and moved back to Virginia to be with her parents, I experienced sleepless nights again. The constant mental barrage grew too loud, too unforgiving. A small amount of alcohol seemed like a harmless crutch to quiet the chaos.

I had to keep it smart. I had to control it.

AA taught me to fight one day at a time. But not one soul there shared the odd torment of being invaded by voices that weren't their own. Their battles were internal; mine were with the other minds all around me.

My fingers hovered as I opened a browser and searched "Jyanette Emery." I told myself this was benign; just checking up on an old friend, making sure she was okay out there. Not stalking. Not obsessing.

But then a Department of Justice press release caught my eye. "Attorney Jyanette Emery joins the Special Investigations

Department," it read with a planned start date early next year. My breath hitched as I stared at the photo—her poised smile, sharp business attire, sharp contrast of white teeth against her dark skin, her hair pulled back in that familiar style I'd always loved.

Washington, DC. The city of dreams and buried hopes.

The truth hit me like a punch to the gut: any faint dream of a second chance with Jyanette was dead.

I took a long, desperate pull from the bottle, the liquid burning down like fire in my throat as hot tears spilled unbidden onto my cheeks.

Couldn't she see? Couldn't anyone see I loved her? That I wanted to build a life with her?

But the madness I attracted—the darkness I fought—ripped her away from me forever. My long-dead fiancée, who died the night I gained these cursed gifts; a woman I dated two years ago, Wendy Wallace, burned alive right before my eyes by a murderer I pursued. A vengeful woman with a grudge, who wanted me shattered, had used her hypnotic skills to kill our unborn child and nearly ended Jyanette's life.

The malevolent forces I battled didn't just want me—it raged against anyone within my reach.

My hand shook as I pushed the bottle back into the drawer, trying to steady myself. I closed the laptop with a click that sounded final.

It was over. I would never see Jyanette again.

Questions swirled in my mind: If I dated April, would she suffer the same fate? Hurt or worse? Was everyone who got close to me doomed?

No wonder I couldn't sleep.

I made a silent vow. When I saw April next, I'd have to tell her everything—my gifts, the dangers, the darkness clawing at my life. She deserved the truth. If I were going to ruin her, I owed her the chance to walk away.

I'd already had more to drink than I planned. Stumbling into the bedroom, I peeled off my pants; I couldn't figure out how to put them on a hanger.

Even the hanger seemed to mock my weakness.

Then I shrugged out of my shirt and collapsed onto the bed, clad only in boxers, sinking into a restless, deep sleep.

5. DEAD RINGER

My cell phone's sharp ringing jolted me awake bright and mercilessly early the next morning. Groaning, I ignored it, willing it to stop so I could sink back into the comforting haze of sleep.

But the insistent sound continued, buzzing until it finally went to voicemail. I rolled over, craving more rest. Then it rang again—relentless.

Enough.

I snatched up the phone on the third ring. The screen flashed "Unknown." My throat was dry and scratchy when I croaked, "Hello?"

"Doctor Wise?" The voice was feminine, tentative yet urgent.

"Yes… who is this?" I demanded, blinking away the fog of sleep.

"It's Anna. Anna Sokolov. Do you remember me?"

Of course I remembered her. With Bill McGee and Kate Yearling's help, we'd rescued her from that brutal sex trafficking ring a year ago. My heart tightened. How could I forget?

"Anna," I softened immediately. "I'm sorry for being abrupt. I was sleeping."

"I know, I know." Her voice quivered. "But I had to call. At school, we're not allowed to have our phones on during class."

"Understandable."

"You gave me your card... you said I should get in touch if I—if I needed you."

"Is something wrong?"

Her voice wobbled as she whispered, "I saw... well, in my mind, I saw a man kill himself. Like I was there."

A chill skittered down my spine. "Anna, when did this happen?"

"Sunday night."

My breath caught. The night Brett Morgan died.

"Can you tell me more?"

"There was this man... he had a strange knife. Curvy, like waves. He pushed it into himself because... because a voice told him to."

My full attention locked on her trembling words.

She went on. "Can you come to the diner after school? I'll be helping Poppa."

Her father owned Mindy's Diner, a well-known business near the highway. I glanced at the clock. 7:30 a.m.

"After three?"

"Yeah."

"I'll be there," I promised. "Anna, please—don't tell anyone else about this until you talk to me, alright?"

Her voice softened. "Okay. Thanks. Bye."

She'd ended the call. I stared at my phone, unease twisting in my gut. Anna had a rare psychic gift—she'd reached out telepathically when trapped by the men who abducted her.

If she truly witnessed Brett's death, if she'd experienced a vision, I needed to know everything she saw, and more importantly—why it had come to her.

Phone in hand, I quickly texted April, despite telling her a second date was her choice:

I had a lovely time last night.

Would like to see you again.

I'll even do some of the talking.

I threw on my robe, stumbled to the kitchen to brew strong coffee, and grabbed aspirin for the headache pounding behind my eyes.

Energized by caffeine, fruit, and painkillers, I was getting dressed when the phone rang again. It was McGee.

His booming voice came over the phone, "Len, you asked about doing a reading on that knife?"

"Yes, I thought I might get a clearer idea—"

"It's gone."

A cold dread blossomed in my chest.

"CSI Simpson said it wasn't where she left it in the van. I thought she misplaced it."

"It never made it into evidence."

I stood frozen as the pieces slammed into place.

"Bill, I've got a bad feeling. Someone might have used Brett Morgan's death as cover to steal that knife."

Silence breathed down the line.

"Why would anyone do that?" McGee finally asked.

"I'm not sure. Back when we were chasing the case last spring, Claude Vandersteen and Antoine Powell hired a burglar to steal that knife. They wanted it because it carried the power of human sacrifice. Claude even created that drug that gave him psychic abilities—"

"The one that made him crazier than a March Hare?"

"Exactly. What if someone's recreated the drug, continued his research? It's our only lead."

"Staten Island is where all that happened. That's not my turf. Maybe you should contact Darren Ward,"

Darren was a private investigator based in Staten Island, who'd helped uncover Vandersteen's dark rituals. It made sense, as both McGee and I trusted him.

"Good idea, I'll call him. I also think we should interview Antoine Powell since he worked with Vandersteen."

"Isn't he Jyanette's ex-husband, right? The abusive one?"

To my surprise, I felt a sudden burst of anger. When Jyanette confessed the things that man had done to her, I had wanted to beat Antoine Powell to death with my bare hands. Apparently, I hadn't dealt with all the emotions of her leaving yet.

"Yes," I muttered, trying to calm down.

"I don't know. He's upstate in a New York prison for his part in the death of Connie Newhouse," Bill said. "I heard he got ten years."

"He deserved it," I spat.

"But Len, getting an interview would be difficult. First, he's in a prison that's an eight-hour drive from here."

I considered this. "Any way to get him down here so I could talk to him?"

McGee considered this. "That's the second problem. I'd have to put in a request through the New York Prison system."

"Can you have him brought down here to Mountainview?"

"I don't know. I'll make some calls." McGee said and sighed. "I doubt they'll do it, but if I can arrange it, the best we can hope for is county lockup in Newark."

"Do whatever you can. It's important."

"I'll get to work on it, Len. Keep me updated if you get anything new, your special way."

"Will do, Bill."

I ended the call and let the silence stretch, weighing the shadows creeping over this case. What had I gotten myself into? Someone with the power to drive people to suicide?

Whatever connection linked that knife, Brett's death, and Anna's visions—it was serious. And I was diving in headfirst.

This wasn't just someone with a run-of-the-mill psychic ability —it was darker, more profound, and terrifying beyond anything I'd ever imagined. It hinted at powers bordering on telekinesis— the ability to manipulate objects with nothing but sheer force of mind.

Or worse—could an entity have infiltrated Brett's motor controls, seized his body like a puppeteer pulling invisible strings?

Neither possibility was promising. Both spelled serious trouble.

And then there was Kate. She'd been at the forensic van at the precise moment the knife vanished.

Could she have taken the knife?

The thought was almost laughable—I knew her well enough to dismiss the idea that she'd steal something. But if not her, then who?

And where on earth could the knife have vanished to? I'd driven her back to her office afterward, and nothing seemed out of place. This meant the theft had to have happened just before she arrived.

Something else gnawed at me—the red pickup truck. I'd spotted it speeding off, a glaring anomaly in that pristine, affluent neighborhood. It reminded me of the same truck that had nearly run me down outside the restaurant when I met April.

The coincidence was too strange to ignore.

With mounting urgency, I input Darren's number.

He picked up on the first ring. "Ward."

"Darren? It's Len Wise."

"Hey, Doc. You in my area?"

"No, Mountainview. But I've got a situation."

"Spill it."

"Remember that fancy knife Claude Vandersteen stole?"

"The fancy one he used to slice up that poor girl, and tried to use it on Erica Marconi? I'd like to forget it. Big thing, all silver and gold, wavy, right?"

"That's the one. The owner's dead—under suspicious circumstances—and the knife's gone missing."

"A death and a theft. Do you think it connects to the Vandersteen case?"

"Anyone involved with Vandersteen needs a closer look. Maybe we should talk to our mutual friend, make sure Erica has someone watching her back."

Darren knew exactly who I meant—Anthony Marconi, the crime boss whose niece I had helped save. Marconi had arranged for Darren to guard me when things turned dangerous.

"Do you think Erica is in danger?"

"I can't say. But if this ties back to Vandersteen's mess, she could be. We need to tread carefully."

"I'm on it. I'll shake up the right circles, check out his contacts at Vanderbilt College."

"Right. He was a student there before he snapped. You might want to check out that abandoned church he used for his rituals."

I heard Darren chuckle. "No can do. The college bought the property and bulldozed everything—the church, the empty school, all of it."

"Good riddance."

"I'll let you know what I find," Darren promised before ending the call.

My gut churned. The pieces were falling into place, but the full picture was far from clear—and whatever truth lay beneath, I was worried about what it could mean.

At noon, I slid into my car and headed over to Bloomdale to catch an Aikido class with my martial arts instructor, Ashwan.

The class was open to intermediate-level students, though I knew I was still very much a beginner. Several men and one woman wearing crisp white clothes sparsely filled the room.

We waited as the quiet hum of anticipation rippled through us.

As the class began, we moved through warm-up exercises that made us look like we were rowing a boat in perfect, synchronized rhythm. Then we clasped our hands together, shaking out the tension, followed by slow, deliberate circles and stretches that coaxed our bodies awake.

It felt good to move, to shake free of the dull ache that had settled in my muscles.

Ashwan stood at the front—a short, compact Asian man with a close-cropped haircut and a round, expressive face. The years etched in his skin suggested he was somewhere between sixty and eighty-five, but his movements betrayed the nimbleness of a man half his age. He thrived in these moments, guiding us patiently, a genuine smile lighting his features whenever a student made progress.

When we did the floor exercises where everyone else sat cross-legged on the floor, I did the best I could with my stiff right leg. This is one reason I stay in the back of the room during classes.

Weeks had passed since my last class, and my body reminded me harshly of that absence. Like any discipline, Aikido required consistency—and between the university's never-ending demands and the chaotic swirl of this semester's events, I'd neglected the dojo.

Ever since Jyanette and I had ended things, motivation had become a foreign currency. Even getting out of bed in the morning often felt like climbing a mountain.

By the time class ended, sweat dripped down my temples, soaking my *gi*. I approached Ashwan, lowering into the traditional bow. "Good class, sensei," I said quietly.

His face turned solemn as he met my eyes. "It is good you have returned," he replied. "You need to come back to regular classes."

"I've been busy," I defended myself, my voice tight. "The university's been demanding."

He stepped closer, lowering his voice so only I could hear. "I am sad to see you have started to drink again."

My heart jolted. How the hell did he know?

His gaze didn't waver. "You must be careful. You walk a hard path, and the drink will not help you."

Without another word, he bowed deeply, then turned and left the room, his footsteps echoing in the quiet.

I stood frozen, gripping my bag tightly, furious and stunned. Who did he think he was, judging me? If I wanted to drink, it was my choice—and I was careful not to when I had work at GSU or when I went out with McGee. I craved the drink to silence the nightmares—the haunting memories that had ruined my sleep in the months since Jyanette and I split.

I simmered with anger as I drove home.

I forced myself to calm down as I got in the shower. The door shut behind me, steam fogging the mirror as I scrubbed away the sweat and fatigue.

As I dressed, my phone buzzed—a text from April.

Today is busy.

Dinner tomorrow?

I replied quickly that tomorrow would be fine. I had work to do: papers awaited me; grades to complete; emails to send to students hoping for good news.

But even as I tried to focus, my thoughts drifted back to Anna's words. Why did she want to meet me?

The chilling confession—that she had seen a man kill himself —in her mind.

I had to ask myself, what could she have to do with all of this?

6. RAT'S TALE

I eased the van into the cramped parking lot, maneuvering it beneath the faded neon sign that blinked a red circular logo above the word "Mindy's" in bright, chipped yellow letters.

Through the diner's glass door, I spotted Carl Sokolov, the owner and Anna's father, stationed behind the cash register.

Carl was about average height, with thick, dark hair receding into a pronounced widow's peak and a bushy mustache that twitched with any word he spoke. Grease stains marred his once-white shirt along the sleeves, silently showing how he juggled every role here: cook, server, cashier, and cleaner.

As soon as I stepped inside, he caught sight of me. "Hey! My Wonder Man!" His thick Ukrainian accent framed the words warmly as he abandoned the register and wrapped me in a rugged hug. Pulling back, Carl studied my face with a sharp glint in his eyes. "You want a booth? Some food? It's on me, eh?"

"No, thanks, Carl," I said, shaking my head. "Actually, I'm here to see your daughter, if that's all right with you."

Carl's face softened with gratitude. "You saved her life from those evil men." His smile wavered, replaced by a shadow of concern. "Anna's been distant—moody. But she still talks about you... all the time. After that mess back in September... when the MPD trouble started? She was terrified for you. Said she couldn't sleep until she knew you were safe."

"I came out of that in one piece," I said.

"Go on back to the banquet room. I'll send her out."

The tension in my chest intensified as I nodded, weaving my way toward the diner's back section. The banquet room was odd for a small-town eatery: maroon carpeting stretched underfoot, focused around a polished wooden dance floor. Crystals from the chandeliers above tumbled broken light across the tables, their surfaces gleaming under the dim bulbs like secrets waiting to be told.

I slipped into the booth McGee and I once used, memories flickering—weeks spent dissecting cases, sharing plans.

Anna entered hesitantly. She looked older than the last time I saw her. Her once-flowing blonde hair was now streaked with dark roots, pulled back tightly into a ponytail. The dark circles under her eyes matched the worry that seemed to ripple off her in waves. She was growing into a woman; I saw strength beneath her fragile hesitation.

I stood as she approached.

"Thanks for coming," she muttered, making her way to the table.

"Please, sit," I replied and gestured at the chair across from me. She tentatively walked over, afraid of making a wrong move. I returned to my chair and patted her hand. I thought in a friendly way, but it made her jump.

"Sorry," I murmured, leaning back. "Didn't mean to startle you."

She stared at her tangled fingers, her voice barely audible. "No… I just need to… talk."

Her mind suddenly poured into my awareness—fragmented thoughts spilling like water from a broken bottle.

God, he's so handsome. He's better looking than I remember…

"Anna," I said, my voice steady despite the overload. "I'm picking up your thoughts right now."

"What?" she gasped.

Did he just read my mind? Please, no… I'll just die…

"Try this," I urged her. "Imagine a barricade—white walls, plain nothingness—all around your mind. It'll shut out the noise."

She bit her lip, guilt flashing in her eyes.

He read my thoughts. This was stupid! God, I am so stupid…

"No," I said firmly, taking her hand gently. "You're not stupid at all, but you have no control. You're pushing your thoughts into my head like water flooding a dam. I'll block it, but you need to focus on what you want to say with your words."

As I released her hand, I closed my eyes and gathered my own mental defenses. I didn't want to drown in the tide of teenage confusion.

When I opened them, Anna's eyelids fluttered open slowly—her breaths even, the hard-won calm etched in her features.

"Better?" I asked.

She flushed deeply. "Better," she whispered, almost shyly.

"What's got you so terrified?" I pressed.

She drew in a shaky breath; the redness fading. "After that… thing last year, I figured out my mind hears other people's thoughts. Like whispers—or shadows creeping in a crowded room."

I nodded knowingly. "That happens to me all the time."

"Really?" she asked hopefully.

"Try the walls. The white walls. It's a shield. It takes practice, but you'll get there."

She exhaled with relief. "Okay. I'll try."

Leaning forward, I lowered my voice. "Now. Tell me about what you saw: the man who killed himself. Was it Sunday night?"

Her eyes brightened faintly. "Yes."

"Was he in a room with glass cases? Filled with weapons? Frost covering everything?"

Her mouth dropped open. "That's it! You… saw it too?"

"I did. Just yesterday. The event really happened—he really did it."

Anna's gaze dropped. "No. The voice… it made him do it. The echo."

I felt a chill up my spine and recalled the words I had heard in my vision.

I am an echo of what was…

I spoke. "I heard a voice too, but just briefly."

She looked up sharply. "No, it was all the time. The entire time."

Does he think I'm pretty…

I glanced away. "Anna, you're leaking again—best not to look right at me."

Her cheeks flamed; she averted her gaze while silently battling to rebuild her mental barriers.

"What do you mean, the entire time?" I pressed.

She traced the lines on the table. "The man talked to the echo. It made him stab himself. I… I felt every second—felt the pain."

"That can happen," I said softly. "Visions pull you in."

"Does it happen to you?"

I laughed lightly, the sound hollow. "More than I want it to."

Her voice dwindled. "Last night I got another one, too. I saw a black woman, tied to a chair... scared stiff. In a nightmare of a room. And there was a man—holding a scalpel."

I shook my head, not sure what to think. "About 9 o'clock?"

"I think so. I was getting ready for bed."

The timing shocked me—April, and I shared the same vision at that exact moment.

I nodded. "Don't freak out, but I saw it too."

"Really?" She dared to meet my gaze for a flicker before looking away. "How is that possible?"

"I don't know."

"I'm scared. If the echo made that man kill himself... could it do the same to me?"

"I doubt it. Any idea who this 'Echo Man' is?"

"A ghost, maybe?" Her voice dropped to a whisper.

I shook my head. "Ghosts cause chaos, but forcing someone to take their own life? That's something else."

Her eyes remained fixed on the table. "I've seen ghosts."

"So have I."

A rare quiet hung between us, broken only by a tentative hope in her voice. "Does that mean I'm not crazy?"

"No," I said, meeting her eyes now—steady and sure. "Not crazy. It means you have a powerful ability, but you don't know how to control it yet."

She frowned, searching for answers in her eyes. "Could I learn to control it?"

I paused, considering the best way to help her. "I could bring you a few books—some that cover the basics of mental discipline and control."

Her lips curled into a reluctant smile. "Great. More homework."

I chuckled softly, relieved to hear some humor despite the gravity of the situation.

She glanced up at me with something almost vulnerable in her gaze. "Could... you... teach me?"

I tightened my mental defenses out of habit. Nothing slipped through, but I felt her thoughts pushing—probing—trying to breach my barriers. It was almost like she needed connection, craved understanding.

"That's possible," I said cautiously, "but we should start with the books. What year are you? Junior?"

Her posture snapped straight as if I'd insulted her. "No, I'm a senior."

A smile crept onto my face despite myself. "No offense. Last year I thought you were a sophomore."

She pouted, voice tinged with irritation. "No, I was a junior."

He thinks I'm a little girl...

I caught the silent thought, an unspoken challenge thrown my way.

"Keep your mental barricades in place," I warned, slightly annoyed she'd gotten through my defenses. "And no, I don't think you're a little girl."

Her face changed, the weight of reality crashing down. "What should I do? I mean... I saw a man get killed."

I steadied myself; I had to present a strong front. "The police are involved. They even called me in to help with the investigation. But if anything like that happens again, call me. Anytime—day or night."

She frowned, doubt flickering. "Really? On Sunday, it was like three in the morning."

My tone remained calm but resolute. "It's not a problem—not with this. Actually, since we're both off for the holidays, we could start some basic mental training. Would that work?"

She let out a sigh heavy with obligations. "I have this week of school left… then my dad wants me working at the diner over the holidays. He needs the help."

"We can work around that," I assured her. "Besides, you have my number now. Was that your cell phone you called me with today?"

She nodded and pulled a bright pink phone from her pocket. "It's new. Poppa got it for me so he can always get in touch."

"Alright. But remember—if you get another vision, like with the Echo Man, you call me. Anytime. Day or night. Do you understand?"

She bit her lower lip, eyes serious, then nodded slowly. "I understand."

I drove home, the weight of the day pressing down on me as I prepared to finish grading the papers scattered across my desk. December's early darkness came swiftly, casting long shadows through the windows by the time it was 4:30.

Just as I settled into my chair, Mrs. Higgins appeared in the doorway of my sitting room, carrying that familiar calm with her.

"I'll be cooking supper for us both," she announced gently.

I nodded, grateful. "Thank you, Mrs. Higgins." As she left, I returned reluctantly to the work, the ticking clock a steady reminder that the evening—and my solitude—would not last much longer.

At 6:00 sharp, her voice called from the dining room, "Dinner's ready, Doctor." I pushed myself up, my muscles aching and stiff from both an earlier, grueling workout and hours of sitting still in one place.

She had set a simple but inviting meal on the kitchen table: a vibrant pasta primavera in bright red sauce with fresh vegetables. Despite her Irish roots, Mrs. Higgins had mastered Italian cuisine with an ease that always impressed me.

She sat down across from me and asked, "Finished with your paperwork, are ye?"

I exhaled deeply, rubbing the ache from my lower back. "I think so. I'll send out the grades to the students tomorrow. Then, at last, I'm free until the new year."

Her eyes lingered on me. "Will ye be seeing that lady again?"

"April? Yes, we're going out tomorrow," I replied, the mention of her name bringing a soft smile to my face.

"That's good..." she said thoughtfully, then leaned forward. "And what about that case McGee has you tangled up in? The man killed by his own knife?"

I nodded, pushing my plate slightly away. "It's complicated, Mrs. Higgins. A real puzzle. Tell me—have you ever heard of a ghost making someone act against their will?"

Mrs. Higgins's face darkened, eyes narrowing slightly as if recalling something unsettling. "Well... according to the old legends, a ghost can make a body do things the living never intended. Take the phantom rat, for example—"

"The tale of a rat, or the rat's tail?" I interrupted, grinning.

"Yer not helpin', Doctor. Many years ago, as the story goes—" She caught herself.

"Which I suppose is better than 'once upon a time,'" I teased.

"Hush now, listen closely. A young man was courting a girl—as young men often do—but one day as he chased after her, love-struck and hopeful, she stopped and pointed to a dead rat in the gutter. Then she said plain as day, 'I'd as soon marry that rat as you.'"

I raised an eyebrow. "Sounds like rejection to me."

"Aye, and the boy took it hard, wasting away until he died. But the story didn't end there. After his funeral, the young woman found herself haunted by a rat—only, this one was no ordinary rat. It came to her by night."

I leaned in, intrigued despite myself. "Really?"

"True indeed, even with her mother and sisters watching over her," Mrs. Higgins said with a solemn nod. "Aye. She received several bites from the beast. They called the priest, but even he could not stop the rat. Finally, she made plans to leave Ireland altogether, to escape the creature. She scraped together whatever money she could and bought a ticket to Australia."

"To run away from the problem," I murmured, picturing the desperation in her eyes.

"Ye must let me finish," Mrs. Higgins warned. "As the ship pulled away from the quay, the crowd watched in horror as an enormous rat with eyes like burning embers galloped to the edge of the dock. It let out a terrible scream before leaping into the water. No one ever saw that rat again, and from then on, the girl was free of the haunting."

She stood, giving a playful bow. I smiled, applauding softly. "A fine story, Mrs. Higgins. But I don't see how it is any help to me."

She smiled quietly, smoothing her apron. "Not yet, ye don't."

I sighed. "You always say that."

"And I'm usually right, don't ye know?" She winked. "And that's why I'm here—to remind ye the answer might hide where ye least expect it."

I spent the evening painstakingly combing through the final galleys of my book, freshly sent by the publisher for a last review. Each page demanded my full attention, every sentence weighed and measured, intent on catching any glaring errors before the story went to print.

Only after hours of this at my desk did I finish. I retreated to my bedroom and flicked on the television, its dull glow casting shadows across the walls. I brought with me my familiar bottle of brandy, sipping with a sense of false comfort.

When I finally shut the TV off and undressed for bed, an unexpected chill ran through me as I glanced at the empty bottle.

How had it gone so fast? I'd always told myself I was in control —that I could stop anytime.

It was the same refrain I'd heard countless times in those AA meetings I used to attend, each person convinced their discipline was ironclad. But we all knew the truth: alcohol doesn't let you quit until the last drop.

Worse still, the craving tugged at me—an insidious, gnawing hunger for more. A flicker of fear tightened my chest as I wondered if control was merely an illusion. I plugged in my phone to charge and crawled into bed, determined to ignore the growing urge.

But as I lay there in the dark, the relentless thought went through my mind over and over: if only I could have more to drink, just a little, maybe I'd feel better. I fought it down and finally slipped into sleep.

But the night was restless. Somewhere between dreams and waking, I heard my phone ringing—sharp, piercing. It blended in a nightmare that included me trapped in my office, drowning beneath an ever-growing mountain of papers to grade, and the pile expanded faster than I could tackle it.

Then abruptly I jolted awake, my heart pounding in the pitch-black room.

Moonlight and streetlights filtered weakly through the sheer curtains, illuminating gently falling snow that muffled the usual city noise.

The phone rang again. I struggled to my feet, surprised at the sluggishness that held me captive—how much had I drunk? Stumbling to my bedside table, the faint light revealed the caller's name on the screen: Anna Sokolov. I had linked her number to the call she'd made the day before.

"Hello?" I croaked, checking the clock: 1:30 a.m.

"Doctor?" Anna's voice trembled with urgency.

"What is it, Anna?" I demanded, suddenly alert despite the fog in my head.

She babbled, her words laced with panic. "I saw something... the voice—the Echo Man... he's trying to make a girl slash her wrists."

My stomach twisted. "Calm down, Anna. Walk me through it."

"I woke up thinking I heard him talking, like he was right there in someone's bedroom. The girl... she's scared. Dark hair, about my age."

A chill shot down my spine. The alcohol dulled my psychic senses, but I latched onto what she said. "Your age? This girl—do you know who?"

"No," Anna whispered. "But he kept saying, 'You were supposed to die.' It was horrifying."

"What else did you see?"

Her voice trembled. "She woke up, sat up in bed, whispering, 'Who's there?' But the voice just laughed and kept saying she was meant to die."

"Did she try to call for help?"

"No. She got out of bed, stumbling like her legs didn't work, you know? She whispered 'Stop,' but kept moving down the hall."

"Could she control herself?"

"I don't think so. The voice kept repeating, 'You were supposed to die' as she made her way downstairs. She nearly fell on the stairs."

My throat tightened. "Then?"

"She went into the basement, pulled the string for a light switch, and there was a workbench covered with box cutters, razors, all the things… That's when I called you."

"Can you see her now?"

"I don't know how. I'll try."

Although my psychic senses were not functional, I knew in an instant who the victim was.

"Hold on for a minute, I have to call someone," I said, putting Anna on hold and inputting Darren Ward's number.

After several rings, he answered with a groggy, "Somebody better be dead."

"Erica Marconi. She's about to kill herself."

"What?" Darren snapped awake. "Where? Who's with her?"

"In the basement of her house. Call someone—anyone—do it now!"

"Are you serious?"

"There's no time!"

He ended the call. Sweat pricked at my temples as I clicked back to Anna. "Anna, I'm back."

"Blood," Anna whispered suddenly. "Oh God, there's blood."

"Is she alive?"

"I'm not sure... There's movement... something..."

"Anna?"

"It's gone—I lost it. I'm sorry. I don't know what I'm doing. Maybe the Echo Man's gone."

"You heard his voice? Like last time?"

"Yes." She sounded crushed. "I feel so useless."

"No. You have a gift. When I started, mine would only get random flashes. But I learned to control it... to summon it when needed."

"What about when you sleep?"

"Sometimes things slip in uninvited."

"Why me? Why these visions?"

We both fell silent as my phone buzzed again—it was Darren.

"Hold on, Anna," I said quickly, switching over. "What's the situation?"

"Len, it's crazy. They found Erica. She tried to slash her wrists, but they stopped her. She's alive, and an ambulance's en route."

Relief flooded through me. "Thank God."

"Thing is—she says she didn't do it."

I whispered, "The Echo Man... This might be possession. Someone forcing her."

"Seriously?"

"Find out if her family will let me visit her. I want to talk to her."

"I'll arrange it, call you in the morning."

"Thanks, Darren."

As the call ended, I returned to Anna.

"She's safe," I reassured her. "You probably saved her."

"There was blood…"

"I know. But you did great for someone just starting out."

"Really?"

"Yes. Thank you for calling me."

"I wasn't sure you'd want to hear from me."

"I'm impressed, not mad. Now, I have an unusual question. Do you have a religious symbol? Something meaningful?"

"A cross. It was my mother's."

"Place it near your bed. If you believe in it—it can protect you."

"Will I be safe?"

"For now. Whoever is doing this, they must be burning through energy fast—I doubt he'll try again tonight."

"I'll do that, Doctor."

"Call me Len, please."

"Okay… Len."

"I'll call tomorrow and drop by some books."

I hung up and stared at my smartphone. Drinking had muted my powers, leaving me useless. If Anna hadn't called, Erica Marconi would be dead.

It had to link back to Claude Vandersteen—the madman who meant to sacrifice Erica to his demonic god, a plan I thwarted.

But had others in his twisted cult succeeded? Worse, had someone replicated or enhanced the drug he'd used, granting remote viewing, telekinesis, possibly even mental possession?

If true, this shattered everything I believed about extrasensory perception.

Yet, Claude's creation drove him insane. What price would the man doing this now pay?

I staggered back to bed, setting my phone on the nightstand—ready for another call. I lay down, sure that I would never get back to sleep, but in a few brief minutes I drifted off.

7. FALLEN FACSIMILE

I woke the next morning with a groggy haze clouding my thoughts and a relentless headache pounding in my skull.

Through the frosted window, a thin layer of snow blanketed the world outside, coating trees and rooftops in a deceptive freshness. It looked pristine, tranquil even, but not enough to slow anyone down today.

Grimacing, I went to the kitchen and poured a cup of coffee, its warmth a minor comfort against my mounting tension. Settling back into my sitting room, I fired up my laptop and dialed Darren Ward's number. The line rang twice before a rasping voice answered, rough and tired.

"Ward," he croaked.

"It's Len Wise," I said. "How's Erica?"

I could hear the faint tap-tap of keys beneath his words. "Alive, thanks to you. I just spoke with her father, Dominic. He says you can visit her in the hospital if it helps."

He hesitated before the next words fell. "Len… do you even understand what happened?"

I braced myself. "Someone's targeting anyone connected to the Vandersteen case."

He sighed, his voice heavy. "Great. Anything you need, I'll help. I'll talk to my contacts at the NYPD—maybe there's something we missed before."

"I appreciate it," I said. "Call me if you find anything."

After hanging up, my eyes drifted to my bedroom, the unmade bed haunting me like a ghost. I saw Jyanette—the way her dark skin gleamed against the crisp white sheets, the mornings when I'd bring her breakfast and we'd eat naked, our laughter mingling with the scent of coffee.

Here I sat, utterly alone. The surrounding silence was suffocating.

Had I not drained that last bottle last night, I might have reached for a drink just to drown the aching emptiness.

But no, there was work to do.

It was Wednesday, just a week before Christmas Eve. Sitting here nursing my wounds wouldn't help Erica or anyone else caught in this shadow.

My fingers trembled slightly as I dialed Kate's number, hoping she'd have access to Stan's files on the Vandersteen case—or at least know where to look for them.

She picked up immediately, her voice sharp but tired. "Hey, how's my chauffeur feeling?"

"Kate, how are you holding up?"

"Drowsy. Bad dreams again. I keep seeing the guy with the knife—the one from Blackshale—coming for me."

A shiver ran through me. "I called you about that very thing."

"Do tell."

I swallowed hard. "Last night, I had a vision of Jyanette tied up, and a man with a scalpel coming at her."

A pause. Then I caught the bite in Kate's tone. "You getting inside my head, Len?"

"Believe me, it came unbidden. I was… kissing someone when it hit me."

"Oh, so you went out with Miss High-and-Mighty-Don't-Touch-My-Stuff," she teased harshly. "Did you get past first base?"

Her jabs, though familiar, stung more than usual today, but I let them slide. "Kate, I know it's been a rough few months for you —"

"Yeah? And now you're stealing my dreams, too?" Her voice sharpened with frustration.

"Kate, I did nothing of the sort," I said, my patience thinning.

She went on, anger simmering beneath the surface. "Just like September, when you pulled those memories out of my mind. My brain isn't your playground, Wise."

"That was different," I argued. "You helped me figure out who set you up."

"I never said you had carte blanche to invade my thoughts whenever you wanted."

The words hit hard. Anger flared inside me. "You're not listening, Kate. That vision forced itself on me—I didn't want it."

Another silence. Then, softer. "It did?"

"Yes. It was unlike anything I've ever felt."

"That is the dream I keep having—the one before he did… what he did to me."

My voice softened. "Kate, you've come so far. Some doctors thought you'd never wake or walk again. They were wrong."

She exhaled sharply. "I want to get off my ass and do some proper work."

"Good, then help me. Stan Frazier worked with me on a Staten Island case—two girls abducted, a cult called 'The Following.'"

She exhaled. "I remember. Stan got stabbed by the perp—Claude Vandersteen—and that's why he quit."

"Can you pull those files for me?"

"Why? What are you looking for?"

"I don't know yet. But anything on Claude's followers or associates might help. I asked McGee to bring his partner down here so I could question him."

"I read the file," she said. "Antoine Powell, right? But he was just one of Vandersteen's followers."

"Can you check if the FBI did any follow-up?"

Kate's voice turned resigned. "So more paperwork, huh? Okay, I'll see what I can do, Len."

I tried to lighten the mood. "What about the holidays? Visiting family?"

"Getting personal, aren't you? No. I'm alone this year. But I'll let you know what I find."

She hung up, leaving me with my swirling thoughts.

I shook my head, the erratic dance of Kate's moods—mad, mocking, vulnerable—a reflection of my turmoil. If she was on antidepressants, I understood why she was a tinderbox of emotions.

None of us should recover alone from trauma that ran deeper than bruises or broken hearts.

Life doesn't spare anyone.

Steeling myself, I dialed Walt Addison—professor of religious studies and chemistry at Vanderbilt College, Staten Island—Claude's mentor and the man whose lab had birthed the sinister blend of henbane and local weeds that fueled Claude's twisted mental powers.

The phone rang several times before Walt answered, cautiously. "Hello?"

"Walt, it's Len Wise."

"Len! I thought you'd forgotten me! I'm on vacation."

"We both are. How'd your semester go?"

"Busy. People keep thinking I'm some kind of chemist wizard cooking up hallucinogens."

"Got some time today? I'll be on Staten Island. I could take you to lunch. I want to pick your brain."

He chuckled. "I never turn down a free meal. What time?"

"One o'clock. You pick the place and text me."

"Will do."

The traffic was a slow crawl as I drove over the turnpike towards the Goethals Bridge. December in New York City has its own brand of madness, especially anywhere near a mall. The Staten Island Expressway—more like Staten Island Parking Lot—tested my patience as I crawled towards the Richmond Road exit.

Finally, I pulled into Staten Island University Hospital and parked in their overfull lot.

I went inside, had my ID checked, photo snapped, badge printed—all routine except for the heaviness settling in my chest.

Dominic Marconi greeted me outside Erica's room, tired but grateful. Her mother stood quietly nearby. Erica lay on the bed, face pale, a bandage wrapped around one wrist.

"Thanks for coming, Doctor," Dominic said, offering his hand.

I shook it. "I'm glad she's going to be okay."

Dominic glanced at his daughter, then back at me. "She says she didn't do this—that something made her do it." His voice cracked. "Do you think that's possible?"

"She's not the only one, Mister Marconi," I said quietly but firmly, meeting his eyes. "Do you have a family priest? Someone your daughter trusts?"

He furrowed his brow. "Yeah. Father Daniels."

"Good." I stepped closer. "Ask him to bless Erica's room. Maybe give her a religious symbol—something she believes in. It might help."

He frowned deeper, uncertainty heavy on his face. "Will that fix it? Will it stop… whatever this is?"

I hesitated, reluctance tightening my throat. "It'll help," I said. "Anything to give her strength."

He nodded slowly, then called over a woman seated nearby. "Isabella, the doctor needs to talk to Erica… alone."

The woman's gentle hand found Erica's uninjured arm. Rising, she glanced at me with a weary nod before they both left the room.

Once the door closed, I sank into the chair Isabella had vacated and faced Erica. She looked so small, so fragile under the harsh hospital lights.

"Seems like I only ever see you in a hospital," I said.

Her eyes bore fear—not just the fear of pain but something darker, deeper. "Believe me, I didn't do this," she whispered.

"I know," I said softly. "You said there was a voice in your head?"

She lowered her gaze to the bandage wrapped around her wrist. "Yeah. It kept saying I was supposed to have died."

"Tell me what you heard."

Her voice was barely audible. "I woke up last night and my room was freezing—so cold I could see my breath. Then that voice started."

"The one that told you that you should have died?"

She nodded. "Yeah, but it was weird. This man's voice, but it was like two people speaking the same words."

"Keep going."

"I wanted to stay in bed, but..." Her eyes flickered up, meeting mine with a sudden brightness.

"You got out of bed," I prompted, "but it wasn't really you moving. Right?"

Her eyes widened. "Exactly. It was like... I was a puppet. Someone else was making me do it." Her voice cracked, tears spilling down her cheeks. "Do you believe me?"

I nodded. "Actually, I do."

"You're the first person who does."

I swallowed the lump in my throat and was brutally honest. "Erica, the same thing happened to another person. He didn't make it."

Fear pooled in her wide eyes. "He... he died?"

I nodded gravely. "He stabbed himself with a knife—the same one Vandersteen almost used on you when he abducted you last year."

Confusion crept across her face. "How did he get it?"

"He was the man who owned it. It's old—a collector's piece. But more importantly, can you tell me more about the voice you heard?"

She trembled, her voice barely a whisper. "I knew it."

"Knew it?"

"Yes," she breathed. "It was him."

"Him?"

She glanced nervously at the door before leaning in and whispering, "Vandersteen."

My brow furrowed. "Are you sure? I was there when he died. I held him as he took his last breath in that church where he held you prisoner."

She shook her head, panic tightening her features. "The voice —I know it was his. It'll haunt me forever."

I clenched my fists, the bitter truth settling in.

That voice… maybe it wasn't really him. Maybe it was something worse—an echo of something he left behind.

A voice from beyond the grave.

An hour later, I pushed open the door of a dimly lit restaurant called "The Road House" on Clove Street. The muffled hum of conversation and clinking glasses greeted me like a familiar, uneasy lullaby.

Through the crowd, I spotted Walt Addison hunched over one of the plain wooden tables tucked into a corner by the vast windows. His frame was unmistakable—stocky, below-average height, with a full beard peppered with stubborn strands of white like frost caught in summer.

I threaded my way through the throng of diners, the air thick with the scent of fried food and beer, my heart picking up pace.

Though his full name was Walter, all of us who had studied with him in Doctor Kohl's parapsychology class that year called him "Walt"—sometimes, fondly, "Uncle Walt." The nickname had nothing to do with Walt Disney, but because of one woman's offhand remark that he felt like a "favorite uncle," a comforting figure in a sea of strange new ideas. Walt wore the affectionate title with quiet pride.

It had been six months since I last spoke with him, but this was the first time we'd actually met face-to-face after our time working with Doctor Kohl. He'd graduated at the end of our first year, but we were closer in age than our classmates, and that made us fast friends back then.

Walt was affable, with a dry wit that could ease any tension—and an intellect that straddled the worlds of religion and chemistry with equal ease. Though he had no psychic gifts himself, the strange realm of parapsychology had called to him like a siren, an odd curiosity merging his passions for comparative religions and scientific inquiry.

As I neared, Walt stood up and caught me in a solid bear hug. I had to bend at the waist to accommodate his shorter frame, the contrast between our heights striking. The warmth of his embrace felt oddly reassuring, like coming home after wandering through a dark forest.

We settled into the sturdy wooden chairs, the hum of the restaurant pressing in around us.

Walt gestured toward the half-full glass of beer in front of him. "You want one? I'm on vacation until January, might as well enjoy it."

His tone was light, but there was an undercurrent of something else—calculation, perhaps even a flicker of worry hidden beneath the casual veneer.

I shook my head. "Maybe a non-alcoholic beer. I'm driving." My voice was steady, but tension crept into my chest like an icy hand.

As if summoned, a young waitress with blonde hair and a slender frame approached us swiftly, cutting through the noise as she called out, "Hey, Walt!"

"Gina!" Walt's face brightened with a grin.

Her eyes flicked to me. "What'll you have?"

"A non-alcoholic beer, please," I said.

She rattled off options until I chose one. Then he ordered a meatball hero, and I got a salad.

She winked at Walt and drifted away like a feather on a breeze.

"You two know each other?" I asked, curiosity nudging at me.

Walt leaned in, voice dropping. "I'm here all the time—just a couple of blocks from college and my place. Plus, I get a discount." He grinned. "And I've dated Gina a few times."

I glanced toward the busy server. "She seems young."

"Twenty-eight. Single mom. We keep it casual. I don't want complications, and she definitely doesn't."

I nodded absently, reflecting on the strange era we lived in. A world where relationships were casual, emotions packaged like fast food. Where people ordered meals on their phones and hooked up through apps.

The thought left a bitter taste in my mouth. Sometimes, I felt like a fossil—a relic who wanted something real: a partner, a family, a home with a mortgage and children's laughter.

Shaking off my spiraling thoughts, I fixed my gaze on Walt. "I need your advice. Strange things have been happening."

He nodded knowingly. "I figured something was up if you were coming out here."

"What do you know about spiritual possession?"

Walt's eyes drifted upward, fingering an invisible bead on the ceiling as he pondered. "Well, all the major world religions accept possession in some form. The idea stretches back beyond Christianity—ancient Egypt, the emperor cults of China…"

"And what about a modern view?" I urged.

He shrugged. "Modern psychologists? Freud killed it. The medieval Church called the spirits demons, philosophers talked about ghosts… Some myths say possession comes from violent or untimely death. Spirits grabbing hold of a living body to finish what they couldn't while alive."

This concept fit Claude Vandersteen perfectly. The man had died from a police bullet during an occult ritual—a human sacrifice to raise a demon.

"That helps," I said, swallowing hard. "Now for a tricky question. You worked with Claude, right?"

Walt raised a hand. "I told the police I didn't know what he was up to in my lab."

"Not what I want to know. Did anyone continue his work... after Claude?"

He leaned back, considering. "He kept extensive notes. The FBI raided his dorm. No idea if they found them."

"Did he work with anyone? Collaborators?"

"That guy, Antoine Powell—his driver, and not much more than an acquaintance. After I learned Claude was making drugs and Powell was a junkie, it made sense." Walt's voice darkened. "Powell's in prison, right?"

"Yes, accessory to murder for the death of Connie Newhouse. I have my police contacts arranging for him to meet with me. Did Claude have a roommate?"

"Yes, Dan Cressley. He's graduated since then. No clue where he is now. Claude was popular; it shocked his classmates when they found out about his dark side. One woman—best student of mine—dated him for two years, then transferred after everything fell apart."

"Any chance she could recreate Claude's drug?"

Walt's face grew serious. "You don't get it, Len. My father taught chemistry, and I've been in this field my whole life. I've seen many compounds—but what Claude concocted? It's beyond me. The plants he used can be deadly if mixed wrong. Synthesizing that drug was incredibly complex."

"But Vandersteen did it."

"Exactly. But only someone crazy enough to experiment on themselves would try. It's got a Jekyll and Hyde danger to it."

"I know, I confronted him when he was in the Hyde persona."

Our talk paused as Gina returned with our food. "You okay for now?" she asked, bright-eyed.

"We're fine, thanks," Walt replied, taking a messy bite of his meatball hero.

After she left, I pressed, "Are you sure no one else has the skill to make Vandersteen's drug?"

Walt sighed, setting down his sandwich. "My best guess? No. I think Claude used 'biological scaffolding'—a complex synthetic method."

"Do you have the equipment for that in the lab?"

"For a university, we're state-of-the-art. Claude was lucky to have tools usually found only in industrial labs."

I stuck my fork in a broccoli spear in my salad. "So, someone would need serious resources and knowledge?"

"Absolutely. Even a chemist with a master's degree couldn't do it without the right gear."

I chewed thoughtfully. "But suppose someone stole his notes, and has the lab and the know-how. Then what?"

Walt shook his head. "They'd still need Claude's brilliance. Mad or not, he was gifted. That's the reason I let him use the lab whenever he wanted."

"Even making narcotics in your lab?"

"I didn't know he was making drugs. I saw the talent and I wanted to nurture it. Without that innate skill, no one could replicate his work."

"What if they had Claude's help—from beyond?"

Walt stopped chewing and looked at me sharply. "Claude's dead. Period."

"But from your religious studies point of view, what if he's reaching out from beyond the grave?"

Walt shook his head. "Len, Joseph Campbell once said, 'Buddhists don't dream of Christ.' Your god shapes the ghosts you see."

"So?"

"Academics say ghosts are psychological constructs. The human brain creates visions that aren't there. Someone might think Claude's visiting. But would it help them recreate complex chemical formulas? Doubtful."

His logic was sound—even soothing—yet a tiny, restless part of me refused to settle. What if someone really could speak to Claude's spirit? What if they learned the secrets hidden in the shadows?

What then?

The question lingered between us, heavier than any drug—darker and impossible to shake off.

8. RESOUNDING REALIZATIONS

I still had one more task before meeting Darren—a lingering doubt I couldn't ignore.

Sliding out of the restaurant parking lot, I followed the familiar signs pointing toward Vanderbilt College. As I neared campus, I veered onto the narrow side road leading to the dormitories and eased the van to a stop beside an overgrown, neglected lot.

Across the street sprawled the large parking area, locked behind a hydraulic barrier. The red-and-white plastic arm was down, blocking entry, and the lot sat mostly empty—an eerie stillness settling over the campus now that classes were out of session.

Beyond the empty expanse loomed a row of red-brick dormitories, silent and formidable.

I stepped out of the van and turned toward the dense thicket of trees and thick underbrush. A narrow path—once a well-traveled road but now choked with weeds and decay—snaked its way through the wilderness.

I carefully stepped over the weathered chain strung between two creaking wooden posts barricading the old roadway.

Up ahead, a pair of rounded stone pillars built with rough-cut stone and mortar marked the path's entrance. One pillar had fallen, leaning at a precarious angle like a wounded sentinel. A faded sign rested nearby, its letters cracked and peeling:

St. Albertus Magnus School for Boys

It was here—within the crumbling, forsaken walls—that I had my final, dangerous confrontation with Claude Vandersteen. He had taken over the empty school building as his headquarters, and the abandoned church adjacent had become his shrine to madness.

I stepped forward into the open field, where I expected to see the grim silhouette of the five-story brick schoolhouse. But the ground was bare, the earth freshly leveled and brown where the building once dominated the landscape.

My gaze flicked to the spot where the stone church had towered, bell tower piercing the sky with its sharply pitched roof. The six-story tower, once the tallest structure on these grounds, was now silent ruins, reduced to jagged piles of battered stone.

A slow breath escaped me, a mix of relief and unease. The place where Vandersteen had sacrificed Constance Newhouse and nearly killed Erica Marconi was gone—obliterated. Still, the memory clung to the air like a shadow refusing to dissipate.

Turning back to the van, a faint hope bloomed: here was a site corrupted by a monster, finally erased from this world. But it could never easily bury the darkness it harbored.

The drive to Darren's office was a quick hop on the Staten Island Expressway—though traffic made it longer than it should have been—and a few meandering back roads guided me to the crowded parking lot of his aging office building.

I spotted Darren's compact car nestled between a sleek black Lincoln Continental and several nondescript vehicles. Finding a tight space, I parked the van and moved toward the entrance.

The building was an odd mix: three stories of white stucco with an overhang on the top floor, decorated with curved red tiles instead of shingles. A matching reddish hue outlined each window frame, and this gave the facade a distinct West Coast appearance that felt out of place on the East Coast.

At the doorway loomed a massive figure that surprised me. It was a man I only knew as Pete. Broad and tall as me but built like a football player, his thick mustache twitched with a scowl as he caught sight of me.

He was the bodyguard of Anthony Marconi, whom I had dealt with in the past. On one of our previous encounters, Pete had pistol-whipped the side of my head, and I had no desire to repeat the experience.

I nodded to him and kept my tone light but edged with caution. "Pete, I hope we won't have any trouble today."

He grunted, eyes darkening. "Louie's hand ain't never been the same since you busted it with that damn cane."

I hesitated.

"You're expected," he growled, stepping aside but never letting me out of his sight.

Pete and Louie had confronted me about a year ago in Maine, trying to strong-arm me off an investigation. Luck, quick thinking, and my sturdy cane had broken Louie's hand—something Pete hadn't forgotten. His presence now was no accident, and tension tightened in my chest.

I climbed the stairs slowly, mindful of my bad leg, each step a small victory of willpower. On the third floor, I found Darren's office and knocked before stepping inside.

Darren sat at his desk as I entered. In a chair, Anthony Marconi was facing away from me.

Marconi, head of the Marconi Crime Family, and I had been on opposite sides when I met him in Maine. But after I saved his niece Erica, and he saved me with a sniper's help against a killer, we had established a shaky alliance. In our last conversation, we agreed that we'd settled our debts.

He rose, his silver-white hair catching the light—a striking resemblance to John Travolta's flair in *Saturday Night Fever*. He extended a hand, which I took cautiously.

To my surprise, he pulled me into a brief hug, and murmured in my ear, "You saved my niece again. You're like her guardian angel."

I stepped back, wary. "Mr. Marconi, you really didn't have to come all this way."

He gestured at the chair, and I sat. Marconi remained standing, urgency etched on his face.

"I need to know what to do to help my *nipote*," he said using the Italian word for niece. "If she's in danger, I have to know what you know."

I glanced at Darren, who shrugged—as if to say, "I didn't know he'd want to see you, but he's the boss."

Clearing my throat, I said, "The problem is, I know very little. A man named Brett Morgan killed himself. Like Erica—a voice—drove him and seemed to take control of his body."

Marconi's eyes narrowed. "What can I do?"

Oddly, there was no gangster bravado, only a concerned uncle's plea.

"Keep someone close to her. Religious symbols will help, if Erica believes in them," I suggested. "This is about energy. Religious symbols carry a protective power."

"Who's doing this to her?" His voice grew sharper.

I met his gaze. "Right now I don't know. Believe me, if I had any solid answers or ways to protect her, I'd share them. Whatever this is—this force I'm dealing with—it's like nothing I've ever faced."

He frowned. "I thought you knew how to handle ghosts and hauntings."

I shook my head. "This isn't a haunting. If it is a spirit, it's capable of possessing someone from a distance. Not even remotely like anything I've ever encountered."

"Let me guess," he said darkly. "Your advice is to nail up crosses and douse her room with holy water?"

"Those items carry an energy that could shield her," I insisted.

He studied me, unconvinced.

I went on. "I promise, I don't know what it is. But I *will* find out."

He looked down at me—a simple command. "Do that. Protect my niece—you hear me?"

"I honestly will. The last thing I want is for her to get hurt."

Marconi nodded, a faint smile breaking his stern demeanor. "I believe you, Doc. You saved her once; I'm betting you'll do it again."

He turned to Darren. "You'll be on top of what he knows?"

Darren nodded, his expression resolute. "Len and I will be in constant contact."

"Good," Marconi said, then turned back to me. "Do what you do, Doc. I'm counting on you."

With that he left, his figure walking slowly down the stairs like a man carrying heavy burdens.

I faced Darren, lowering my voice. "You could've warned me."

"He asked me not to tell," Darren said with a shrug. "What could I do?"

"I ran into Pete downstairs," I muttered, tension tightening my jaw. "Last time we met, it was... rough."

"Sorry, Len. Marconi's worried. He doesn't know what to do."

I shook my head, frustration burning. "Neither do I."

Darren leaned in, eyes serious. "Is there a history of people being forced to act beyond their control?"

I shrugged. "There are many tales of possession by evil spirits, but they don't fit into the scientific framework I work with."

"Isn't it enough that you were told it happened?" he pressed.

"No," I said firmly. "My way of working focuses on residual energy—trauma's imprint. It creates echoes, not spirits. When a psychic sensitive enters a location, their energy awakens these echoes. These manifestations feed on the living's mental energy—hence cold spots, manifestations, all of it."

"So the idea is," Darren mused, "there has to be someone to drain energy from. Like a vampire sucking blood."

"Not exactly the image I prefer," I replied dryly. "I've encountered possession before, but it's rare. This is different. Somehow, the consciousness reaches out remotely, to people far away."

"That's what happened with Erica," he said quietly. "This whatever-it-is used her energy to push her toward killing herself."

I shook my head. "That's not how it should work."

"So how does it work?" Darren demanded.

I rubbed my chin, the weight of uncertainty heavy. "I need more research. For both our sakes."

The room felt colder somehow, the threat still looming—unseen, unfathomable, and far from over.

On the drive back to New Jersey, a knot of irritation tightened inside me. The frustrating absence of answers gnawed at my thoughts like a relentless itch I couldn't scratch.

I phoned McGee to see how things were progressing on his end.

"Hey Len," he said on answering his phone.

"Any luck setting up an interview with Antoine Powell?" I asked.

"Actually, the NYPD has been quite helpful. They are transporting him to county lockup here in Essex County. They might let you see him as early as tomorrow."

"Good. I'm trying to get some answers, and so far, I've got nothing."

"Do you really think he can offer any help?" McGee asked. "I mean, he was basically just doing what Vandersteen told him to do."

"He might know other people who worked with Vandersteen, giving us a new place to look."

"Or he might know nothing," McGee stated.

"I won't find out until I see him."

"Just don't get your hopes up," McGee said and ended the call.

My mind churned over the unsolved mysteries and looming questions concerning Powell, but there was no escape from reality —I had to get ready for my date with April. The clock was ticking, and I knew she wouldn't appreciate being kept waiting.

I texted April, asking her where she wanted to meet.

She quickly replied with an address and the name of the restaurant: a place called Corsica 99—and a time.

Arriving home, I had some time before our date, so I poured myself a cup of coffee and settled at the kitchen table to do a final review of the galley proofs my publisher had sent.

In this digital era, I found it baffling and somewhat archaic that they still insisted on proofreading physical pages. With multiple sheets spread out before me, I meticulously scanned for errors.

Surprisingly, despite all the rewrites and editor revisions, I caught several typos and inconsistencies that had somehow slipped through—a reminder that the mind often fills in blanks without registering mistakes.

Glancing at the clock once more, I knew that the night crept closer. I wanted to research spirit possession or drop a quick email to my mentor, Dr. Fritz Kohl, but my date wasn't something I could skip or be late for.

Not a good way to start a new relationship.

Reluctantly, I put away the pages, picked out a suit, and changed quickly. On my way out the door, I decided this time, no alcohol—not again. Drinking had dulled my psychic senses before, and the attacks on Brett Morgan and Erica Marconi had caught me completely off guard. I couldn't let that happen again.

The drive felt longer than usual; the city blurring past in a haze of headlights and street lamps. Parking near Corsica 99 was a challenge; spots were scarce, but luck favored me with one on a nearby street.

I rushed to the restaurant entrance and stepped inside. The space was cozy, dimly lit, and quieter than I expected for a Friday night. I noticed a curious decoration on the far wall: a bicycle with a large metal "F" mounted on one side and a "D" on the other. With the wheels between them, it cleverly spelled out "FOOD." A small smile crept over me at the oddity.

At the back of the room, April waved me over. She looked effortlessly beautiful in simple black pants and a loose white blouse. Notably, she wasn't wearing her glasses. I guessed she'd switched to contacts for the evening. She lifted a paper bag from under the table, and I immediately suspected it held a bottle of wine.

"Oh," I said as I slid into the seat across from her, "I'm not drinking tonight."

April pouted adorably. "Oh, come on. Have a little. This place is BYOB, and there's no way I can finish an entire bottle myself." Then, with a teasing smirk, she added, "Besides, I've heard New Jersey is pretty strict about open bottles in cars, Doctor."

"Very formal," I replied with a raised eyebrow. "What happened to 'Len'?"

"Sorry," she grinned. "Len it is."

The server approached, placing two glasses and pouring the wine. I picked up the menu and scanned the items. The dishes sounded exquisite, but the prices made my stomach tighten.

Dating wasn't cheap—I'd forgotten that.

With Jyanette, it had mostly been quiet nights in, cooking and talking. Those days seemed far away now.

April took a delicate sip and fixed me with a look so intense I felt exposed. "How was your day? Any progress on Brett Morgan's case?"

"None whatsoever," I admitted. "Though I suspect there was almost another murder last night."

"Murder? Didn't Morgan kill himself?" she asked, her brow furrowing.

I hesitated, recalling how she'd pressed me for details at the crime scene. "I told you, we're investigating all scenarios."

She waved a hand dismissively. "Sorry. I'm juggling four other cases since Monday. We handle forensic work for the entire county, so we're in, process the scene, and move on fast. Actual lab analysis is a different story."

"Do you do that too?" I asked.

She smiled. "I'm assigned to the lab later this week."

"That keeps you busy," I commented.

April sighed, took a slow sip of wine, then admitted, "Crime scenes are the hardest part, especially during the holidays. Traffic's a nightmare, and we have to cordon off busy areas. People get angry."

I took a sip of the wine, cursing myself softly for giving in so easily. So much for staying sober.

"You sound frustrated," I observed.

"A little," she said, leaning back with her glass in hand. "Most people with regular jobs don't understand our hours or what we do."

"I'm a voluntary consultant," I explained. "I only get involved when something's unusual."

"So that suicide case is unusual, right?" Her eyes lit up with curiosity.

"Did I say that?"

"You have a terrible poker face, Len," she said with a sly grin. "You think it wasn't suicide."

"Have you found any evidence to suggest otherwise?" I challenged.

"Great, turn the tables on me." Her throaty chuckle filled the space just as the waitress returned to take our orders. After noting them, she refilled my glass, which I now realized was already half empty.

When had that happened?

April swirled her glass thoughtfully. "There's something curious about the room where Morgan died. It had temperature and humidity controls—probably because of the knives he stored. The system kept a log of huge temperature fluctuations that night."

"And did you find anything significant? Maybe a temperature drop near the time of death?" I pressed.

She deflated slightly. "How did you know?"

"It matches a chilling experience I had with a second victim last night."

"Another suicide?"

"No. Someone tried to kill themselves, but the family stopped them."

April leaned back, suspicion knitting her brows. "How did you find out about that? Were you called in, like at Morgan's house?"

"I have my ways," I said tightly, unwilling to reveal Anna's part in the rescue.

Her dismissive gesture returned—a newly adopted quirk that somehow softened her sharp edges. "There you go, all mysterious again."

"I thought you liked that about me."

She considered this and took another sip of wine. "Do you think someone's making people kill themselves? Is that what you're saying? That sounds pretty far-fetched."

"Not as much as you'd think," I replied quietly. "A few months ago, I was involved with a case where a hypnotherapist was programming people to be her puppets."

"Oh my God! Is that what this is about?"

"I don't think so. But right now, it's just theory. I don't have concrete evidence."

She flushed faintly. "How about that strange thing when we kissed? Was that what you do? Things like that?" Her voice dropped playfully.

"That never happened before, and I have no explanation," I confessed.

She leaned her head on one hand, challenging me with her eyes. "So, level with me—what exactly do you do?"

"It's not as exciting as it sounds," I admitted. "You probably imagine me finding lost treasure by reading the ether, but it's a lot more like what you do."

"Fingerprints and trace evidence?" she guessed.

"Sort of," I smiled. "I detect unusual energies, strange vibrations, and interpret them with my mind."

Her gaze sharpened. "Is that what happened at Scudder House?"

I took a deep breath and swallowed, surprised she had brought this up. "Scudder House was an anomaly—both times I went. You did some digging on me."

"'The super-psychic of Scudder House,'" she teased with a grin. "Yes, I looked you up online. Any smart young woman would, when dating a mysterious man."

I leaned back, raising my hands in mock surrender. "Well, it couldn't have been too bad. You agreed to meet me again."

She sighed, the playful mood dimming. "I'm still deciding. Your fiancée died in a car crash—"

"That accident crippled my leg," I interjected.

"Then there was the woman who burned to death while you were at the scene."

I met her gaze steadily. "Did you dig through police files too?"

"No, just Google," she admitted. "And your name came up with the Assistant District Attorney."

Suddenly, I was on my feet—how and when had that happened? I was breathing hard, a flare of anger threatening to overwhelm me. My voice dropped to a low growl. "Thanks for inviting me out. Seems I've lost my appetite."

"Len," she whispered, reaching to touch my hand.

I looked at her, eyes wide, apologetic.

"I just wanted to know. Please stay," she pleaded softly.

Slowly, I sank back into my chair, struggling to keep the raw wounds inside from showing. "Some things are private, and still painful," I murmured.

"I see that," she said gently.

The waitress arrived with our entrees, refilling my glass as I fought to compose myself.

"I didn't mean to pry," April apologized. "You didn't tell me much about yourself, so I did some research. Investigations are what I do, after all."

"Few people accept what I do. I don't enjoy having my life opened up to scrutiny."

"I'm sorry. I had good reasons. If I was going to date you, I needed to know. Admit it, you didn't share a lot on our first date."

"Sorry," I said, unsure why the apology spilled out. After all, I'd never searched into her past.

"I just wanted to know more about you."

"I overreacted," I confessed. Together, we ate in a comfortable silence, the tension easing.

She savored the salmon and asked, "Did you really find all that stuff at Scudder House?"

"I was part of a team. I served as a medium."

"A medium?"

"Yes. I allowed entities, or residual energies from the house, to act through me."

"What was that like?"

"I remember nothing I said during the experience. My team recorded everything, and later, the recordings helped us locate the treasure Elias Scudder had hidden behind a false basement wall."

"And you didn't get a cut? Not even a finder's fee?"

I smiled ruefully. "I'm afraid not."

She cut another piece, stabbing it with her fork. "That sucks," she said, chewing thoughtfully.

I laughed. "No worse than you being around all those priceless swords for Brett Morgan."

She frowned, a shadow flickering across her face. "I was verifying evidence at a crime scene."

I leaned in, eyes locked on hers. "Yes, but you were around those swords and knives... some of which were worth a fortune. Like I said, our jobs aren't all that different. I found artifacts at Scudder House, but the beneficiaries were the college that funded the research. The money and valuables were never mine. They were just... there when I did my job."

She studied me with a trace of skepticism lingering. "I don't know. Every kid dreams of finding treasure. I know I used to. You found one but didn't get to keep any of it."

I shook my head resolutely. "I didn't want any of *that* treasure, I assure you."

Her eyes narrowed as she leaned closer, voice dropping conspiratorially. "Was there a curse on it?"

I hesitated, the memories surfacing unbidden: the deaths that had stained the house's history, even as recently as August, when I confronted a trapped ancient entity that had poisoned the land with its malice.

"Yes," I admitted finally, the tension between us thickening. "In a way, there was. An even better reason not to take any of it."

The silence settled briefly before we resumed eating. The food was exquisite, each bite better than the last, and April kept refilling my wine glass. With each sip, the warm alcohol dulled my heightened psychic senses, letting me relax against the usual sharp edge of caution.

I told her about my sister and my twin brother—he had become a magician in Las Vegas.

Her eyes sparkled with surprise. "You're an identical twin? That's hilarious—so am I."

"Really? What does your sister do?"

"Housewife," she shrugged, a faint smile teasing her lips.

"Still in South Dakota or… here?"

"Far away," she said, leaning in and narrowing her eyes playfully. "Twins, huh? You know, that means I have to think long and hard about you."

I frowned, confused. "Why?"

"Because," she said with a sly grin, "if we have kids, they'd probably be twins too." She laughed softly, then leaned back. "Don't know if I can handle that."

I chuckled at her forwardness. "You're projecting pretty far ahead. We're only on our second date."

She leaned forward, eyes locked on mine. "A girl has to think ahead and figure out what she's getting herself into."

The meal concluded perfectly—the portions were just right, leaving neither of us hungry or bloated. I glanced at the check; it was, predictably, impressive.

But she'd brought the wine, and I told myself that was what credit cards were for. I signed, stood, and helped her with her coat. Together, we stepped out into the biting December cold.

Christmas lights blinked softly along the streets and storefronts, casting festive colors onto the snowy sidewalk.

"Where's your vehicle?" she asked, her breath puffing mist into the frosty air.

"Across the street," I said, nodding toward my van.

"Can I see it?" She followed me as we crossed.

I pressed the button on the fob, and the doors unlocked with a comforting beep.

She slid into the passenger seat gracefully. The ease of her movements contrasted with mine—I had to open my door and use the mechanical device that turned and lowered my seat so I could climb in comfortably. Once settled, I fired up the engine, welcoming the warm murmur of the heater.

"Brr," she purred, pulling her coat closer. "Pretty cold for December."

"I hope January won't be worse," I shrugged.

She glanced around the cabin. "Nice ride for a college professor." Her finger traced the hand controls by the steering column. "Are those because of your bad leg?"

I nodded. "Correct. They're the accelerator and brake controls."

"How did you afford this? Is it like a large monthly payment?"

"It was a gift, actually. I helped solve the murder of a well-off family's son," I explained.

Her eyes widened. "Really?" She turned to glance at me, a passing car illuminated her face, revealing a small scar on her chin I hadn't noticed before.

I caught the detail immediately and grinned. "I didn't notice until now, but you have a little scar on your chin."

Her hand went up instinctively. "Oh, that... chemistry experiment gone bad. Kinda blew up in my face."

Slowly, I raised my hand and placed a thumb gently on the tiny indentation—the scar so small it was almost invisible. "You also look very different without your glasses."

She smiled and leaned into my touch, warmth spreading across her cheeks. "I was hoping you'd notice. Makes things easier."

"Easier for what?" I asked, heart quickening.

She leaned closer, voice dropping low. "Let's see."

Our lips met softly at first, tentatively and searching, then with growing hunger. The heater hummed between us, and so did the quiet swell of desire. Her mouth was eager, pressing hard, sucking at my lips and teasing my tongue. Her hands roamed—caressing my face, tracing my arm—then slipped lower to more urgent places.

I reciprocated fully, fingers slipping under her layers, stroking, savoring her soft sighs. She was so responsive, so alive beneath my touch. I swallowed down the months of loneliness; the tension coiling deep in me.

My hand edged beneath her top and under her bra, cupping her breast. As I stroked, she moaned, "Pinch it."

Not usually one for theatrics, I complied, pinching gently. Her body shivered and she let out that throaty chuckle again, sighing with approval.

Then, with a sudden movement, she took my arm, pulling it out from beneath her clothes, and leaned back, fixing her bra into place.

"That was nice," she breathed.

"Yeah," I groaned, ache blossoming in my chest as I sank back, trying to steady myself.

"Len," she laughed softly, "we can't just do it in your van."

"No," I admitted, though the thought had flickered through my head. "Could you come back to my place?"

She sighed, leaning forward to rest a hand lightly on my leg. "That's a good idea... but not tonight. I'm on call tomorrow, and I don't want to rush this." Her eyes met mine, sincere and tender. "I don't want our first time to be in a hurry."

"Okay," I murmured, hiding my disappointment behind a soft smile.

She kissed my cheek—a quick, warm peck. "Just because you're on vacation doesn't mean I am. Besides, like I said, I have to be careful what I'm getting myself into."

I grinned. "How am I doing so far?"

She nodded, her grin widening. "So far? Very nice. Good night, Len."

"Good night, April."

She opened the door and stepped out into the freezing night, boots crunching softly on the snow. Across the street, she slid into her small white car and drove away, taillights fading into the darkness.

As the door closed behind her, I thought about her name— Simpson. Definitely not Jewish. My parents would like her, I decided. At least, bringing a date to one of the Chanukah evenings might focus my mother's attention away from me—and maybe, just maybe, make the visit bearable.

Except for my outburst over Jyanette earlier that night, the second date had been an apparent success.

I turned on the headlights, checked my mirrors, and merged smoothly into the street. As I approached a traffic light, it flicked green, but something—a sudden hesitation—made me slow just a fraction.

From the left, out of nowhere, a pickup truck barreled through the red light.

I slammed on the brakes, tires screeching as the van skidded violently. My wheel jerked hard to the right, narrowly missing the truck.

The pickup spun sideways, crashing into a streetlight with a thunderous clang, missing me by mere feet.

My breath caught in my throat as recognition hit me—it was the same truck that had almost struck me two nights ago. The one fleeing the Morgan crime scene.

Heart pounding, I sat frozen behind the wheel, the sudden danger lingering in the frosty night air.

9. ANSWER BACK

The light pole twisted grotesquely, a shattered relic hanging by fraying electrical wires stretched to their breaking point.

Suddenly, with a deafening snap that seemed to reverberate through the frozen night, one cable gave way. The pole crashed down, smashing onto the truck below, the roof caving inward by several crushing inches.

A live wire spiraled free, thrashing wildly as it hit the icy puddle beneath, sparks leaping and sizzling as electricity danced erratically over the melting ice.

Darkness swallowed the entire block instantly—the street lamps flickering out and plunging the street into utter blackness.

My breath came in ragged gasps as I fought to steady myself. My van was untouched but lurked awkwardly sideways in the road. Shaking off panic, I shifted gears smoothly and edged it safely to the curb.

I grabbed my phone and hit the button labelled *Emergency*.

"9-1-1, what is the nature of your emergency?" The calm, familiar voice of CeeCee, the Mountainview dispatcher, crackled through my van's speaker system.

"CeeCee? It's Len Wise." Relief flooded me—thank God it was her that picked up. "There's been an accident. Pole down, power cable thrashing in the street, arcing everywhere."

I peered at the street sign, illuminated faintly by my headlights despite the blackout, and gave her the cross streets.

"CeeCee, I don't know about the driver."

"Len, let the police handle this. Broken electric cables are highly dangerous. Stay in your vehicle."

"I know, CeeCee, I saw the safety video. But this cable—it's live, and the fire's starting under the truck's hood." A plume of smoke curled into the night air, thick and ominous.

"Len, stay inside your vehicle unless it's on fire. A fallen cable may electrify the ground around you. I'm sending cruisers now."

"Understood." I ended the call, but my eyes couldn't look away from the thickening smoke drifting upward from the hood of the truck.

The situation shifted in an instant. The rule was clear: stay put if you're safe inside a vehicle, insulated from the ground. But fire changes everything. If the truck blazed, the driver could already be in mortal danger.

My heart hammered as I assessed—I didn't know if he was conscious.

I grabbed two pairs of latex gloves from the console—leftover from crime scene visits—and slipped them on, double layering for extra protection. Not ideal like electrician gloves, but better than bare skin.

I left my cane, although the wood couldn't conduct, the metal sword inside it could create a circuit all by itself.

I cut the engine, grabbed my keys, and swung my door open and controlled the mechanical swivel chair to lower me out of my van, but stopped it before my foot touched the ground.

I steadied myself, because I knew the ground might be electrified. The only solution was to jump down, but that meant landing cleanly—both feet together—to avoid creating a path for the current to pass through.

I pushed off and straightened up as my feet hit pavement simultaneously, a shallow drop cushioned by the rubber soles of my shoes. I had chosen the right footwear by sheer luck.

My weight removed from the seat, triggering the device to retract and the door to close automatically behind me.

Now I needed to get to the truck.

Every step forward was cautious, deliberate—a shuffle, feet close and light, following the precise method I'd learned from the safety video I'd watched. No sparks, no tingling; maybe the ground was safe, or my shoes were insulating well.

Still, I didn't relax.

I moved toward the truck, glancing warily at the jagged wire sizzling nearby and the growing fire beneath the hood. If the gas tank leaked or the live wire touched metal, the truck could erupt in a plume of fire any second.

I could see the unlocked passenger door just ahead. The older vehicle had manual locks, and I could see the knob was up. I pressed my gloved hand to the handle and yanked it open, heart pounding against the frosty night.

Inside, a young man slumped by the wheel. Thin—alarmingly so—with a scruffy beard and a heavy denim coat lined in fake fur. Dazzling white flashes illuminated the swirling smoke inside the cab. With my gloved hands on the doorframe, I pulled both legs up onto the running board at the same time, breaking my contact with the ground.

My fingers were numb from the cold despite the gloves. A seatbelt strapped him in, and I pressed the release, but the latch held firm.

No time to hesitate—I pulled my keys and used one key as a small lever to wrest the latch open. The electric flashes flickering outside added to the urgency, but the latch wouldn't pry open.

I took the next step and jammed the key in the belt's fabric. It took several attempts, but I finally created a hole and slowly sawed through the fabric using the jagged side.

Precision and force: I sawed the polyester webbing through several strokes until it gave way. Slowly, I slid the young man sideways toward the open door.

But moving him out was only half the battle. We both needed to touch the ground at the same time or risk electric shock.

With a tremendous effort, I lifted him and cradled him in my arms, surprised by how little he weighed, almost as much as a child. He was even thinner than I had thought, shockingly so.

We might have a chance.

With him in my arms, I jumped the short distance to the ground, my right knee screaming in protest as I landed hard but stable.

After several deep breaths, with every part of my body aching, I shuffled my feet forward, heading for my van and safety.

HURRY...

It was impossible. The alcohol I'd foolishly consumed hours ago should have dulled and numbed my usually sharp and reliable precognitive senses.

Yet the voice echoed inside my head, chillingly clear, and it wasn't even my own.

It sounded like Kate Yearling, crisp and urgent, slicing through the fog of my daze.

A surge of panic and adrenaline slammed through me. I quickened my pace, every muscle screaming in protest as I lugged the unconscious man toward the van.

The wail of sirens grew louder, closing in fast, heightening the tension knotting inside my chest.

I reached the van but knew, without a shred of doubt, that there was no way I could get us inside without my swivel lift seat.

There was no time. No options.

So I pushed on, carrying him behind the van, where a thin patch of snow-covered grass stretched beside a weathered wooden telephone pole.

It was the only haven I could see in the chaos unraveling all around us. Carefully, I set him down, heart pounding as my fingers tremblingly brushed the icy ground.

Then, a blinding flash tore across the sky.

I collapsed over the man instinctively, pressing my body down as the truck exploded, a cataclysmic boom that shattered the silence like thunder. The pickup blasted upward in a fiery arc, crashing back down in a shower of flaming debris—deadly as a fireworks display from hell.

Metal shards and searing fragments rained down, battering my van, then clattered and scattered across the deserted street. But somehow, miraculously, the van stood firm between us and the inferno, a fragile shield holding back the flames and destruction.

My heart hammered in my ribs as I lifted myself off the man and stared at the blazing wreckage. I pulled myself to my feet using the telephone pole until I was fully upright. My hands shook violently, but we were alive—against all odds, still breathing.

Suddenly, two MPD police cars screeched to a halt, lights flashing red and blue, anchoring themselves a cautious distance from the snapped utility wire still sparking ominously across the road.

An African-American woman slipped out of the driver's side with measured calm and strode toward me. Officer Tylissa Booker —an ally I'd worked with before. Relief washed over me like a balm.

"You all right, Len?" she asked gently.

"Had to get out of the van," I panted, voice ragged. "Smoke… the truck—it caught fire."

She nodded, taking in the scene with sharp eyes. "Is that the driver? How is he?"

"Unconscious. Pulse's holding steady."

She radioed her partner, requesting an ambulance, her tone crisp and professional.

"What happened, Len?" she pressed.

I swallowed hard, forcing the words out. "I had dinner a couple of blocks from here. At the intersection, that guy ran the red light. I slammed the brakes. He hit the utility pole—it snapped."

Tylissa's gaze bore into me, her tone serious. "Len, I have to ask —have you been drinking?"

Lie. A simple word that fought to bubble up with ease, but I couldn't. Not this time. Not to her. My throat constricted, my eyes flooding with shame.

"Yes," I whispered, voice barely audible. "But I'm not drunk."

She was steady, her expression unreadable as she said, "You know I have to do the Breathalyzer."

"I know, Tylissa," I admitted, the weight of the inevitable pressing down.

Her eyes flicked back to the smoldering heap of wreckage. "You probably saved his life, Len."

I nodded slowly as more sirens tore through the night, the ambulance coming, bringing a flicker of hope into the dark chaos surrounding us.

The EMTs worked swiftly, their presence cutting through the chaos as they handed me a threadbare blanket before carefully loading the unconscious man into the ambulance.

The wail of the siren grew louder as they prepared for the trip to Mountainside Medical Center. I sank into the cool vinyl bench of the patrol car's backseat, grateful at least to be out of the cold and wrapped in the feeble warmth of the vehicle's heater.

A sharp jab of pain shot through my right leg—the fact that I have no knee, combined with the rough landing from jumping out of the truck and the agonizing shuffle afterward, was unforgiving.

Every muscle screamed in protest.

Tylissa crouched by the open back door, holding a breathalyzer tube with gentle insistence.

"Blow steady," she instructed, her eyes sharp and unblinking as she watched the device analyze my blood alcohol content. The machine beeped sharply; she pulled it away and read the small screen with intent focus.

"Point zero seven nine," she announced, her voice steady but tinged with seriousness. "You're just under the legal limit of point zero eight, Len."

I let out a breath I hadn't realized I was holding. "Well, there's that, at least," I said, relief washing over me.

Her eyes flickered with a mix of concern and reprimand. "What if I'd tested you the minute I arrived? Instead of waiting twenty minutes? What would I have found then?"

Her words hung heavy in the cold air.

I could only nod. No argument would serve.

"Len, you know how tough the DUI laws are nowadays. I don't want to see you land in hot water."

"Thanks, Tylissa," I murmured, grateful for her honesty and care.

She glanced toward the road where the distant rumble of a utility truck declared the power company's arrival. "'Bout time they showed up. As soon as they shut down that line, you can get back in your van and leave. Was your van damaged?"

I rubbed at my aching leg absently. "I'm not sure. Debris hit it when the truck exploded."

"I'll wait until you get moving, then give you an escort through the mess."

I nodded.

She finally spoke in a lighter tone. "I heard you were hanging out with my boyfriend today."

My head snapped up in surprise. "Darren? Did he finally get enough nerve to ask you out?"

Her grin was wide, genuine. "He did, and I gotta admit, I'm liking it."

"He must tower over you by a full foot," I joked.

"Thirteen inches to be exact," she boasted. "But we make it work."

"Good. Both of you deserve some happiness."

Tylissa's face shifted, growing more serious. "Who did you have dinner with?"

"A new forensic investigator working for Doug Millbank. April Simpson."

Her brow furrowed. "Don't know her. Then again, I don't work a lot of murder scenes."

"You'd notice her. She's tall."

Her expression darkened further. "You mean like Jyanette."

A sudden sting behind my eyes caught me off guard. Tears stabbed sharply. "Yeah," I whispered, voice ragged.

Tylissa's gaze softened as she watched me. She stepped away to talk to the officer in the other car, silently giving me space.

And there I sat, eyes wet, blubbering like a child. So much for my "man of action" routine—it was clear I was an emotional wreck beneath the surface.

After a long moment, she returned quietly. "You okay?"

"Yeah," I replied, forcing a smile. "Just a momentary thing."

"I should have had the EMT check you for shock," she said gently.

"I studied medicine, Tylissa," I responded, trying to keep my voice steady. "I'm not in shock."

She narrowed her eyes skeptically. "Well then, I'm gonna say it: you sure you're ready to date? Seems like you ain't over Jyanette."

I exhaled, the truth spilling out. "I'm lonely, Tylissa."

She nodded in understanding. We both turned to watch as the power company truck pulled smoothly to a stop several poles from the still-sparking downed cable. A worker went up in the articulated telescoping arm, and moments later, the erratic flashes stopped.

He waved to us before descending.

Offering her hand, Tylissa helped me out of the patrol car. "Okay, check your van, and I'll follow you home. The others will manage traffic till the electricity's back."

Surveying my van, I spotted a small dent on the driver's side sliding door, a souvenir from flying debris during the explosion. Aside from that, it had escaped with minor damage.

I used my lift chair to get in, started the engine, and eased off the shoulder. The wheel held steady. No strange noises from underneath. Relief buzzed in my chest as I navigated the familiar roads home.

Pulling into my driveway, Tylissa waved and sped off. I parked in the roundabout, headed inside—a hollow, heavy feeling sinking deeper into me.

Hours had passed since dinner, and though I was more sober than after my time with April, a persistent lightheadedness lingered.

Maybe I was wrong. Maybe I was in shock after all.

The downstairs was dark—no surprise. Mrs. Higgins often went to bed early with a book.

I shrugged off my coat, creeping down the long hallway toward the kitchen.

On a special shelf stood a bottle of Irish whiskey, reserved by Mrs. Higgins for rare "wee dram" moments. I poured a small glass, the liquid catching the dim light. The burn from the first sip loosened the tight coil of tension in my chest.

Replacing the bottle, I shuffled toward my end of the house, cane tapping rhythmically on the polished blonde wood.

My eyes lifted to the intricate woodwork—a testament to the repairs Mrs. Higgins and I had labored over since last September, when a gunman attacked the house.

Professionals handled most of the restoration, but I contributed hours of spackling and painting, erasing the scars of that violent night. The cost had been steep, despite insurance.

I pushed open the door to my sitting room. The night's chaos lingered inside me—each ache in my back and legs a reminder.

I settled into my desk chair, booted up my laptop, and took another sip of whiskey.

I sent a quick email to Doctor Fritz Kohl:

> **Dear Fritz,**
>
> **Need information on spirit possession. Seems like a spirit is making people hurt themselves. Something to do with that cult leader I mentioned —Claude Vandersteen. Could use any insight you have.**
>
> **Len**

I sent it off, then sifted through my inbox, deleting clutter. An unexpected message caught my eye—from asimpson@gmail:

> **Dear Len,**
>
> **Now that I know you teach at the same school I go to, I found your email on the GSU website. I must say, you're much more handsome than the photo posted there.**
>
> **I had a pleasant time tonight—especially the part in your van.**
>
> **Just wanted to make sure you got home all right.**
>
> **Stay in touch,**
>
> **April**

I smiled, admitting quietly I'd enjoyed that part too. Was it strange April investigated me so thoroughly? She said she wanted to make sure I was real—more effort than Jyanette ever showed.

Then again, Jyanette had always been one of a kind.

Some days, missing her left me hollow—an ache stretching cold where my heart should be.

I thought back to our last meeting at Mountainside Medical Center. She lay there, fragile and broken, tears staining her face.

"I need to get far away from all this," she had whispered, her dark hair tangled against the pillow.

"From me as well?" I had asked, heart twisting.

"Don't you see? All we'll ever do is remind each other of what we lost. I can't bear it, Len. I just can't."

Tears had streamed down her face—and mine.

"I love you, Jyanette. I always will."

"And I'll always love you," she whispered. "But I need... help... right now."

I took her hand gently. "Your mother will know what to do." Her mother, descended from an African healer, was the one who could mend her shattered spirit after losing our child.

I bent forward and kissed her forehead. "I'll let you rest."

"Goodbye, Leonard," she whispered.

And that was the end. She returned to Virginia, to her family, leaving me to search for happiness alone.

The whiskey glass sat empty on my desk. I tried to pinpoint when I'd finished my drink. My fingers itched to pour more, but I knew Mrs. Higgins would notice.

I had only needed one glass to calm my nerves.

I could stop anytime I wanted to.

Couldn't I?

The night had been strange—fractured fragments of dreams pressing into my mind like unwelcome intruders. Faces from my past hovered just beyond recognition, drifting like ghosts at the edge of sleep, elusive and haunting.

When morning finally came, it was with a shuddering ache that seized not only my head but every muscle in my body. I tried to move, only to recoil at the sight of my right leg: swollen grotesquely where my knee used to be, the pain sharp and unyielding.

I leaned heavily on my cane, a ritual I wished I didn't need, and dragged myself into a robe before gingerly shuffling toward the kitchen for coffee.

It was Thursday, and aside from the case, I had nowhere to be —an entire day to be still. Maybe that was the best thing I could do right now.

My phone sat on my desk, screen glowing with missed calls and waiting messages. I must have left it on silent during dinner with April, forgetting to restore the ringer—probably because of the accident, or maybe the whiskey that helped numb the pain.

The most recent voicemail was from Bill McGee.

"Len, it's Bill. Antoine Powell escaped from county lockup last night. Call me."

I stared at the screen; the words sinking in like a weight. Then I noticed the multiple calls from Anna Sokolov, all between 1:00 and 2:00 in the morning. A pit opened in my stomach as I played the first message.

"Doctor... um... Len, this is Anna. I'm having this vision— like before. It's a black man in a cell, and this guard comes and lets him out. The Echo Man is talking to the guard telling him what to do. Please call me. I don't know what to do."

More missed calls, then the next message, her voice trembling with fear.

"Len, please call me. That guard—he's being made to do things. He's taking a sheet and wrapping it around his neck. Call me. You said you would answer! Where are you?"

I skipped through several more missed calls and landed on the last message, her voice raw with distress and tears audible beneath her words.

"Len, it's Anna. The guard—he hung himself. Wrapped the sheet around his neck, pulled until he choked. And then the vision faded. But the voice, I heard it. It was there the whole time, talking to him. I'm scared. Please call me."

Panic edged into my chest as I hit the dial button, but the call went straight to voicemail. A bitter curse escaped my lips; Anna was still in school, and she couldn't have her phone with her. She probably wouldn't hear from me until after classes ended.

I left a hurried message, my voice tight with guilt.

"Anna, it's Len. Sorry—the phone was on silent. I was in a car accident last night, and I wasn't thinking straight. Call me as soon as you get this."

Then I called McGee back. There was no ringing—he picked up instantly. The urgency in his voice was like a live wire crackling through the line.

"Len, did you get my message?"

I hesitated for a second, then said, "I heard. Antoine Powell escaped?"

"Yeah," he snapped. "And I've seen the damn video."

"What happened?" I asked, leaning closer to the receiver, already feeling the weight of dread settling in my chest.

"In the dead of night, supposedly a quiet hour, the guard—and listen, it's county jail, so they only had one guy watching three prisoners—he just... walks over, unlocks Powell's cell, and escorts him right out of the building, like it's some routine transfer or something."

"That's insane," I said, the disbelief rising in my voice.

"Wait, it gets worse. After that, the guard walks back *talking to himself.* Then—get this—he goes into Powell's cell and uses the bedsheet to hang himself. Len, this isn't just an escape. Something's seriously wrong."

I swallowed hard. "It has to be Powell. Bill, he's the Echo Man —somehow, he made that guard release him, and then... convince him to kill himself. I need to see that video."

"Did you see anything—your special way?"

"No," I admitted. "I got sidetracked—a car accident pulled me away."

"I heard about that, you saved a guy's life, right? But how could Powell pull that off? He displayed no abilities before, and there's no way he could get Vandersteen's drug in prison."

"That's why I need to see the video," I said, feeling the knot tighten in my gut. "It's the explanation that fits. He's the only one who'd want to take out the people Vandersteen knew."

"Are you saying he's planning to go after someone else? Tonight?"

My voice caught on the edge of panic. "I think so. And if he does, we're running out of time."

"Well, I've put out a three-state All-Points-Bulletin on him. Come by this afternoon—see if we can figure out a way to stop him."

"We need to move fast," I insisted, the weight of the situation heavy in my voice. "Or tonight—someone else will die."

10. RICOCHETING REBUKES

I finished my shower and shaved, the sharp scrape of the razor a brief relief against the numbness creeping through my swollen leg. Wrapping myself in my robe, my phone cut through the quiet with an abrupt ring. I padded into the bedroom and snatched it up.

Kate Yearling's voice came through, clipped and a little tense. "Len, I found those files you asked about, but it's… sketchy at best."

"Hit me with it," I said, already sitting on the edge of the bed.

"Better face-to-face. Can you swing by the Task Force office in Morris Plains?"

"I'm meeting McGee this afternoon. Vandersteen's partner escaped county lockup last night."

"Antoine Powell?" She sounded surprised. "That's weird."

"Why?"

"I had a dream about him last night."

I frowned, skepticism stirring. "Really? What happened?"

Her voice dropped, serious now. "I don't really remember... just that it felt important."

"Well, Kate, I've got almost nothing to work with. Anything could be a lead at this point."

The next question came hesitantly. "Is any of this tied to Brett Morgan's death?"

"Yes."

A long silence fell between us.

"There's something you're not telling me," she finally said.

I couldn't help but repeat her earlier words. "Better to do it in person."

"Touché," she grunted with a reluctant chuckle. "Can you be here in an hour and a half?"

"I'll grab some coffee and head out."

"Geez, Len, it's only ten in the morning. Just waking up?"

"I had a late night and I'm still officially on vacation, Kate."

"I've been on vacation for months. It gets boring real fast."

"See you soon." I ended the call before I said more.

I didn't want to bring up the voice I'd heard last night—that haunting message from Kate in my mind—until we were face-to-face.

Dressing quickly, I leaned heavily on my cane as I shuffled to the kitchen. The swelling in my leg made every step a sharp reminder of the previous night's rescue.

"Ah, Doctor, let me get you some coffee," Mrs. Higgins said kindly as I limped into the kitchen.

"Thanks, Mrs. Higgins," I murmured, lowering myself carefully onto the chair where we often shared meals.

"You're moving like you're in pain," she observed, pouring cream from the big refrigerator to lighten my drink.

"I was in a car accident last night, on my way home."

Her worry carved deep lines into her face as she set the steaming mug before me. "Was it your fault?"

"No. A pickup truck ran a red light, slammed through a utility pole. I had to pull the driver from the wreckage before his truck exploded."

"That's frightening," she breathed. "And very brave."

"There was a live electrical cable on the ground. It took everything I had to carry him away in time."

She sat beside me, eyes narrowed with concern. "But now you're moving like you're an old man."

"I feel like one," I admitted, nursing the coffee. "I'm going to have to be more regular with my Aikido classes. Last night hammered my leg pretty hard—I had to jump to the pavement."

"You've carried a heavy burden on that leg for a long time," she whispered, reaching out to touch my free hand.

I looked up, surprised at her insight.

"I noticed, too," she said, a flicker of disappointment in her eyes. "You took a dram of whiskey last night, probably to calm yourself."

Wincing, I said. "I'll replace the bottle."

"I don't care a whit about the bottle," she said firmly. "I'm worried about you. You're called to do important things, but the drink will only hold you back."

My temper flared. "I really don't need a lecture this morning, Mrs. Higgins."

She didn't budge. "No lecture. Just a reminder that you have to choose the path you walk. And alcohol won't bring Jyanette back. You'd think after Cathy, you'd have learned that lesson."

Her words hit me like a punch.

Cathy—my fiancée, long dead—the memory burning fresh despite the years.

On the night when my abilities first surfaced, I had been driving with her to her parents' home in Mountainview. The rain pounded against the windshield as we joked about starting our residencies at Rutgers. Her radiant smile was a brief lighthouse before the storm.

The road ahead blurred into something terrifying—a red-skinned demon looming in the rain. I jerked the wheel, losing control, smashing through the guardrail.

Glass exploded around us as we tumbled down the mountain. Pain seared through my legs. When we landed, I was trapped, helpless, as Cathy's blood dripped and her life slipped away.

"Cathy, don't go," I had whispered, but the silence that followed was final.

My uncontrolled mental powers grew from that broken moment, and I buried myself in drink to silence the voices... and the pain.

Mrs. Higgins sat across from me, unwavering.

I said, "You have no right—"

"No, I don't," she snapped back. "Nor do you to neglect the people who need you by drowning yer sorrow. You've lost, yes— one woman dead, another gone. But this is your path. Get back on it before someone else dies."

She rose and stormed out, leaving me stunned and strangely sober.

Staring after her retreating figure, I realized Mrs. Higgins had just taken me to the woodshed.

Back in my study, I opened my laptop with shaking hands, grateful for an early email from Fritz Kohl in California:

Leonard,

There is more than one type of spirit possession.

You speak of an entity temporarily inhabiting

people, which suggests—based on our studies—a case of spirit attachment. This spirit consciousness clings to a living person and feeds on them to manifest such phenomena. This implies someone with very strong psychic abilities. I'm sending a research article about this to you.

Fritz

I downloaded the PDF to my phone for later and closed the laptop. Before heading out to meet Kate, I remembered my promise to Anna Sokolov. In my bedroom, I found the books— *Psychic Self-Defense* and *The Training And Work Of An Initiate* by Dion Fortune. Old, steeped in Christian mysticism, but perfect for beginners.

These two books would be a good beginning.

Clutching them, I grabbed my cane and leather bag, steeling myself for whatever awaited at Morris Plains.

I slipped out through my private entrance, desperate to avoid running into Mrs. Higgins again.

The cold air hit me immediately, and I regretted leaving my heavy winter coat hanging in the entrance hall. The chill bit into my skin as I made my way to my van, shivering despite the adrenaline coursing through me.

I drove toward Morris Plains, my mind racing with the implications of Doctor Kohl's cryptic email: spirit attachment.

Over the four years I'd studied under Kohl, we had dissected nearly every historical and mythological account of supernatural entities influencing humans. The sheer volume was staggering. From the ancient Egyptians and Babylonians to the Greeks and Romans, spirit possession was a pervasive belief—one that had transcended time and culture.

Tales echoed from the sands of Arabia with Jinns, from Jewish folklore with the Dybbuk, and beyond—every civilization had stories of disembodied spirits taking hold of the living, bending them to their will.

Full possession meant the entity supplanted the host's mind entirely. I'd faced that horror firsthand with the demonic Ashtoreth, who had taken over a fragile old man, endowing him with terrifying strength and nearly costing me my life. The demon had shattered the man's psyche until only the demon's consciousness remained.

But spirit attachment was different. I had read little of the paper Kohl sent, but I still understood the main points. Rather than overtaking the body, an incorporeal entity would latch onto a living person, subtly exerting influence, slowly draining their energy to sustain its dark existence. It never fully possessed the host's body, but whispered insidiously, nudging them, making the host believe the disturbing impulses were their own.

The host became a living battery—a puppet for a parasitic presence.

But how did these spirits manage more extreme acts? How did Brett, Erica, and the guard suddenly lose control of their own limbs, compelled to harm themselves? The thought chilled me—it was a terrifying mystery.

Then there was Claude Vandersteen—creator of the drug *Miracle*. His creation granted psychic powers matching or surpassing my own. What happened to people gifted with innate psychic abilities when they took his drug?

The question nagged at me.

As I parked my van across from the Morris Plains train station, the weight of the situation pressed down on me like ice. Antoine

Powell swirled in my thoughts. He was Jyanette's ex-husband and had taken me at gunpoint to my confrontation with Vandersteen.

His loyalty to Vandersteen stemmed from the fact that he was a drug addict and Vandersteen had been his supplier.

Could Powell be the vessel for Claude himself? If so, why kill Brett Morgan? And how did he steal the knife when he was still in custody at the time?

Or was Brett's murder a plan to get us to pull him from a high-security prison and bring him to county lock-up, where, by controlling one man, he could regain his freedom?

The FBI New Jersey Task Force offices sat above a nondescript retail drugstore and dry cleaner, windows concealed by heavy drapes that shielded their work in shadows.

Climbing the stairs, I passed through a door into a corridor. Ahead, a glass-walled research lab held two people in white coats and surgical masks, absorbed in their instruments—a spectrometer and chromatograph—analyzing evidence sequenced from crime scenes. Machines hummed quietly, their complexity beyond my understanding.

I turned left toward Kate's office. She opened the door at my knock, and I stopped, noticing immediately how pale she looked —much paler than the last time I'd seen her. Freckles dotted her skin, and dark circles shadowed her eyes. Her flaming-red wig framed her face perfectly, yet her exhaustion was unmistakable. Tension radiated from her.

"How are you holding up, Kate?" I asked quietly.

She sighed, stepping back to let me inside. "Still struggling with sleep. Therapy warned me nightmares would return after a stretch with none. Now they're back—regular and relentless."

"It's tough to take a step back after moving forward like you have," I said, settling into the overstuffed green chair beside her psychiatrist's divan.

"Sometimes," she muttered, "it feels like two steps back, and then two more." Kate rummaged through a pile of papers, slipping on a pair of designer glasses. "There's so much to wade through, and I still owe you that profile."

I noticed the glasses. "New?"

"Yeah. Surviving that messed-up night left me with some lasting damage—minor, but enough to need reading glasses now," she said with a wry smile.

I nodded, then hesitated before speaking. "Kate, I need to ask you about something that happened last night."

She frowned, concern tightening her features. "What?"

"I was in an accident—"

The remaining color drained from her face. "Oh God—"

I was immediately worried. "Kate, what is it?"

She swallowed hard, her voice small. "The truck..."

My brow furrowed. "How did you know it was a truck?"

Her mouth thinned into a line. "What happened?"

"I had to rescue the driver—I was—"

"Running out of time."

Relief flickered in my chest that she understood. "Yes. I heard your voice telling me to hurry."

Her eyes locked on mine, the door of fear slightly ajar. "You did?"

"It was unmistakable."

She stumbled over her words. "It... had to be... you. Just your mind playing tricks, pulling a friendly voice out of thin air."

I leaned forward, the intensity sharpening my tone. "Kate, it had to be more."

"You're psychic, Len. But even you have moments when your brain spins illusions," she said firmly.

I mulled over her words. "Maybe..."

Kate let out a slow breath of relief and turned toward her paperwork. "Can we focus on Vandersteen?"

I nodded. "What have you uncovered?"

"After Staten Island, after Claude stabbed Stan Frazier, the FBI looked into him and his so-called 'Following of Astarte.'"

"Was there ever a following? The raid only caught Claude and Powell," I said.

Kate opened a folder, scanning the contents. "The FBI interviewed people, but they didn't dig deeply."

"Why not?"

"Because Claude was dead, Erica was saved, and the police arrested Powell," she said, waving vaguely. "Here's what they found: Claude ran a booming business making pharmacological hallucinogens for his peers."

"I know. The chemistry professor at Vanderbilt, Walt Addison, told me he didn't know about Claude's double life—only that he was working late hours."

Kate raised one skeptical eyebrow. "That's not what students reported during interviews. Rumor had it Addison looked the other way because he got a cut of the drugs."

I frowned. "I've known Walt a long time—he studied with Doctor Kohl, too. I can't see him as dishonest."

Kate's head shook slowly. "Students from Claude's dorm claim Addison shared the same recreational habits as his students."

The possibility sent a jolt through me. If Walt took *Miracle*, would that unlock latent psychic abilities? Could he have been an unwitting host for Claude's influence instead of Powell?

If that were the case, if he were Claude's host, wouldn't I have sensed it? Then again, he'd been having a beer when we met. Could alcohol have inhibited my reading of him, the same way it was for me when I drank?

"Addison said the FBI collected Claude's notes on his experiments," I said.

Kate nodded, flipping through more papers. "I have the notebooks and scanned them in for analysis. I've reviewed them thoroughly. Want to see?"

I shook my head. "No. My concern is who else might manufacture that drug, and how Powell could have gotten it."

"Why?" Kate asked.

"Because that drug gives whoever takes it telepathic abilities—and who knows what else. But more than that, it drove Vandersteen insane. He wasn't just experimenting; he was tampering with the mind itself. That's dangerous."

"Maybe it was the dosage he was taking," Kate countered smoothly. "I've reviewed his formulas. At lower doses, that substance could be useful—perhaps even beneficial."

"You understand his chemical formularies?" I asked, incredulous.

"I majored in chemistry when I received my Bachelor of Science," she said almost casually. "It all got put aside when I began psychotherapy and hypnotherapy. But I could make sense of Claude's notes."

My jaw tightened. "Kate, that drug is a poison—to anyone who touches it."

Her gaze didn't waver. "According to the FBI interview of his former roommate, Claude had women, quote: 'coming and going at all hours'. End quote." She sounded almost amused.

Leaning back in the chair, I said, "I guess when you can make designer drugs, you're pretty popular. Did the FBI find anyone else tied to 'The Following'?"

She rifled through her papers, pulling out a faded eight-by-ten and sliding it toward me. The photo showed a clean-cut young man, his features easy to forget—except for the eerie calmness in his eyes.

"That's Dan Cressley. Claude's old roommate." She flipped through more sheets. "Mixed reports, really. Some say Claude obsessed over ancient religions, pushing people to join him in bizarre rituals. Cressley moved out because Claude painted a pentagram inside a ritual circle right on their dorm room floor. He said it creeped him out."

I made a note on my phone. "Do you have photos of the others the FBI interviewed?"

"Just Cressley. And that's actually his student ID photo enlarged."

"We need to warn anyone who was close to Vandersteen or Powell. These suicides—they all circle back to him."

Kate leaned in, eyes sharp. "You think Vandersteen is reaching out from the grave to get revenge?"

I met her gaze but kept silent.

"Oh, come on! You can't really believe that."

"Maybe not," I said evenly, "but I *can* believe three people all hearing the same voice, urging them to kill themselves."

"Could be guilt. Or hallucinations," she argued. "Len, people's minds play tricks on them all the time."

"Claude created a drug that enhanced mental capacity. When I faced him in the snow, we communicated telepathically." I tapped my temple for effect.

She regarded me with a new seriousness. "I know you can do that. You did it to me."

"Yes." I nodded. "That ability—direct mind contact through eye-to-eye connection—is all I can do most of the time. Vandersteen taunted me mentally from a distance that night."

Kate's skepticism surfaced. "How could a drug do that?"

"There are plant alkaloids that the ancients linked to prophecy," I explained. "The priestess at Delphi, for instance, used henbane and ethylene in the water to induce trance states. Claude combined those with jimsonweed, which grew right across the street from his dorm."

Kate frowned. "Jimsonweed's pretty common."

"Exactly. But Claude synthesized a molecule mimicking those plants' effects, a biosimilar with the poisons removed," I said.

Kate nodded slowly. "I read his notes. He claimed it was safe."

"Perhaps, but it was highly addictive, and it drove him mad eventually," I said grimly.

"That matches the interviews. People close to Claude saw him unraveling. June Steen, who dated him briefly, said she refused all those 'weird drugs.' She was a science major, left school soon after."

I smirked bitterly. "Probably she didn't want to be remembered as the girl who dated the crazy guy." I added her name to my phone.

Kate's eyes sharpened. "So your theory is someone's recreating Claude's drug, and using mental manipulation to compel victims into suicide?"

I shrugged. "Let's say I agree with that."

"What's the other theory?"

"That someone on the drug is a host for Claude's consciousness —making victims hurt themselves."

Her stare turned icy. "That's insane."

"Kate, the only reason I get called in is *because* it's insane."

She sighed, brushing a hand nervously over her wig. "And sometimes, I have to admit, maybe we need to listen to you."

"All the signs point to Powell, but how could he get the drug?"

"People get drugs in prison all the time," Kate said.

"Then he has to be working with someone with a full lab that can create it for him."

She leaned back. "Alright. What do you need from me?"

"Contact info for the people the FBI interviewed. I want to know if any are still nearby."

She nodded, scribbling. "Got it."

"Also, see if you can locate sources of medical-grade henbane."

Kate already had her pad out. "I'll check with the company supplying our lab."

"If we can track down someone who ordered it, it might tell us who's making this stuff now. I also need to figure out who Powell would target next."

She met my eyes, steady and serious. "If you want my educated guess, you're at the top of that list."

"I'm aware of that." I nodded, then sat upright. "But it could also be Stan Frazier. Claude stabbed him, but he survived."

Kate grabbed her phone. "He only lives ten minutes away. I'll call him."

She dialed, and I watched her eyes narrow. Why hadn't I thought of this before? Stan had to be on Powell's hit list.

"Hey, Stan. It's Kate," she said warmly into the phone. "I'm here with Len Wise, about Claude Vandersteen." She chuckled. "Yeah, that bastard. Can you come by and give us some insight?" She paused. "And yes, I know it used to be your office. You tell me that every time."

She hung up. "He'll be here soon. You free?"

"Got an afternoon meeting with McGee, but no set time."

Kate grinned. "Forgot you're on vacation."

"I'm working until we crack this. Two dead already, Brett Morgan and the guard at the county lockup. We were lucky that Erica Marconi was rescued by her family the other night."

"If we think like profilers—"

"Since you are one," I reminded her.

She ignored the jab. "What do the incidents have in common?"

"All happened in the dead of night. Usually between one and three a.m."

She wrote rapidly. "If someone's using Vandersteen's drug to gain mental powers, when would they have to take it for the drug's effects to peak?"

"If orally, they'd have to take it between nine p.m. and midnight."

"An hour or two before those incidents," she mused, continuing to note details.

"But Claude took it constantly. Powell admitted to me that the comedown was brutal."

Kate's pen paused mid-air. "Look at you—drug vernacular and all. So withdrawal was harsh, every time?"

"Powell told me back then that he only took it once."

"So you think he's taking it now."

I nodded. "Yes, and in doses as large as Vandersteen was doing."

"Good point. Why *now*?" she tapped her pen rhythmically. "Claude died back in March. Why has this started only recently?"

I considered. "Maybe Powell needed someone to master the formula. Or, let's say he's been receiving it for a while, he needed to build up tolerance to get the full effect."

Her eyes brightened. "What else?"

"Or he only found the time to act within the last week. That makes little sense. Powell was in prison, so he had all the time in the world."

"Claude was a college student, right?" Kate said.

"Yes."

"And the semester ended last Friday?"

I sat straighter. "If the person making the drug is a student, maybe they didn't have the time to ramp up production until classes were over."

Kate nodded thoughtfully.

"Any other theories?" she asked.

"Claude came back to ruin his victims' Christmas?" I suggested.

"Like Scrooge and his ghosts? I doubt it, but I'll write it down."

We kept exploring possibilities—the winter solstice, ritual timings—but none seemed convincing.

A sharp knock echoed through the office. The door creaked open, and Stan Frazier strode into the room.

He was a towering figure, broad-shouldered and imposing, with hair streaked auburn and gray, cut short into a practical style. His thick mustache twitched nervously, like an untrained caterpillar crawling across his upper lip.

Clad in worn denim pants, a crisp dress shirt, and a heavy winter coat with a hood, he was nearly as tall as I was—but undeniably more rugged.

Without hesitation, Stan bypassed me and approached Kate, who stood and threw her arms around him in a quick embrace.

"How you feelin', girl?" he asked, his voice rough but warm.

"Better," Kate replied. "Len pulled me into a case and asked for a profile."

I rose from my chair as Stan turned, crossing the room toward me. He grasped my hand in a firm grip. "Len Wise, the Wonder Man. How are you holding up, professor?"

"I'll be better if we can finally put Vandersteen's legacy to rest," I said.

Stan's eyebrows shot up, disbelief flickering across his face. "I thought we'd buried that little creep for good. You mean I got stabbed for nothing?"

I met his gaze steadily. "How's your recuperation coming along?"

"Around nine months, and I still get twinges now and then—but civilian life is treating me right," he said with a half-smile.

"Not bored yet?" I asked.

"Working on the house, finally ticking off the list of chores I promised the missus years ago. We even went on a cruise—nice to breathe fresh air for once. But this, what's the deal with Vandersteen? You didn't, y'know, raise him from the dead, did you?"

I shook my head. "Not in my skill set. But there've been some strange suicides, or what might be murders. Three victims—all connected to Vandersteen: Brett Morgan, an officer working for the county, and an attempt on Erica Marconi."

Stan frowned deeply. "Marconi I know—but why the officer?"

"He freed Antoine Powell."

"Another name I know. Who's Morgan?"

"The previous owner of the knife Vandersteen used on you."

"That thing?" Stan's hand absentmindedly rubbed his shoulder, the place he'd been stabbed. "Man, that blade was nasty."

"The knife disappeared after Morgan's death," I explained.

Stan frowned, his face tightening with unease. "Powell on the loose and that knife out there doesn't sound good."

Kate cleared her throat. "Len wanted to see if you knew anything."

"And to put you on alert," I added. "If Powell or someone else is targeting people who brought Vandersteen down, you're on their list."

"Shit." Stan exhaled, his voice low and strained. "I thought we'd settled this. His cult was just a story."

Kate spoke firmly. "There could be followers we don't know about. I'm working that angle into the profile."

"I've got that PI on Staten Island checking things out," I said.

"Darren Ward?" Stan's lips curved in recognition. "Met him. Seems solid."

"He's digging into known acquaintances for me."

Kate's voice was cautious. "Len, is this private eye in any danger?"

"Not right now. He wasn't involved in Vandersteen's takedown. But a warning wouldn't hurt."

Stan turned to Kate. "Got the files? How many people did the FBI team interview?"

"A few—only three stood out as important: Professor Addison, Dan Cressley, his former roommate, and June Steen, a woman he dated from chemistry class."

"Why them?" I asked.

Kate shook her head. "The agents sensed dishonesty. Dan never mentioned he took Claude's drugs. June claimed they'd dated briefly, but others said they were together for two years—and she often did things for Claude."

"And Addison?" I pushed.

"The people in charge barely looked into the details around Addison," Kate said plainly.

Stan sighed, shaking his head. "I guess it seemed pointless. After all, Claude was dead."

Kate nodded. "Our office was in turmoil, searching for a new commander."

Stan's jaw clenched. "Still, I expected more thoroughness." He leaned back against a chair, troubled. "But yeah, we've always been short-staffed."

"If needed, I could help with follow-up interviews," Kate offered.

"From a distance," I warned her. "I don't want the killer to notice you if they are hunting people."

"Len, I'm tired of being stuck in this office," she protested.

Stan grinned. "Len's right. Let me handle it—I've got time, and I'm already a target. Besides, it'll give my wife a chance to miss me."

I warned him, "Carry a religious symbol if there is one you believe in."

Stan snorted. "What are we fighting? Vampires?"

"The power of faith can provide protection," I said seriously. "If we're confronting something disembodied, I'll take any advantage I can get."

Kate grinned. "That's a little unscientific, Len."

"Maybe," I admitted. "But we're treading unknown ground."

Stan exhaled heavily. "Alright, but let's all try not to end up dead."

11. MIRROR IMAGE

On the way back to Mountainview, I slipped into Mindy's Diner to drop off the books with Carl Sokolov. It was still too early in the day to call his daughter, and the unanswered questions about her gnawed at me.

Was there a way to confirm whether she was being manipulated? Night after night, visions disrupted her sleep—fragments of images and emotions she didn't understand. But why were these visions coming to her?

I knew I'd have to spend time with her during the upcoming break. The books were a start—but nothing compared to the one-on-one techniques Doctor Kohl had drilled into me. Meditation, mental shielding, reinforcing the basics.

Anna's gift was powerful—maybe too powerful. Her abilities were growing, developing, and if she could learn control, she would become a formidable asset.

But all this excess mental power had a downside: spirit attachments. Bright flames attracted psychic energy-thriving entities, and Anna's was brighter than most. If we didn't put mental protections in place, these entities would latch onto her.

Once I parked in the MPD lot, I pulled out the paper Doctor Kohl had sent me—a detailed explanation of spirit attachment. Earthbound entities that clung to the living, forced to replay their unfinished business in the physical world.

With Claude Vandersteen, I knew, revenge was a brutal motivator. The paper called these beings "psychic parasites" that drained their hosts' life force. For a moment, I thought of Stan's vampire analogy.

Maybe he hadn't been far off.

The report warned that paranormal investigators and inexperienced psychics were most at risk, lacking the mental defenses to repel these creatures.

People who dabbled in the occult were vulnerable, but Claude hadn't dabbled—he'd plunged headfirst into communion with an ancient demon.

What worried me most was the drug Claude took—*Miracle*—that seemed to distort the body's aura. Everyone has a protective aura, an energy shield invisible to most but strong enough to keep spiritual predators at bay.

I theorized Claude's drug had severely weakened his aura, leaving him wide open to psychic attack. That vulnerability was what Astarte—the entity he worshipped—had exploited. In destroying his natural defenses, Claude surrendered control.

That meant anyone using the *Miracle* drug would be just as vulnerable, ripe for possession or worse.

Was Powell possessed? Was that how he'd escaped so easily, led out by the guard who was supposed to watch him?

I had to focus on finding the human host, probably Powell, sever the bond, and make sure no other "echoes" of Claude remained.

It was the only logical path forward.

I headed to the back door of the Mountainview Police Department. In the locker room, festive Christmas lights twinkled softly, a stark contrast to the storm brewing inside me.

Walking into the executive offices, I spotted a small artificial tree at an empty desk—an attempt at holiday cheer amidst the chaos.

CeeCee Carter was on dispatch, headset in place. She removed it and smiled. "Hey, Len, glad to see you had no ill effects from that accident last night."

"Some scary moments," I admitted, "but I saved the driver. Do you know if he's okay?"

"Last I heard, he's still in the hospital," she said quietly. "They said he's not in good shape."

I sighed, eyes dropping to the floor. "He seemed young— maybe mid-twenties. No obvious major trauma, but far too thin. Do we have his name?"

CeeCee grabbed a sheet of paper. "Daniel Cressley."

Icy dread crept up my spine, icy fingers clutching at my chest. I fumbled for my phone, scrolling through names from the FBI report Kate had read earlier. There it was—Dan Cressley: former roommate of Claude Vandersteen.

"Len? You okay? You've gone pale," CeeCee asked, concern creeping into her voice.

I forced a shaky nod. "I'm fine."

But my mind raced. The truck that almost hit me last night— the same one from two nights ago—now connected to Claude's roommate.

Could Cressley be the host?

Just then, the door to McGee's office opened, and Bill popped his head out. "Len? I've been waiting for you."

I turned, probably still pale and jittery.

"You alright?" he asked, concern written on his face.

I met his steady gaze. "The guy in the truck that nearly ran me off the road last night was Vandersteen's college roommate."

Bill frowned. "This case keeps getting weirder."

I followed him into his office, every movement mechanical, like clockwork in a broken machine. He sat at his desk, his face serious.

"I read the report about your accident last night," he said.

I exhaled softly. "Not surprising."

"I was sorry to hear you'd been drinking."

I bristled slightly but admitted, "I had a little wine."

Bill raised an eyebrow. "A little? More like most of a bottle, I'd guess. Look, I'm your AA sponsor, not your mother. I'm here to help, Len. But the program only works—"

"— if I work it. I know, I know," I said, unable to meet his eyes. "I have it under control."

"Sure, Len," he replied skeptically. His voice dropped. "You show up at a crime scene smelling of alcohol, you're off the case—and out of this department. Is that clear?"

"Bill, I would never—"

He moved his hand in a dismissive gesture. "Save it. Let's stick to the case. You said the guy who ran the red light was Vandersteen's roommate? Do you think he's part of this?"

I clenched my fists. "I don't know, but two nights earlier, the same truck almost hit me crossing a street."

"Where were you headed?"

"I... had a date."

Bill's eyebrows rose. "Really?"

I nodded. "The new forensic technician on Doug's team."

"The tall one? What was her name, May?"

"April," I corrected.

"I knew it was a month. Was she your date last night?"

"Yes. Our second."

"Let me get this straight—you had two dates with her, and the same truck nearly hit you both times?"

"I also spotted his pickup leaving Brett Morgan's house."

"Really?"

"It was around the time that the Kris knife disappeared."

"Then he shows up and tries to run you over? Think he's following you?"

"I would've noticed. Felt a tail."

"Could he be following April?"

I paused, considering. "If so, how'd he know I'd be there?"

Bill shrugged. "Maybe he got lucky."

I stared at the ground, piecing the puzzle together. "That means April could be in danger."

"Any connection between her and Vandersteen?"

"None that I know of."

"Then her name's at the bottom of the list—at least for now," McGee said firmly.

I filled Bill in on my meetings with Walt Addison and Kate Yearling. He brightened when I mentioned Stan Frazier would be helping.

"How did Stan look?"

"Good. Retirement suits him."

"I miss the guy. Gabe Petrie's a bit too high-strung for me," Bill remarked.

"Petrie was a solid asset last September. But Stan's in real danger. Claude stabbed him and he almost died. I think Claude would want to finish him off."

Bill's face darkened. "What about Cressley? Could he be the one behind this?"

"I'm going to visit him at Mountainside Medical Center."

"I'd come but I'm buried under paperwork."

"Local crime spree?" I joked. Mountainview was usually quiet —the worst complaint being noisy student parties.

Bill chuckled bitterly. "Had a 911 call Saturday night because a fast-food joint ran out of popcorn chicken."

"They called 911?" I gasped.

He nodded solemnly. "Believe it or not. I have to admit, being lieutenant means more paper pushing than fieldwork."

"Any luck locating the knife Brett used?"

Bill shook his head. "Still missing. Maybe you could track it down, your special way?"

"If you can get me the sheath, I might have a chance. They're energetically linked—but that knife has a bloody history."

Bill nodded. "I remember. Last time you tried to read it, you picked up on every death."

"With the sheath, I could isolate the energy."

"I'll see what I can do."

"I'm also worried about Anna Sokolov."

"Carl's daughter? How is she?"

"Her abilities are evolving rapidly. She's had visions—of Brett's suicide and the attack on Erica Marconi."

Bill pursed his lips thoughtfully. "Sounds like you've got a helper."

"I'm worried. Why those visions? When I spoke to her at Mindy's, I could read her thoughts effortlessly."

"You're probably the only one who can."

"I plan to work with her next week—to help her build barriers. Energy-hungry entities often prey on psychic gifts."

"Think that's what the 'Echo Man' is?"

"Still figuring it out, but Doctor Kohl suspects a spirit attachment. A living host has to fuel Claude's thirst for revenge."

"Which you think is Powell."

"Yes, but someone has to make the drug for him, and that could be Cressley."

"Do you think Cressley knows where Powell is hiding out?"

"If he's his supplier, he'd have to."

Bill nodded grimly. "Then talking to Cressley at the hospital is the next move."

"That's the plan." I stood up but hesitated. "Do you think Kate has been acting strange?"

Bill frowned. "Haven't seen her in weeks. She's made remarkable progress."

"Miraculous, really," I confirmed. "But last night, I heard her voice in my head."

"How's that possible?" Bill asked.

"I don't know. But it saved me from that exploding truck."

"I'm not the expert on that—you are." Bill's expression grew hard. "Well enough of the niceties. You came to see the video from lockup."

"It might help to see how Powell escaped."

"That's the thing—he didn't escape. He was just… let out," Bill said, his voice low and heavy with disbelief. "Come on."

He led me briskly down the corridor toward the AV room, a large space that doubled as the computer hub and, occasionally, a secondary conference room. The stale scent of old electronics and faint traces of disinfectant hung in the air.

At one desk sat Ben Galland, dressed in his crisp uniform, his posture rigid as he noticed our entrance. His eyes flicked up, sharp and alert.

"Galland, can you pull up the tape of Powell from last night?" Bill ordered.

"Yes, sir, Lieutenant," Galland replied, fingers tapping the keyboard with practiced efficiency.

The large monitor flickered to life behind him, casting a pale glow. A grainy, black-and-white image filled the screen— flickering and distorted, but unmistakable. We settled into a pair of worn chairs as the footage rolled.

The camera focused on a bleak cellblock with several cells lined in harsh fluorescent light. I spotted the blurry figure of Antoine Powell immediately—a tall, gaunt African-American man with thinning hair. I remembered him well: once sporting only a thin mustache, but now a close-cropped, scraggly beard covered his face, framing his hollow cheeks.

The timestamp glared at the bottom: 00:21.

"Galland, can you speed it up to the time of the incident?" Bill requested.

Galland nodded silently, accelerating the footage. The blurred figure shuffled to his bunk but kept drifting back to the bars, peering out into the empty hallway like a man haunted by anticipation.

"Any idea why Powell's just standing by the bars instead of lying down?" McGee asked, his brow furrowed in puzzlement.

"No clue," I said. "But it's like he's waiting for something... or someone."

"Here it comes," Galland said quietly, as a second figure—a uniformed officer—stiffly marched into view. The timestamp read

02:30. The same time of night that Brett Morgan had died by his own hand.

The guard approached Powell's cell, keys jangling in his hand before the lock clicked open. Neither spoke a word; Powell followed silently, resigned to his fate. The pair exited the cellblock, Powell's figure wandering away and eventually slipping beyond the camera's reach.

"Switch to the outside view," McGee commanded.

"Yes, sir," Galland responded.

The screen abruptly shifted, now revealing a shadowy shot of the courthouse's exterior, nestled in the heart of Newark's empty streets. The two men emerged beneath the harsh glow of a flickering streetlamp, and Powell simply walked away. Soon he drifted out of sight—vanished into the night like a wraith.

"Did they say anything?" I asked, leaning forward.

"Doesn't look like it," McGee said grimly. "The whole thing's a nightmare. But it gets worse."

Galland brought up the cellblock footage again, the eerie stillness settling back in. The cell stood wide open, the barren bunk exposed.

"Didn't the other prisoners see anything?"

"They were all asleep, Len. Look—here comes the guard back."

The officer reappeared in the frame, muttering to himself with unease, his shadow long and distorted on the cold concrete.

"Is there audio on this thing?" I asked, voice tightening.

"Yes, sir," said Galland. "But he only speaks in whispers—talking to himself."

"Whispering?" I repeated, eyes narrowing.

We watched, horrified. The guard slipped into Powell's cell again, pulling the thin sheet from the bed like a coffin shroud. His fingers trembling, he rolled it into a dense, makeshift noose.

All the while, his muttering rose into a desperate litany of arguments with himself.

Then, with terrifying calm, he tied the sheet to the top bunk, the crude knot digging into the metal frame. Slowly, deliberately, he wrapped the loop around his own neck.

I felt a cold sweat break out as the guard leaned forward, his face turning a grotesque shade of crimson, veins bulging as his breath hitched. His body convulsed, flailing weakly as the noose cut deeper, until finally—mercifully—he went still, hanging from the cloth.

"Wasn't there anyone to help him?" I blurted, voice cracking with shock.

"Len, it was the middle of the night. Only one man was on duty," McGee said grimly.

"I've seen enough," I said, chest tightening with disgust and helpless rage.

The screen went black.

Bill looked at me, eyes dark. "He was a fifteen-year officer, a veteran, and a husband and father of two."

I shook my head slowly, swallowing the bile settling in my throat.

"I want to find whoever did this," I said, voice steady but cold. "And make them pay."

"Let me know anyway I can help," Bill said, and looked at me seriously. "And if you want to talk about the drinking, you know I'm here."

I nodded, steeling myself. "Thanks, Bill. With everything happening, staying sober is the only way forward."

"If you slip, call me. Any time."

I gripped my cane, steadying myself as I left the office, the weight of the case—and the unknown—pressing down harder than ever.

It took barely ten minutes to reach Mountainside Medical Center, a sprawling monolith of glass and steel crowned with a labyrinthine, multi-level parking garage.

As I stepped inside, the main atrium opened up like a cathedral, soaring over five stories high. Each floor wrapped around me in elongated balconies, dotted with silent onlookers peering down like vultures.

At the very top, an expanse of glass and steel framed a breathtaking panorama of Mountainview—calm and unsuspecting beneath the soaring concrete and glass.

Approaching the main desk, security swiftly checked my police ID before nodding me toward the fifth floor, where Dan Cressley was being treated.

My footsteps echoed down the sterile hall until a nurse blocked my path. She was of average height, brunette, dressed in pink scrubs, and her face bore a tight, almost pinched expression.

"Can I help you?" she asked, eyes narrowing.

"I'm here to speak with Dan Cressley," I replied coolly, pulling out my MPD identification. The word "CONSULTANT" emblazoned across it in large, bold letters—vague enough to deflect questions, a label I'd always appreciated.

Her eyes flicked over the card. She scoffed, lips curling. "Another one? We've had everyone up here—from cops to forensics."

"We're just trying to figure out what happened with his vehicle," I said.

"Let me guess, you're a shrink?" Her tone was biting.

"Just someone the police asked to speak with him," I said evenly.

She let out a half-smile. "Sure sounds like a shrink to me."

I nodded, unconcerned. My brother always said, "There's no need to run when no one's chasing you." Or in magic terms, no need to rush sleight-of-hand if no one can spot it. If she wanted to believe I was a psychiatrist, then so be it.

Leaning closer, she lowered her voice. "Honestly? He's malnourished, and some of the stuff he says... well, he could probably use a shrink."

"Trouble?" I asked.

"Talks about a dead friend who haunts him. Crazy shit."

I nodded, feigning sympathy. But deep down, I understood better than anyone exactly what Dan meant.

She pointed me toward the room. Inside, against the faint hum of a muted TV, I found Dan tucked in a corner, the lone patient in the room. No guard stood by the door—there was no need for one. He hadn't committed a crime; only survived a wreck.

Stripped of the heavy winter coat I'd seen him in the night before, Dan was skeletal. The robust man in Kate's photo had vanished—now his sharp cheekbones and sunken ribs poked hungrily beneath thin, hospital-issue fabric.

He looked up, eyes wide and hollow. "Water, please," he rasped.

I fetched a cup, placed a straw to his lips, and he took a slow, shaky sip.

"He told me you'd come," he murmured, puzzlement flickering across his face. "I thought you'd be more muscular."

"Do you know me?" I asked.

"You're the one he's always thinking about," Dan said, his gaze sharp.

"Who?"

"You know who," he said. "He sees you like Goliath—big, unwieldy. And he's like David, wanting to bring you down." His index finger tapped his temple. "But his weapon… it's here."

I frowned, heart tightening. "So Claude's been talking to you. How long?"

"Since he died," Dan sighed, voice flat. "He tells me things. Makes me do things."

"Like trying to run me over?"

Dan chuckled, a dry, rattling sound that collapsed into coughs. "That was just to scare you. Claude knew you'd feel it and get out of the way."

"And if I hadn't?"

His shoulder shrugged weakly. "Then you'd be dead. Either way, Claude didn't care. But he figured you'd be okay. Like when I tried to broadside you—when was that?"

"Last night," I said, realizing the fog in his memory. "You don't remember?"

"I've been in and out," he admitted, waving a dismissive hand.

"Want something to eat?" I offered.

"I can't." His face snapped with anger. "Claude won't let me. I eat, I throw up. Every time."

"They might help you here."

"No one can," Dan sneered. "Claude told me you'd come."

I stood warily. "I didn't come to talk to you about Claude. I wanted to ask you about Antoine Powell."

"Powell," he snorted. "Why him?"

"Have you been supplying him with *Miracle?*"

"I'm not supplying anything to anyone. Claude was the chemist, not me. I don't know how it's made," he said and gazed up at the ceiling. "I took it a couple of times, though."

"What was it like?"

He sighed, a soft sound coming out of that frail body. "It was like being one with everything. Man, talk about mind-expanding. But, coming off of it, the withdrawal was too harsh. I stuck to the other stuff he made."

"How did Claude avoid the withdrawal?" I asked, knowing the answer.

He smiled, a grin like a skull. "He never stopped taking it."

"So where is Powell getting it?"

"Claude told me you'd want to talk about Powell. He told me you'll find him."

"Where?" I asked.

"At the place where it happened."

I frowned. "If you mean that old school Claude used for rituals, it's gone. Torn down."

He chuckled, a hollow sound. "That's what you think? You're easier to fool than I thought."

I could see I was getting nowhere. Cressley was just too far gone.

"Thanks for talking to me, Dan," I said. "I hope they help you."

"Oh, we'll meet again, Doctor." His grin was a bony rictus, terrifying. "One last time."

I left using my cane, unsettled. This wasn't what I'd expected, but there was no doubt I'd found one vessel Claude attached himself to. But did Cressley possess the ability to kill those people?

Heading down in the elevator, I resolved to tell Bill to put surveillance on Cressley.

If Dan was Vandersteen's spiritual battery, would keeping him at the hospital end the killings? And what about Cressley's prediction that I would find Powell?

I thought of a way to separate Claude from Cressley. What could we do? Exorcism?

I thought of a procedure a demonologist had once given me: BIND—AGREE—LOOSE. Bind the spirit, get agreement to leave, and then release. It had worked on a possessed patient once.

Another time, I'd channeled a spirit guide to banish an ancient deity. But this was different.

None of this was straightforward.

The elevator door opened to the lobby, yanking me back to reality.

I'd need to revisit the site of the old school, confirm what Dan meant by "the place where it happened." The school and church were rubble now. Was there another? I had no answers yet.

As I headed for the parking lot, my eyes lifted to the balconies above. Suddenly, a commotion broke—a chorus of raised voices and a woman's shout. Danger sliced through the sterile air. My blood froze.

A voice I recognized—the nurse in pink scrubs—was yelling.

Then I saw him: Dan Cressley, bursting through the double doors, hospital gown flapping as he strode onto the walkway. The nurse followed, calling out for orderlies.

But Dan looked nothing like a weak, malnourished patient. There was a fire in his eyes. He locked eyes with me and flashed that skull-like grin that sent a jolt down my spine.

Without warning, he climbed onto the balcony railing with unnerving agility.

"No," I whispered.

Two hefty orderlies rushed out, hands reaching for him.

Delirious with joy, Dan threw his arms out wide and leapt.

Time slowed—the air thickened as he plummeted, arms out wide, a smile on his face as he fell and fell…

A sickening impact; bones snapping and flesh tearing only a few yards from me. Screams erupted from every level.

Security shoved me aside as medical staff rushed to his broken form, but even before touching him, I knew.

He was dead on impact.

I slumped onto a nearby bench, heart pounding. The one thing that chilled me beyond the fall was the look on his face—pure joy.

That was not the face of a man falling to his death.

It was the face of a man finally breaking free.

12. BOUNCE BACK

The hospital staff swiftly cordoned off the lobby, their movements tense and professional. I glanced around the space, my heart heavy as the reality settled in.

Finally, I pulled out my phone and called Bill, even though the hospital security team had already alerted the police.

Minutes later, Bill arrived with his aide-de-camp, Galland—who wasted no time coordinating with security and questioning witnesses. The air seemed charged, thick with unease.

Leaning in, I lowered my voice and told Bill everything—the strange message Dan claimed Claude had passed to me from beyond the grave, the twisted narrative pieces barely fitting together.

"There's nothing you could have done, Len," Bill said quietly, his eyes shadowed with frustration.

Nearby, a somber crew worked methodically, slipping Dan's broken body into a body bag. The finality of it hit me like a punch.

Bill's sharp gaze met mine. "So, he delivers his ghostly communique and then kills himself? Or did Claude or his surrogate make him do it, like the others?"

I shook my head slowly, trying to piece together the puzzle in my mind. "No, this feels different. I think Dan was finally free of Claude. For the first time."

Bill's lips pressed into a thin line. "There'll be a full investigation."

"Exactly why I called you," I replied, voice tight. "I wanted to get my statement down while it's fresh."

"You mentioned you thought Dan was Claude's host. Now he's dead. Does that mean we're in the clear?"

I let out a long, weary sigh. "No. It means... I was wrong. And that it has to be Powell."

Bill's jaw clenched. "Great. Back to square one."

"The problem is we have no way of knowing where Powell is."

His brow knitted with concern. "I put out an APB on him when I found out he escaped."

"Any luck?" I asked.

"No," Bill said, annoyance creeping into his voice.

"I am sure he went outside your jurisdiction," I said.

"Psychic insight?"

"Just a guess."

"Well, if that's the case," Bill said. "Call that PI friend of yours."

"Not a bad idea," I admitted.

Bill glanced at the towering glass windows, the sunlight fading rapidly. "It's getting dark. Do yourself a favor—put everything off till tomorrow."

I stared out at the long, creeping shadows swallowing the daylight. Another cold December night and another death, both of which burdened my soul.

"Bill… another person could die tonight," I stated, the dread settling deep.

"And it'll be you if you don't have backup," Bill warned. "Claude nearly killed you once while he was alive."

I had to admit he was right.

He pulled out his phone. "I'll get a warrant to search Cressley's place. You said you saw a truck like his drive away from Brett Morgan's around the time that knife disappeared?"

I nodded. "You think he took it?"

Bill shrugged. "That's why I want the warrant. To find out."

"Can you check the truck's registration?"

"Already done," he replied. "According to his driver's license, he lives in Bloomdale."

I frowned. "That's just the next town over."

Bill's eyes darkened with resolve. "Being in Bloomdale keeps him close—ready to monitor you."

I swallowed hard. "Or hit me with his truck."

Bill exhaled loudly. "I'll get the DA moving on that warrant. No promises we'll get it today."

"Let me know when you have it. I want to be there when you go in."

"I'm still trying to get you that sheath from Morgan's estate, but the lawyers are stonewalling."

"Tell them it'll help recover the knife. That should pique their interest," I offered.

He smiled briefly. "Good tactic. I'll keep you posted."

I nodded and headed toward the parking lot. Settling into my van, I glanced at my phone—several missed texts. I'd had it on silent.

The first was from Anna:

Tried to call you.

You didn't pick up.

Pretty freaked out. Call me.

I checked the call log—she was right. Multiple attempts.

Next text was from April:

Schedule opened up.

You free tonight?

I typed back quickly:

Might be on call.

Break in the case.

Don't know if I'm free.

I started the engine to warm the van.

Suddenly, a reply from April:

It would be our third date.

You know what that means.

I stared at the screen, heart skipping. Did I? After my third date with Jyanette, we got intimate for the first time. Was April hinting at that?

The dating game always left me guessing.

Our brief tussle in the van had stirred something too—enough to make me want to take things further. I typed:

Will let you know soon.

I called Anna using the van's Bluetooth.

A shaky voice answered: "H-hello?"

"Anna, it's Len Wise."

"Oh God, Len. I was so scared," she blurted out, breath ragged. "I tried calling last night. When you didn't answer... I thought the Echo Man got you."

Her voice cracked, tears spilling through the pain.

"Anna, calm down. Breathe. I'm safe," I soothed, guiding her through deep breaths. "Focus only on the air going in and out."

As I drove back toward town, she steadied, listening as I coached her mind away from panic.

"Better?" I asked softly.

"Yes," she replied, voice steadier. "Thank you."

"It's meditation techniques. I'm going to teach you more when I see you. It'll help keep you grounded."

Pulling into my driveway, I parked the car, leaving the engine and the heat going. "Now—tell me everything again."

Anna recounted the harrowing vision: a cell where the voice she called the 'Echo Man' forced the guard to release Antoine Powell.

"I saw the video. Anna, do you know if Powell, he was the prisoner, was talking at all?"

"No. And it was the weirdest thing, he looked like he expected the guard to take him outside and let him go."

"Did you see which direction he went?"

"No because once he made a left out of the building, I didn't see him anymore. All I saw was the police officer,...um... the guard. Len, then he—then he—"

"I know Anna. You don't have to tell me"

She murmured, "It was horrible." I could hear the raw emotion in her voice. "It's happening every night. I don't know how to stop it."

"Anna," I said gently, "this isn't a curse—it's a tool. You're getting crucial information."

"But I felt him die," she whispered in a voice filled with pain.

"I understand. The same thing happened to me." I'd experienced a vision of a man burning to death, and for a moment it felt as if I were the one on fire. "Tell yourself to remain the observer."

"How?" Anna's voice trembled, a fragile murmur laced with desperation.

I swallowed hard, steeling myself before answering. "Remind yourself it's just a vision. You're a witness, not a participant. It's like watching a movie, no matter how real it feels." I paused, searching for words that might ease her fear. "Look, Anna, I had to learn these techniques—years of practice just to get control of my mind. You're not alone in this."

She exhaled a shaky breath. "I might need a good night's sleep before even trying," she admitted, her tone so innocent that I couldn't help but burst into laughter, the sound bubbling up uncontrollably from my belly.

"I'm sorry," I blurted, trying to mask my amusement. "I know you're serious, but... that was funny."

Anna's voice softened, less frantic now. "I guess. So, what do I do next?"

"Start with your breathing. When you get flustered, slow it down—inhale steadily, exhale calmly. And build those mental walls I talked about, like a fortress around your mind," I encouraged. "We'll get into more advanced stuff once you're on vacation. By the way, did you get the books I sent?"

"Yes. I'll dive into them tonight," she said, determination creeping back into her voice.

"Good—you'll find some useful techniques in the *Initiate* book."

"Thanks, Len," she sniffled, a cracking vulnerability beneath her resolve.

"You're not alone, Anna. I'll keep my phone close tonight. Call me if anything happens—anything at all."

"Okay. Bye," she said softly before ending the call.

I slipped the phone in my pocket, shut off the van, and stepped into the chill of the evening, my breath forming clouds in the frosty air. The winter coat I'd left on the coat rack this morning still waited for me inside. Pulling my jacket tighter around me, I went in. The warmth of the house felt good as I closed the front door.

Mrs. Higgins was in the kitchen, a comforting sight as she nursed a cup of tea. "Oh, you're home! Would ye care for some tea?"

"Thank you, Mrs. Higgins," I replied, grateful for the simplicity of the moment.

"Will ye be here for dinner?"

I smiled, feeling a flicker of humor amidst the chaos. "I'm not sure. Either heading to a crime scene or maybe a date."

Her eyes sparkled with curiosity. "That science woman again?"

I sighed. "Yes, but there was a twist—the man who crashed his truck last night took his own life in the hospital."

"What?" Her voice cracked with shock.

I nodded. "McGee's working on a warrant to search his apartment. We think he might have stolen the missing knife."

Mrs. Higgins clucked her tongue with concern. "You're never home, I worry for ye. But I'm making shepherd's pie, and there'll be extra—for when ye get hungry."

"Thanks, Mrs. Higgins. That means more than you know."

I took the cup of tea and went into the living room, as Mrs. Higgins had a fire going. I sat with the cup warming my hands and phoned McGee. "Think you'll get that warrant tonight? I might have a date."

"Looks like tomorrow," Bill admitted.

"By the way, do you know the significance of the third date?" I asked.

"How the hell would I know?" he laughed. "Laura and I met on the job—we skipped the dating part and just got married and had kids."

"I gotta find out about this stuff," I muttered.

"Or just relax, have fun, and see what happens," he said. "That's a good plan."

"Thanks, Bill."

I hung up and texted April:

I'm free if you still are.

Sitting back in my chair, doubts bubbling beneath the surface. Was I ready for this? April seemed to like me—especially that night in my van—but was I ready for something real?

My phone buzzed with a text from April:

Sounds good!

Why don't I bring takeout?

You like Thai?

Send me your address.

I quickly sent my address with a note to come through the side door. She let me know she'd see me in forty-five minutes.

I headed to my end of the house, straightened up the sitting room and made my bed, tossing things into drawers or under blankets with hurried efficiency. Limping down the hall for the vacuum, I called out, "Mrs. Higgins, do we have any candles?"

Her voice floated back, "A few. Why?"

"My... um... date's coming," I said, feeling my cheeks heat. "She's bringing me take out."

"Oh? I might have just the thing," she said with a chuckle.

As I vacuumed, Mrs. Higgins appeared carrying two tall white candles, elegant candlesticks, and a plain tablecloth.

"Romantic setup?" I asked with a smile.

She raised an eyebrow. "If she's bringing food, we set your desk for dinner." She moved my laptop bag off the desk and covered the surface with the cloth, placing the candle holders at each end and lighting the flames.

I held the larger cylindrical candles she'd brought. "What about these?"

"You'll put one at that small table over there," she said.

"And the other?"

"In the bedroom, of course," she teased, shaking her head. "Honestly, you have the romantic instincts of an undertaker."

"Hey!"

"Light it. If you end up in there, you'll be grateful. If not— blow it out when you go to bed."

I nodded slowly. That made sense.

She gathered the vacuum, smiling. "Enjoy yourself, Doctor."

When she was gone, I lit the bedroom candle. I trusted Mrs. Higgins' advice. After all, What did I have to lose?

Dimming the lights just enough, I let the candles' glow take center stage and put on some smooth jazz through my speaker system.

A knock came at the door. I opened it to find April bundled up in a heavy coat and wool cap, glasses perched on her nose, two large paper bags in her hands.

"Need help?" I asked as she pushed past and set down the bags.

"No, I'm good," she gasped, pulling off her cap. Her long blonde hair cascaded down her back—a golden waterfall.

I stepped forward to help with her coat. Beneath it, she wore black velvet stretch pants and a red top that exposed her arms. The neckline had a bow that appeared as if one tug could open it.

There was no hint of a bra.

"You look… nice," I said, quickly shifting my gaze to hang her coat.

"Not much of a compliment, but I'll take it," she smiled. "Terrible choice for the weather. I'm freezing."

She moved close, the soft scent of florals filling the air.

"You smell good," I admitted, hugging her. The warmth of her pressed against me, sending a thrill through my body.

"Thank goodness for the locker room at the lab," she said. "I hoped you'd be free."

"I see you're wearing your glasses."

"Had to work late—no contacts."

I leaned forward. Our lips met—and suddenly, the world dropped away.

A flash of a dark, cold stone room filled my mind, tight and claustrophobic—only eight by ten feet. Painted on one wall was a fresco of a naked woman, about three feet tall, sculpted with such detail her skin seemed alive—supple and soft.

But her legs twisted grotesquely into birdlike talons. In one hand she held an ankh; in the other, a Kris knife. Crimson letters above her read: *The Following of Astarte*, and below her, it said: *The Goddess is made flesh.*

We both gasped, stepping back as the vision faded.

"There it is again," April whispered—the same eerie glimpse from our first date.

"What did you see?" I asked, heart pounding.

"A dark room, naked woman with claws for feet, a strange painting."

I nodded slowly. "Me too."

Her eyebrows lifted. "Is that going to happen every time we kiss? Because that could become a real problem later in the evening."

"I hope not," I whispered, though the knot in my stomach betrayed me.

Why were these strange, disjointed visions breaking into my mind at the worst potential moments? I swallowed hard and focused all my mental energy on reinforcing the barriers I'd built around my thoughts. The intrusive images throbbed insistently at the edges of my consciousness.

"I like the candles," she said, her voice cutting through the rising tension. "So, this is your place? Do I get a tour?"

She pulled herself against me, and I felt a jolt. She was standing close enough that I suddenly knew my initial guess was right—she wasn't wearing a bra.

A flush crept up my neck as my gaze tried to settle on her face instead of anywhere else. The flickering candlelight painted soft shadows across her skin, making it impossible to focus solely on words.

"Not much to see here," I muttered, trying to sound casual. "Just the sitting room, bedroom, and bathroom. You want to see the house?"

She tilted her head, a playful glint lighting her eyes. "This is all I need tonight. Can I take a peek at the bedroom?"

I nodded and gestured to the open door connecting the rooms. She slipped through it gracefully.

"Nice," she called back after a moment. "You even made the bed." She returned, grinning. "And a lit candle in there. Feeling confident, are we?"

I swallowed hard, grateful the dim candlelight masked the creeping redness on my cheeks. "I… um… it's not… I mean…"

"Relax," she teased, tossing back her hair. "I'm just giving you a hard time." Her eyes flicked toward my desk, where two more candles burned on a carefully folded tablecloth. "I think I know where to set up dinner."

I grabbed one bag; she took the other. I pulled out multiple containers of food while she uncorked a bottle of wine.

"'I didn't bring wine glasses," she admitted.

"We don't need them," I said, disappearing into the bathroom. I returned holding two small glasses—usually used for water when I brushed my teeth.

She twisted the bottle's screw top and quickly filled one glass. "I'd better pass," I said, the weight of my case pulling at me. "I might get called in."

Her eyebrow arched in mild disbelief. "At this hour? I thought I worked long days."

I shrugged. "My case has people dying in the middle of the night."

She took a small sip, studying me. "Anything new you can tell me?"

"Not much yet," I admitted quietly. "Mysterious deaths, late at night, staged to look like suicides…"

Her eyes sparkled with excitement. "So you really think they're *not* suicides?"

I allowed a small smile. "Didn't we talk about this on our last date?"

She hesitated, her brow furrowed. "But now you have proof?"

"Not yet," I confessed. "Still just theories. What food did you bring?"

She pouted, unapologetically adorable. "I never get to hear the fun stuff."

The containers opened to reveal crispy spring rolls and a salad laced with ginger. We sat facing each other; she set out paper plates, plastic utensils, even chopsticks. I bit into a spring roll, savoring the fresh vegetables, when she lifted the wine glass toward my lips.

"Come on, one taste," she urged. "I have to know if you like this wine."

I gave in reluctantly and took a long swallow. The wine was surprisingly smooth—full-bodied, lacking acidity.

"I really shouldn't," I muttered, but she filled my glass again.

"I want us both to be relaxed," she said, locking eyes with an intensity that melted away my resistance. "After all, the night has just started."

Changing the subject, I asked, "Tell me about your day."

She cautioned me as I spooned curry onto my plate. "Careful with that one—that's the hot one. I had two cases today. Both took hours," she began. Her voice grew animated as she sketched out the crime scenes she'd analyzed miles away. Her boss, Doug Millbank, oversaw the entire county's investigations, keeping the team busy, but she was clearly finding her place and proving herself.

During a lull, I interrupted with a compliment. "I like your blouse."

She smiled brightly. "It's my Christmas outfit." She pointed to the bow on her shoulder. "See? You can unwrap it easily."

I blushed and looked down, prompting a carefree laugh from her. "You're so easy to embarrass. I'm going to have so much fun with you."

I met her mischievous eyes. "Are you?"

"Oh, yeah." She drained her glass in one gulp.

"Did you get into any trouble over that stolen knife?"

She shook her head. "Missed the bullet on that one. Millbank forgot to lock the van, so I got off."

"That's lucky. It wasn't your fault—you were with me when it went missing."

"I still think that FBI woman took it," she insisted.

"Kate Yearling? She didn't have it on her. Where could she hide it?"

"She could've stashed it somewhere on the grounds and come back after everyone left," she said. Then, teasing, "Why are you defending her? Should I worry about competition?"

I smiled. "Kate? We just work together."

She pouted dramatically. "That's not the impression I got."

"Relax. You're the only one I'm dating."

"Okay," she said, appeased. "By the way, I brought my cards."

"Your cards?" I repeated, eyebrows raised.

"Tarot," she said matter-of-factly, fishing a small cardboard box from her handbag. She opened it, dumping the slender cards into her palm, then held the stack out. "Here—shuffle them, get your energy on them."

I took the cards, feeling something intangible but familiar in their weight. Perhaps it was the wine dulling my senses or the mysterious energy she hinted at. I shuffled them with practiced hands—adding in fancy moves I'd learned when I did magic tricks with my brother years ago. The cards were longer than typical playing cards, making the task awkward.

"Now what?" I asked once I'd spread them out.

"You pick six cards and lay them in a row."

I selected six at random and placed them carefully across the tablecloth.

"Not bad," she murmured, taking back the deck to put it away, pointing at the first card. "This shows how you feel about yourself."

She flipped it over to reveal a hooded man on a cliff, staff in hand, holding a glowing lantern.

"The Hermit," she said. "You're looking inward, searching for answers. It often suggests loneliness—feeling disconnected from others." She met my gaze. "I'll help with the loneliness."

"Please do," I whispered. "What's next?"

"What you want most right now."

She turned the next card: a red-robed woman seated on a throne, sword raised, crowned in gold.

"Justice, inverted," she explained. "You seek fairness, but it's being denied."

"Not bad," I agreed. "Sounds like me."

"The third card symbolizes your fears."

She revealed another red-cloaked figure, taller with a crown, brandishing a golden staff with intricate crosses.

"The Hierophant, inverted," she said. "Resistance to old spiritual beliefs."

"You're good at this," I admitted.

She smirked. "Told you. The next card is what you have going for you."

I flipped it, and it showed a golden wheel surrounded by mythological creatures.

"The Wheel of Fortune," she said. "Good fortune—but mostly not from your own doing."

"I'll take whatever help I can get," I sighed.

"The fifth card shows what's working against you."

She flipped the card—it depicted a tall tower struck by lightning, two figures falling.

"The Tower. It could mean demons of despair unleashed from ancient hiding places."

My jaw clenched, shadows deepening. "Sounds like my usual nightmare."

"Forensic investigators don't get all the fun," she chuckled. "The last card is your likely outcome."

She turned it over. A skeletal figure grasping a scythe. Bold text at the bottom: DEATH.

My mouth went dry. "I think I can interpret that one myself."

She frowned. "It's not literal death. Could mean the end of a project, plan, or relationship."

I drained my glass to avoid giving her a look.

Suddenly, she rose. "Come on. Dance with me."

"Uh—what?" I blinked in surprise.

She stood with open arms. "I mean it. I love the jazz you chose."

I pushed myself up using my cane and moved toward her.

"Leave the cane," she commanded.

I set it aside and limped closer. "You have me at a disadvantage."

Her smile deepened as she pulled me close. We swayed gently, rocking with the music. She hummed softly; I did my best to follow the rhythm without toppling over.

I locked eyes with her and frowned.

"What's wrong?" she asked, smiling up at me.

"Your scar," I said, turning my head slightly to catch it better. "I can't see it."

Her fingers dabbed her chin. "It's the light. It's really not that big."

"I noticed it when we kissed in the van," I admitted.

She stepped back, her hand still near her chin, eyes gleaming with mischief. "If you're going to examine me, I should make it interesting."

With a sudden tug at the bow on her shoulder, her blouse slipped open and fell to the floor.

I gasped, my breath catching at her pale, naked skin. Without hesitation, she stepped out of the fabric, pressing close again, her nipples hard in the flickering candlelight.

"You're beautiful," I whispered, my voice rough with desire. I traced my hand along her bare back as we continued to dance.

"That was the right thing to say," she teased before kissing me. The kisses started soft, then deepened—more intense than before but different, more deliberate, more arousing. She pulled my jacket off my shoulders, letting it fall to the floor.

She unbuttoned my shirt with strong fingers, her eyes dark with need.

Before I could react, she yanked it free from my trousers, almost tearing it as she threw it across the room with a fierce, urgent motion.

Then she pulled me close, pressing her naked chest against mine. The warmth of her skin, the soft curve of her breasts against my bare chest—it ignited a wildfire of desire deep within me, leaving me breathless.

Still swaying slightly, she turned so her back pressed into my chest, her every curve aligned with mine like puzzle pieces. Her hands guided mine up to rest on her breasts.   The memory of the night before flashed through my mind—how she liked a sharp pinch. Tentatively, I gave her one, quick and teasing.

"Ouch," she gasped, her voice sharp, sudden. "Not so hard."

My cheek brushed against her ear. "Sorry. You liked it last time."

"Did I?" Her voice held a playful challenge as her hands slid over mine, soft but sure, directing the pressure and placement. "Well, tonight, I want everything gentle."

Gentle sighs and murmurs of encouragement punctuated her whispered instructions. My heart thundered in my chest. She held me spellbound; I would have obeyed her every command without hesitation. The heat pooling in my veins made it nearly impossible to think straight.

Then, softly, she took my right hand and guided it lower, toward the catch of her velvet pants—

Suddenly, a sharp beep shattered the moment.

"Shit!" she muttered, pulling away reluctantly. At first, my racing mind couldn't place the noise; I thought I'd done something wrong.

She moved swiftly to the door, grabbed her purse, and pulled out a small pager and her cell phone. Her eyes flicked to the screen, and she thumbed rapidly across the keys, urgency etched on her face.

"Can you cut the music?" she commanded.

I reached for my device to kill the smooth strains of jazz playing softly.

"Hey there," she said into the phone, voice steady but tight, retrieving a small notebook and pen from her bag. She moved toward the table where candlelight danced across paper and ink. "Yeah, it's me."

I stood shirtless in the dim room, trying to rein in my breath, watching her—the tall, impossibly beautiful April—her skin almost shimmering in the flickering glow. She took notes with a focused intensity, the playful fire gone, replaced by professionalism.

It was a stunning contrast.

"I'll get there as soon as I can," she said, ending the call. Her eyes met mine, a shining mix of frustration and something more —lust, regret, exhaustion. "This sucks."

"It's the job," I said, swallowing my disappointment.

"I was told I had the damn night off," she snarled, a shadow crossing her features. "And you—God, you got me so worked up."

"Same here," I admitted, trying to steady myself. "What do you need?"

"I have a change of clothes in a bag in the back seat of my car. Can you grab it?"

I nodded, pulling my shirt back on as she watched, still bare from the waist up, the candlelight tracing every curve. She moved to put the phone away and offered me her keys with a faint, tired smile. "I'll change in the bedroom."

She slipped past me, clutching her purse and blouse as she disappeared into the bedroom. I grabbed my heavy coat and stepped into the chilly night air.

Her car waited in the roundabout near my door—the small, unassuming hatchback, jokingly dubbed an SUV, though it looked better suited to city streets than backcountry trails.

Using the key fob, I unlocked the door and retrieved the bag of clothes from the back seat. As I shut the door, my eyes caught a small sticker on the rear window:

Vanderbilt College
Dormitory C

A sudden chill ran down my spine. She'd never mentioned Vanderbilt—the same college Claude Vandersteen had attended.

Did April know Claude?

The sticker, the cold air, the creeping suspicion—they crushed the embers of desire, leaving only a knot of unease in my gut. I headed back inside, carrying the bag.

In the bedroom, only the flickering candlelight illuminated April's silhouette. She stood in a tiny thong, every inch of her lean hips smooth and bare—almost boyish in contrast to her generous chest. The sight nearly stole my breath again.

She took the bag from my hands, pressing a quick kiss to my lips. "You're a gem."

I tried to focus, to shake the creeping distrust. "You never told me you went to Vanderbilt."

She pulled out a pair of loose scrub pants, slipping them on as she spoke. "What?"

"There's a Vanderbilt College parking sticker on your car—the kind for Dorm C."

She shrugged casually. "It must've been on the car when I bought it."

I pressed on, cold gnawing at my spine. "When'd you buy it?"

She pulled a bra from the bag, sliding it over her breasts and adjusting the straps. "Back in May, maybe. Got it on Staten Island from some girl."

"Staten Island?" The name felt like a weight.

"Yeah. She was moving, sold it cheap. Why?"

I cleared my throat, searching for a casual tone. "I—guess it doesn't matter."

Everything screamed otherwise—something was off. Without the wine and the haze of desire, my instincts screamed warning, but I pushed the thoughts aside.

"Good," she said, folding the clothes she'd been wearing and tucking them back into the bag. "I hate leaving you hanging, but believe me, I'm just as pissed as you are."

I nodded, though suspicion tightened its grip. Not the best foundation for what I hoped could be a beginning.

She grabbed her coat from the rack, moving toward the door. Just as I stepped close, she turned, pressed a searing kiss to my mouth—a kiss that could've awoken the dead.

"We'll finish this another time," she promised softly, before slipping out into the night.

The door clicked shut behind her. I swallowed hard, fighting to steady my breathing.

I blew out the candles and cleaned the remains of our dinner from the table, eyes lingering on the half-full bottle of wine.

With a mixture of hesitation and habit, I poured myself a glass —the warm liquid sliding down my throat while my mind spun with unanswered questions, shadows darkening the night.

13. REFLECTIONS

The next morning, I forced myself out of bed, every muscle protesting after a night riddled with unrest.

It hadn't just been dreams—they were nightmares, vivid and relentless.

Every time my eyelids closed, my mind dragged me back to that forsaken, abandoned church on Staten Island where I'd faced Claude Vandersteen. The memory was a scar etched deep: the place where Claude had sacrificed Constance Newhouse, poised to kill Erica Marconi before I intervened.

In my dream, I moved deliberately—slowly, painfully slowly—through the dim narthex. A door slid open on its own, an eerie invitation I couldn't resist.

There around the chancel stood robed and hooded figures, motionless and solemn, their shapes barely discernible in the low candlelight. Next to them were candles mounted on five-foot-tall metal braziers, much like the one I had lit for April in my bedroom. Their flickering flames barely pushed back the oppressive shadows that clung to the walls, casting these cloaked forms as gigantic, flickering giants that seemed to loom closer with every breath.

In the cold center of the scene sat the stone altar. On it were three women: Erica Marconi, my deceased fiancée; Cathy Garber; and Jyanette Emery.

Their vulnerability was stark—they were completely naked— Jyanette's dark skin contrasting with Erica's pale complexion and Cathy's sun-kissed tan. The floor was littered with debris, remnants of the long-removed pews, and a pair of small propane tanks with red-glowing heaters peered toward me like angry eyes.

Then, the nightmare morphed. Those propane tanks transformed into eyes—the burning, unforgiving gaze of a giant Claude Vandersteen looming above, his sinister laughter reverberating through the space.

My heart exploded into frantic beats as I jerked upright in bed, drenched in sweat.

Each time I tried to sleep, a new variation of this hellish scene replayed itself. Sometimes, Erica alone rested on the altar—the only real moment I'd witnessed. Other times, it was just Cathy… or Jyanette, isolated and exposed.

But this time, the nightmare shifted—the robed figures were alive. They chanted and swayed in rhythm as I moved through the church, unlike the mannequins I'd seen in reality, which concealed a recorded chant.

Among the living was Dan Cressley—who I'd met when he was gaunt and ill, now back to his full weight and in prime shape. Was he truly one of the Following, Claude's twisted congregation? The faces of the others remained shrouded beneath their hoods.

Suddenly, Claude rose—his grotesque figure bursting from the ground beneath the altar, Brett Morgan's knife gripped high and poised to strike. Before I could barely gasp, my phone's sharp ring shattered the nightmare.

My eyes snapped open to see the glowing screen: 5:00 a.m. A text from April:

Finally, going home.

Just wanted you to know I'm alright.

I figure you'll see this when you wake up.

I exhaled, a tight knot loosening somewhere in my chest. No more sleep came to me that night.

I turned my attention to the manuscript sprawled across my desk—the story of hypnotherapist Anika Vanya, a case that had consumed me. I kept labeling it a "novel" and altered the names, hoping to avoid legal issues, though the truth weighed in every line I wrote.

Two hours passed before I headed to the kitchen for coffee, the familiar hum of the coffeemaker grounding me. Yet the residue of that nightmare clung stubbornly.

Oddly, I'd drunk the last of the wine the night before—the same wine that usually dulled my psychic sensitivity—yet even that couldn't mute the vivid dreams.

The stone altar haunted me most—the real one, the place of sacrifice. The gigantic Claude, the knife-wielding attack: none of that had happened. And the chanting figures—no, in reality, they had been nothing more than carefully arranged mannequins, a grim theatrical set-up.

The FBI's raid had uncovered just one real adherent of the Following, Antoine Powell—convicted and now an escaped convict.

A thought hit me suddenly: Jyanette didn't know her ex-husband was free. Would he bother her, maybe attack her? Should I tell her? Could I?

Maybe it would be better for McGee to deliver such news. A text from me might reopen wounds too fresh.

But I missed her. Deeply.

Despite last night almost ending with another woman, my mind wandered to Jyanette—the one I couldn't forget. I hesitated, fingers trembling, before typing:

Jyanette, it's Len Wise.

I'm sorry to bother you.

I wanted to let you know that Antoine Powell

has escaped from prison.

I thought you should know.

I hit send before second-guessing, heart pounding in the silent kitchen. I poured coffee, clutching the warm mug just as my phone buzzed with a reply:

Len. I didn't know.

Thank you for telling m*e*.

I quickly texted back, trying to sound steady:

Congratulations on your new job.

Her answer came cold and sharp, cutting through my fragile hope:

Thank you.

It would be best if we didn't communicate.

The words hit me like a blow. My chest tightened, and stinging tears pooled in my eyes. The woman I still loved despised me now. I sipped my coffee and typed a single word in response:

Understood.

Slipping the phone into my robe's pocket, my gaze drifted to the whiskey bottle on the shelf—a bottle Mrs. Higgins kept under her watchful eye. A single shot could drown this pain, make the ache in my chest vanish, if only briefly.

Just then, Mrs. Higgins burst through the swinging kitchen door.

I spun around, grabbing a paper towel from the dispenser.

"Ooh, Doctor! Yer up early," she said, eyes scanning the table. "Is yer friend still here?"

I exhaled deeply, rubbing the paper beneath my eyes. "No. She had to leave last night. Got called in on a case."

"Sorry to hear that," she said softly, concern etched across her face. "Are ye all right?"

I blew my nose. "I just told Jyanette about her ex-husband."

She didn't move, watching me carefully. "I take it that didn't go well?"

"She thanked me... but said we shouldn't communicate." The raw admission brought fresh tears. Why couldn't I be stronger?

"That can't've been easy," she said gently.

"I still love her. I miss her. This time of year makes everything worse. Last Christmas..." I trailed off. "You remember the good times we all had."

"I do. But she's probably sufferin' as well," she offered quietly.

I nodded, gripping my coffee. "I'm heading back to my office —to make sense of this case. At least no suicides last night."

"Are ye sure?" she asked, watching me as I passed.

I checked my phone—7:30 a.m. "I'll call McGee to be certain."

The weight of the world bore down as I made my way back to my sitting room. I dialed McGee.

He answered on the first ring. "McGee."

"Len here. Nothing about suicides last night?"

"Nothing at all here in Mountainview. Good news. We'll be able to check out Cressley's apartment in a couple of hours."

"Will Bloomdale police be involved?"

"It's necessary. I'm calling the captain once I'm in. I'll coordinate everything."

"Let me know where and when."

"I'll text you."

He hung up, and I returned to the manuscript, wrestling with the tangled threads of a case and a haunted past, both impossible to escape.

Hours later, I stood before a weathered brick brownstone in Bloomdale—an aging relic clinging stubbornly to life just off Montgomery Street.

Dan Cressley had been renting two rooms on the third floor of this four-story building, a structure indistinguishable from its identical neighbors. Builders erected rows of these nearly identical brownstones in the 1950s to house the influx of factory workers flooding into the city. Those factories dominated Bloomdale's economy for decades, but when they shuttered and scattered, the city's heart withered.

The damage wasn't just economic. The Garden State Parkway sliced the town in half like a jagged knife, deepening the divide, both physically and socially. This neighborhood where Dan lived now teetered on the edge of bleakness—mostly government-assisted tenants drifting in and out of Section 8 housing.

The hallways bore scars of neglect: dirty floors, flickering or dead bulbs that left the landing in shadow. The elevator was long out of service, so I climbed the stairs, each creak and groan beneath my shoes and cane echoing the decay.

Yet, just down the street, the irony was stark: a vibrant town hall stood in contrast, and beyond that, a park bursting with life —a cruel juxtaposition.

I noticed the familiar figure of a police officer stationed at one doorway, his dark blue uniform a reassuring anchor in the gloom. I flashed my consultant ID without hesitation. He nodded curtly and stepped aside. This was exactly the mood settling over the place—stark, wary, fraying at the edges.

Inside, the apartment was no better. The walls' sickly yellow paint reminded one of vomit and old warnings. There were only two cramped rooms: a living room that also served as a kitchen and a bedroom with a small attached bathroom.

Cooking facilities meant little more than a card table cluttered with a hot plate, a toaster oven, and a small cube fridge beneath. The arrangement screamed mere survival.

Dan had told me he couldn't eat, so these appliances puzzled me. I cracked open the refrigerator door, peering inside. Energy drinks, protein shakes, half-empty cans of beer—the contents whispered of a liquid diet, a fragile attempt to sustain himself, maybe even to fight a losing battle against his own body.

My eyes caught on a large white classroom-style clock affixed to the wall. It seemed oddly out of place: pristine, modern, and glaringly oversized with a face at least a foot across. It was as if time itself were being marked and monitored—but for what purpose?

Bill was already combing through the room. He turned towards me as I came in. "Hey Len, good to see you, we could use your help."

"What's the latest on Antoine Powell?" I asked.

Bill shook his head. "Galland went through the video from street cameras, the Newark Train Station, and even the Bus Depot. Nothing. Powell just up and vanished."

"He has to be somewhere," I said.

"I've got a five-state APB out on the man. So far, no luck," he said with a frown. "We also haven't found that knife anywhere in this place. Can you sense it? You know, the way you do?"

I shook my head, stepping back from the fridge, feeling more frustrated than ever. "No. Nothing. Not the knife. In fact, I'm not picking up any energy readings at all in here."

Bill's jaw tightened. "I'll search the bedroom. You try to conjure your voodoo."

I couldn't help but smile faintly. Bill intended his comment to be tongue-in-cheek. Unlike others in the MPD who used words like "witch-doctor" to mock me, Bill's faith hadn't wavered. He understood, trusted my abilities, even if he didn't always comprehend them.

I took my place on the one hard-backed chair, closing my eyes to slip into the altered state where I could tune into the unseen.

It wasn't easy this time.

Thoughts swirled, unwelcome intrusions: memories of April, bare-breasted in the candlelight; fleeting regrets about my spiraling drinking; the cold message of Jyanette's text. These "cloud thoughts" usually drifted by; today they clung like shadows.

With a slow, steadying breath, I pushed them back, trying to clear my mind. But my training with Doctor Kohl had never prepared me for this barrage. Today was different. The resistance was stronger; the distraction nearly overwhelming.

I loosened my mental grip, letting go of control, opening myself to whatever might emerge.

Suddenly, the vision exploded into life: Claude Vandersteen, leaping up from the dusty floor of an abandoned church, a gold-and-silver knife raised high. The blade twisted in the flickering candlelight, shimmering with a sinister promise.

I shoved the image of Claude aside as if warding off a blow. It was too vivid, too intrusive—a ploy by my own fears.

I slowed my breathing, and let the noise in the room fade, focusing on the residue of energy here. This was a spiritual struggle, fierce and painful, the imprint of a will crushed beneath a stronger force. I needed to know the truth behind this psychic battlefield.

Descending deeper, I felt the room transform. Opening my eyes, the vibrant colors of the room had drained away, replaced with sepia browns and grays. Suddenly, a translucent figure of Dan appeared before me—less skeletal than in flesh, but already worn thin—dressed in loose pajamas, his voice slicing through the silence.

"Why are you bothering me? I've done everything you asked," he shouted, pounding the empty air as if demanding answers from the shadows above.

Unlike many visions where the words refuse to form, here the voice was clear as day. Dan's bitterness, his desperation hammered in the echoes.

He froze mid-room, as if receiving an unseen response.

"I didn't know," came his plaintive reply.

But I caught only half of the conversation. If this was the turning point—the moment that bent Dan toward his fate—I had to hear both voices. I let myself sink deeper, matching my breath to his energy, attempting to blend with his fractured mind.

Dan repeated his question in slowed, stretched syllables: "Why are you bothering me? I've done everything you asked."

Then came the whisper, layered, fragmented: "When you said the words to join the Following, you vowed to be my sword…"

There it was—the chilling tether that had bound him.

The voice belonged to Claude Vandersteen. Yet, it carried an unnatural echo, as if two voices spoke nearly in unison but never quite aligned—like a sinister duet, disturbing in its dissonance.

"I didn't know," Dan's voice trembled again, sluggish and low.

"You must strike against those who hurt me…" the spectral chorus insisted.

Frustration boiled over. "I can't eat, I can't think," Dan cried, desperation thick in his tone. "How far do I have to go until you leave me alone?"

"Until you join me…" came the bitter reply.

Dan stood silent for a heartbeat, then whispered almost mournfully, "But you're dead."

"Go to bed. We will speak tomorrow…"

I glanced up at the enormous clock, its ghostly hands overlaid atop the real ones, fixed at 2:30 a.m. The hour was unmistakable. The events from my vision were unfolding in the dead of night— the same time as the attacks we'd been investigating.

Dan retreated to the bedroom, the weight of realization pressing down: that death might be the only escape left.

McGee's footsteps broke the trance as he walked through the vision, prompting me back to reality. I blinked, forcing my mind into the present.

"Anything?" McGee asked.

I drew in a breath, shaking my head with a mix of frustration and revelation. "Nothing about the knife. But I know one thing."

"What's that?"

"Whoever Claude Vandersteen is using… it wasn't Dan."

McGee narrowed his eyes. "Why?"

"Because Dan heard the same voice as our victims heard. If he was the host—fully possessed—it would be deeper, more... ingrained, like part of him."

"So, this 'spirit attachment' you talked about—it's different from possession?"

"In a way, yes. Possession obliterates the host's identity, swallowing them whole. An attachment, though, is more like a partnership—two minds agreeing to merge and accomplish shared goals. Dan had pledged himself to the 'Following of Astarte,' swearing fealty. That's why Claude could speak to him so easily."

"There really were members of this cult?"

I shrugged, lips tight. "All evidence points that way. I imagine Antoine Powell was top of that list."

"Then why weren't they at the big confrontation? At the sacrifice—when you faced Vandersteen?"

"Maybe Claude told them to stay away. The drug he took to enhance his psychic abilities could have given him a glimpse into the future. He'd know that if he fell, his followers could seek revenge for him."

"So, we need to dig into Claude's old college circle. Find anyone else he might've been in contact with?"

"Exactly. Darren Ward can focus on that. We need to root out every connection Claude made."

"That professor from the college said those ties were few, mostly casual."

"Dan suffered torment at night for months before these recent attacks. It wasn't sudden."

Bill exhaled sharply. "Do you think the host has to build up control—kind of practice before the actual attacks?"

"Maybe. Or perhaps the host is dosing a different amount of the drug Claude developed, trying to get it right."

Bill's jaw clenched, the weight of uncertainty thick between us. "The big question is: how do we stop the next attack?"

I hesitated, swallowed the knot in my throat, and confessed, "I honestly... don't know."

14. SPLITTING IMAGE

A s I drove back to Mountainview, my phone buzzed with a message from April—she was finally awake.

I instinctively reached for the phone, but didn't want to risk distractions while driving. I spotted a dimly lit parking lot up ahead, pulled off, and killed the engine to use my phone safely.

Before I could, the disembodied voice in my Bluetooth console informed me a call was coming in from Thomas Wise.

I accepted the call from my twin brother. "Hey, Tom, how are things in Vegas?"

"Wonderful, naturally." His tone was upbeat, but with an undercurrent of something urgent. "Listen, Jules and I are flying out for Chanukah this Saturday."

Jules—that was Julia Tannenbaum, the woman Tom lived with. I had dated her back in high school and was the one who gave her that nickname.

"That's the Saturday before Christmas. The traffic will be a nightmare!" I warned him.

Tom was pragmatic. "Lenny, it's all I could spare. The casino is adding extra shows between Christmas and New Year's. It's crunch time, and anything family-oriented is in demand. You'll be there, right?"

I sighed, frustration tightening in my chest. I had to see the family at some point. If Tom and Julia were there, maybe it would ease some of the pressure.

"Yeah, I guess I'll be there."

His voice dropped to a more serious tone. "It would mean a lot to me, Lenny."

I softened. "Okay, okay… I haven't gotten my monthly guilt trip from Mom yet."

"Thanks, buddy. See you then."

The call ended abruptly. But why was it so damn important? Tom had never been one to value Jewish holidays much, and even if he did, Chanukah wasn't exactly one of the important ones.

Still, why fight it? I'd show up and be polite.

Switching back to the Bluetooth, I dialed April.

"I thought no one talked on the phone anymore. It's all texts," she teased as soon as she answered.

"I'm an old guy," I replied, earning the throaty chuckle I adored.

"That means I owe you a night of unbridled passion."

"That makes two of us," I said.

She exhaled. "But not tonight. I'm pulling overnight. Either at a crime scene or stuck in the lab."

"What happened last night? You were late."

"A shooting at some dive bar down in one of the Oranges. The place was a mess—fingerprints and DNA everywhere. I didn't get home until five."

I had seen the message she sent earlier. "I was awake too… bad dreams."

"You mean I could've come over and finished what we started? You should've told me."

"I'm regretting it now."

She laughed and then sighed. "Don't worry, Sunday I'm off."

"I have family Chanukah plans Saturday night. My brother insisted."

"Sunday then. Maybe you can arrange dinner in your room, and unwrap me again."

"I'd love to finally be alone with you. Naked, of course."

"That was my thought exactly." She giggled again. "I need coffee. Keep in touch."

She hung up before I could say anything else.

I restarted the drive, calling Kate on a whim.

She answered without pleasantries, "I don't have your profile yet. Still digging."

"And hello to you too, Kate," I said. "Do you know the name of the girl the FBI interviewed from Vandersteen's chemistry class? I want to pass it along to Darren Ward."

"June something. June Steen. Stan's already looking into her. Didn't you save her name?"

"I forgot. I'll check when I get home. Can you text me Stan's number?"

A rustling of papers. "Sure. You guys get all the fun, driving around, interviewing suspects."

"Hours in the car really fill my day."

"Keep me in the loop, professor. I need some excitement in this lonely paper-pushing life."

"Don't waste guilt on me. My mother is an expert."

A theatrical sigh. "I'll call when I have a preliminary report."

"Thanks, Kate."

I ended the call as I pulled into the driveway. Back in my sitting room, I pulled my notes and found the name I'd been looking for—June Steen. Kate mentioned she'd dated Claude and was one of the few interviewed by the FBI.

That placed her in danger, especially after what happened to Dan.

If Claude or Antoine—or whoever Claude was using—was targeting those he blamed, June could be next.

Or worse, what if she was the host?

I used my phone to call Stan.

"Hello?"

"Stan, it's Len Wise."

"Hey, Professor. Checking on me?"

"I'm tracking someone from Vandersteen's past—June Steen."

"I've been on it too. Turns out she left Vanderbilt. Still trying to find where she transferred."

"I'm worried she might be the next victim."

"Guess I'll bump her to the top of the list. It's tough, Professor. No FBI badge means I have to ask people nicely, not order them to do things."

"Have Kate push for a warrant, say it's for witness protection."

"Good call. I'll move on that."

"I'll call Darren for backup; he's got connections in Staten Island."

"Anything else?"

"Just keep me posted."

"Will do."

Ending the call, I felt useless—there were probably others I hadn't considered. The problem was how little I really knew about Claude.

I pulled out a yellow legal pad and started piecing it together.

Claude was brilliant—a prodigy who made designer drugs for classmates, showing no moral compass from the start. Creating a substance that heightened mental abilities and opened a doorway to converse with demons… that was a dangerous addiction.

Later, he'd taken the drug *Miracle* for months, developing a dependence. Was it the drug combined with Astarte's influence that destroyed his conscience? Did Astarte teach him how to kill without regret?

If someone had Claude's notes and could manufacture the drug, were they on *Miracle* regularly, losing their grip on reality like he did?

I stared blankly at the notes, exhaustion dragging me down. I needed sleep.

I emailed Darren, asking him to investigate June Steen and verify the church where I fought Vandersteen was truly gone and buried.

I had a fleeting memory of kissing April—and of seeing that bizarre fresco of the naked goddess that Claude had sculpted in the catacombs beneath that church.

That gave me pause. The catacombs under the church.

Were those underground tunnels destroyed with the building? When I visited the site, I saw the church wrecked, but I hadn't checked if anyone filled in the underground parts.

Part of me wanted to call Darren immediately, but the fog of fatigue was relentless.

I stripped down to my boxers and T-shirt, slipping into the bedroom. Suddenly, a sharp tingle prickled the back of my neck.

My heart hammered. I scanned the room, letting down my mental barriers to sense any threats.

Something is wrong…

I sensed the buzz and tried to locate the source, but it was too faint to catch. There was an energy here, unseen but chilling—an unfamiliar presence that wasn't good.

Great. My precognition was more frustrating than helpful.

If I lay down and slipped into an altered state, I might either pin it down or simply fall asleep—both acceptable.

Under the covers, I focused on my breathing. Sleep claimed me almost instantly.

Or so I thought.

I was back at that cursed church—moving through the narthex, into the sanctuary.

The scene was hauntingly familiar: the ring of hooded figures circling, and Erica Marconi lying naked on the massive stone altar raised three steps above the floor.

The chanting filled the air, voices hauntingly recorded by Claude himself. For the first time, I noticed the dirge wasn't just random Latin—they were singing "Ave Astarte," a strange mix of praise I hadn't caught before.

I'd replayed that night endlessly in my mind—but this detail was new.

I knew what would happen next: Claude's demonic jack-in-the-box scare, to rattle me, just like the night before.

I turned and twisted in the dream, desperate to anticipate his attack.

Why did I keep returning to this place in my dreams, with only subtle changes? There was no logic—unless someone or something was forcing me back.

And each time, Claude won. Unlike reality, where I had defeated him, here he defeated me over and over.

I edged closer to the ring of hooded figures, my heart pounding against my ribs.

Among them was Dan—not in his prime, robust and healthy, but the frail, malnourished shadow he'd become the last time I'd seen him. A dark hood covered his gaunt face, but I recognized the hollow eyes that seemed to pierce right through me.

Another figure shifted slightly. I caught sight of worn brown loafers before raising my gaze—and froze. Walt Addison turned his face away, his lips moving in sync with the eerie chanting that crackled from the recording.

His presence here made no sense.

Desperately, I scanned the others. Antoine Powell loomed with an empty, dull stare that felt more like a warning than recognition.

Brett Morgan—short, stocky, sinewy—stood rigid, muscles coiled as if ready to strike. What was he doing here, gathered like prey in this macabre ritual?

One of the hooded figures pivoted to walk away. My eyes caught a glimpse—a rounded female silhouette beneath the robe. A name surfaced unbidden in my mind: June.

My voice was tentative, but urgent. "June?" I called out, hoping to conjure her into the circle.

By now, I had stepped inside the ring, the oppressive silence swallowing me whole. The figure nearest turned sharply. I gasped —Claude's twisted grin was unmistakable.

"You cannot stop me," he sneered, his voice dripping with madness.

Suddenly, Brett Morgan's hand shot forward, a gleaming knife flashing in the dim light. The blade plunged into my stomach with cruel precision, hot agony exploding through me.

I jolted upright in bed, a guttural roar tearing from my throat. Sweat slicked my skin as I clutched my belly, panting hard. Darkness surrounded me.

The glow of my digital clock on the nightstand confirmed the time—past 5:00 p.m. I'd been asleep for over two hours.

Everything had happened so fast, the nightmare morphing into a living nightmare. This time, Claude's assault had felt alarmingly real—almost fatal.

Trembling, I swung my legs over the bed and stood, moving toward the bathroom. I grabbed a comb, forcing my tangled hair back into place as I tried to steady my racing heart.

The disturbing additional elements in the dream—the circle of victims, and the woman cloaked in mystery—gnawed at me.

June Steen seemed likely; after all, Dan had been there, and she was one of only a few Claude had ever been close to back in his Vanderbilt College days.

But why was Walt Addison there? Was he another intended victim? And more chillingly, who was serving as the host for Claude's dark influence? If Dan was gone—and it hadn't been him—then who had taken his place?

June? Walt? Antoine? My mind churned with suspicion I'd tried to avoid. The circle of people familiar with Claude was frighteningly small, and with every death, it was growing smaller still.

The nightmare was closing in, and so was the truth. I had to uncover who was behind Claude's malevolent grip—before it was too late.

Fully dressed, I made my way to the kitchen, my cane tapping steadily on the worn wooden floorboards.

The house felt different somehow—Mrs. Higgins had strung colored lights around the windows, their soft glow casting flickering, rainbow-hued shadows that filled the room with a sense of magic, almost as if the old walls were hiding secrets waiting to be uncovered.

As I stepped into the kitchen, the warm, comforting scents of fresh-baked bread and a hearty, savory soup curled around me like a gentle invitation, teasing my senses and momentarily pushing away the lingering weight of the troubling dreams.

"Ah, Doctor! Yer here, are ye?" Mrs. Higgins greeted me from behind the stove, her voice carrying a spark of cheer that felt almost out of place in my foggy mood.

I managed a smile. "Yes, Mrs. Higgins. I had a rough night— needed a nap to pull myself together."

Her brow knitted in concern. "Ye don't look very rested, if ye ask me."

I exhaled, feeling the frustration rise. "Bad dreams won't let go. I keep seeing that old church—confronting Claude Vandersteen again and again. But no matter what I do, he keeps winning. It's like a loop I can't break."

She frowned, her hands pausing in their work. "That'd haunt my sleep too. Are ye here for dinner? I made bread and soup. Simple, but good."

"Thank you. And I see you've got the lights up already. I suppose a tree will be here any day now?" I asked, trying to lift my spirits with small talk.

Mrs. Higgins wagged a finger at me with a playful sternness. "Doctor, ye know well it's family tradition to only put the tree up on Christmas Eve."

Snapping my fingers, I brightened. "Right! Jyanette and I helped decorate it last year."

She chuckled softly. "Aye, that ye did. Maybe yer new lady will help this time?"

I hesitated, the weight of memories flickering in my mind. April had mentioned her family was in South Dakota—maybe inviting her for Christmas wouldn't be such a bad idea. The thought of having her to myself overnight, away from the chaos, was tempting.

"I'll ask," I replied cautiously.

After finishing my coffee, Mrs. Higgins gently nudged me out of the kitchen. "I'll call ye when dinner's ready," she said warmly.

I retreated to my office, pulling up the research paper Dr. Kohl had sent me. The paper delved into attachment and possession in meticulous detail but offered little beyond the obvious: religious symbols that made the bearer feel protected.

A frustrating lack of concrete solutions.

With time on my hands, I opened my laptop and scoured online forums and articles. The results were disappointing. Most "experts" offered spirit removal for hefty fees—four hundred dollars to be "relieved." I was sure the only thing being relieved was the client's wallet.

Another site recommended crystals, burning sage, and essential oils. Scientifically, these engaged the senses—vision stimulated by sparkling crystals; olfactory nerves fired by the pungent smell of burning sage; touch and smell combined in essential oils to awaken mental energy. But I doubted these gentle rituals could repel whatever malevolent force I was facing.

Religious artifacts, candles, oils—these focused the mind, activating specific brain regions through sensory input and ritual. But an avenging spirit powered by someone like Claude Vandersteen required more than comforting symbols.

Mrs. Higgins's voice echoed down the hall, pulling me back.

Closing my laptop, I followed her call and joined her at the kitchen table. She had spread out dinner before us: rich lentil soup steaming beside a crusty, dark loaf of bread.

As we ate, I filled her in on the developments and asked for her thoughts.

Her story about a possessed rat lingered in my mind—I still didn't see how it fit.

I told her about the faint, unexplained buzzing I'd sensed in my bedroom. She looked puzzled.

"That's curious," she mused. "I don't mean to pry, but did ye and yer lady friend… um… y'know?"

I shook my head. "Nothing happened. She had to leave before it could go that far."

"Perhaps her presence pulled something to you?" she suggested.

"More likely, Dan Cressley is the key," I said grimly. "He'd been tailing me, staking out the Brett Morgan crime scene. We believe he stole the sacrificial knife. He might have spotted April there and possibly followed her as well."

Her eyes widened. "Is she in danger?"

"Anyone who went to that house could be," I answered.

She nodded solemnly as she spooned more soup. "What is this Claude fellow after?"

I shook my head. "Revenge is part of it, but it's not the entire story. Claude sought power—a pact with a demon. That's why he killed Constance Newhouse and tried to sacrifice Erica Marconi. Brett Morgan's death secured the knife, vital for the ritual. The guard's death allowed Powell to escape. Dan's death silenced someone who knew too much."

"And the girl?" Mrs. Higgins asked softly.

"Erica? He targeted her to kill herself, but her family stopped her before it went too far."

"It sounds like there's pleasure in the killing—does the host enjoy it?" she pondered aloud.

I nodded. "Taking a life can be a 'high' for a serial killer. Maybe that's the lure."

"Cruelty, then," she said, slicing another piece of bread.

"The drug Claude created changed him," I added. "Even Antoine Powell said that. If we could find him, that would help."

"Aye, but cruelty had to be there first," she said, her eyes sharp. "An orange, when squeezed, only gives orange juice."

I frowned. "I don't follow."

"When life squeezes ye, only what's inside will come out," she explained. "Pressure reveals what's already there."

I smiled. "Very apt, Mrs. Higgins."

She grinned. "Thank ye. If yer talking about serial killers, isn't that Yearling woman an expert?"

I nodded, glancing at my watch. "She is. She said she might have a profile soon. Good thinking, Mrs. Higgins."

"Just doing me part," she replied, standing to clear the table.

I rose unsteadily, pushing myself up. "Let me help."

"Nay," she said firmly. "There's folk dyin'. Ye need to work, not get in me way."

I grinned weakly. "Fine. I'll return to my dungeon."

"Do that," she said with a warm smile.

I strode briskly down the hallway. I pulled out my cell phone, thumb fumbling to input Kate's number as I moved.

"Are you always this demanding?" came her voice, laced with playful irritation but underscored by something sharper.

I couldn't suppress a short, mirthless chuckle. "Is this your usual way of handling the cops? Rough and ruthless?"

A pause. Then: "You're worried, aren't you?"

I swallowed hard, the knot in my stomach tightening. "I have to admit it. Last night, there wasn't even an attempt. That only means the odds are worse... that whoever this is will try again tonight. And maybe—target someone new."

Kate's voice hushed, almost conspiratorial. "I agree. You know the typical profile for a serial killer, right? White male, usually in his twenties or thirties, a recluse."

I cut in, dryly. "So, basically—Claude Vandersteen in plain English."

"He fits the profile, yes. But here's the thing: most serial killers have a sexual fixation. Though Claude never sexually assaulted either victim, Connie Newhouse was naked when he killed her."

The memory struck me. "And Erica... she was naked too, preparing to be the next victim."

Kate's voice dropped even lower. "Right. But those suicides—they don't share that element at all."

I nodded, stepping into my sitting room and shutting the door with a soft click. "That's one more unsettling fact."

She was quiet for a moment before speaking again. "Let's entertain your idea—the suicides aren't just suicides. They're the work of someone else, someone controlling their bodies. A 'host,' if you will. And this host would be fiercely loyal, probably feeling deeply wronged—so much so that the only way to right those wrongs is revenge. Revenge for Claude. That's why they strike back at the people they believe hurt him."

A chill ran down my spine. "It puts a whole new spin on the revenge angle."

Kate sighed. "Yes. And it means I agree with your gut—there's a good chance this killer will strike again tonight. The murders have been 'successful' so far. Whoever is doing this feels unstoppable now. The hunger, the compulsion to kill, will only grow."

My voice was tight. "Any more details? Something concrete I can use?"

She paused. "You've suggested that Antoine Powell is the one behind this, yet the murders don't fit his profile. I know he has a history of violence, abusing his wife. But this is much more ego and isn't a spur-of-the-moment impulse. Whoever is doing this is targeting the people."

I rubbed my forehead. "Honestly, that doesn't help much, Kate."

"This isn't a solo act," she said, a hint of frustration creeping into her tone. "It feels like a serial killing duo."

"Yes, Antoine Powell under the influence of Claude Vandersteen."

"That's not what it seems like to me. There is a feminine side to this, the desire for power and control. There is a history of husband-and-wife serial killers, and this is more like that. In those cases, the woman often takes a submissive role—helping select victims to please the male partner. There was that husband-and-wife pair back in 1978 who killed ten teenage girls. The man had sexual motives, but the woman was complicit."

"So you think the host is a female working with Powell?"

"It fits the profile. It's a team effort—except in this case, the sexual element seems absent. If your theory about the host is correct, then it suggests a submissive female under the thumb of a dominant entity, maybe Powell, maybe Claude's ghost, whispering in her mind. The team dynamic works."

A sudden thought hit me hard, like a hammer: "Then the logical suspect is June Steen."

"Any idea where she is?"

I sighed. "No. Have you had any luck with the warrant for Vanderbilt College records?"

Kate's voice dipped with exhaustion. "No. Len, I have to ask, if there's an attempt tonight—what can you do?"

"I don't know."

Silence settled between us. Then she teased, "Not your usual confident self, Doctor."

I swallowed hard. "This isn't like anything I've faced before, Kate. It's uncharted territory. But... I'll do everything I can."

"I'll be at the office tomorrow with the full profile for you. Sorry for the delay. I'm only human."

A pang of guilt hit me. "Kate, I'm sorry. I shouldn't have pushed you so hard."

Her voice cracked ever so slightly. "It's frustrating. I finally get to work a case, and I feel like I'm falling short. Maybe everyone was right—I came back too soon."

I softened. "Ease up. You're tougher than you think. What you've told me helps more than you know."

Breathless, she replied, "That'll have to do. Keep me updated."

The line went dead. I sat at my desk, staring at the phone, the weight of helplessness pressing harder. Finally, I set it down and opened my laptop.

A new email from Darren flickered on the screen:

Len;

Checking into June Steen. Something feels off.

Need to dig through court records.

I visited the abandoned school, like you asked.

Nothing left but stone pillars at the driveway. The church is just rubble now.

Darren

I reread his words, heart sinking. The abandoned school, the ruined church—symbols of decay and lost hope. What did the courts have on June Steen? Did they arrest her? A history like that would make her an ideal vessel for Claude's dark influence.

What could I do now? If Claude was planning another strike tonight, how could I protect anyone? Who would be next? Anna had visions—terrifying glimpses of his attacks—yet all I had seen was the aftermath, stale and cold.

But tonight was different. I was sober—clear-headed. No alcohol to dull my senses, no distractions. A silent promise to myself.

Tonight, I was going to confront Claude—not in the physical world, but in the only battlefield that mattered now: the mind.

15. ANSWERED ATTEMPT

Waiting to face a madman in my dreams was torture —a nerve-wracking limbo where time stretched and reason frayed.

I fought the rising tide of anxiety by burying myself in mindless busywork, then slipping into the easy numbness of scrolling endlessly through social media feeds. I updated profiles with meaningless details, as if that minor act tethered me to normalcy.

After all, who would believe me if I told them the truth? That tonight, I would confront a killer in the dark, or worse—a ghost lurking just before it struck again.

No one would believe a word of it. That was why I had disguised my investigation into a pyrokinetic as a novel, changing every name and place. The last thing I needed was unwanted scrutiny too close to my cases.

At 10:30, I brewed a cup of chamomile tea—a feeble attempt to calm my rattled nerves. By 11:00, I was finally in bed, my body ready but my mind restless.

I tossed and turned, gnawed by the fear that I might not be prepared for the attack Claude was surely planning. Could I stop him? Was I ready?

Eventually, exhaustion edged me toward sleep, aided by a meditation technique that steered my mind into a sharp, focused calm. But even then, the boundary between dreams and consciousness felt thin.

Fleeting images pressed at me—the abandoned church flickering with candlelight, the heat of propane tanks burning like twin, furious eyes; a circle of robed figures chanting in Latin, their masked faces disturbingly familiar.

I tried to focus on the woman in the robes. Tall, shadowed beneath billowing fabric that concealed her figure, she hid her identity as if desperate. Was she slender or stout? The loose garment masked everything, making her shape nearly impossible to discern.

Each time I reached for her face, she turned, eluding me like a wraith.

Then sleep deepened, and my mind slipped beyond the borders of dreams.

Suddenly, I floated silently in an unlit room—someone's bedroom; I deduced—perched high in the corner by the ceiling. Below, a king-size bed held two sleeping figures in the semi-darkness.

I had done this before, drawn into such visions as a spectator, invisible and untouchable. It helped when I knew who I was watching.

One figure was a white-haired woman, the sheets pulled up tightly to her chin, fragile and still. The other—a broad-shouldered man with a heavy mustache—was Stan Frazier.

Was this where Claude would strike? If so, being here meant I could watch—and intervene.

Stan stirred and lifted himself from the bed, careful not to wake his wife. He wore checkered flannel pajamas, a quiet defense against the winter chill. His movements were deliberate, subdued. He opened the bedside drawer and unfastened a leather holster, pulling out a thirty-eight caliber revolver. Silently, he closed the drawer and put on worn slippers.

Pulling a battered robe over his shoulders, gun in hand, he crept into the hallway.

I followed effortlessly, passing through walls like a shadow tethered to him.

Downstairs, Stan flicked his wrist with practiced ease to open the pistol's cylinder, confirming each loaded chamber, before snapping it shut.

The staircase led to a cozy living room—a carpeted haven with walls adorned by family photos and paintings, sturdy wood furniture, and a scuffed leather recliner. A sectional sofa faced a large flat-screen TV, promising normal domestic comfort.

He prowled through the rooms: the kitchen with its oaken cabinets and modern appliances, the dining room with a heavy table for six and a gleaming china cabinet, then back to the kitchen where he opened a door to wooden steps descending into the basement.

He grabbed a flashlight from a drawer and clicked it on, casting a narrow beam into the darkness below. A flick of a switch illuminated a dim underground workspace, cluttered but orderly.

The flashlight's beam swept across a workbench covered in tiny clear plastic drawers and metal boxes, tools sprawled in disarray.

Stan wheeled a chair over, sitting amid the tools, switching off the flashlight and setting both gun and light on the bench.

"Damn, I'm getting jumpy," he muttered.

The voice exploded in the silence.

No, you're not...

I heard the voice, and apparently so did Stan. He leapt up, swinging the flashlight wildly as I scanned the room myself.

Unlike previous times I had experienced this out-of-body technique where I could sense spectral presences or residual energy, there was nothing—only Stan and the cold emptiness.

"Who's there?" His voice was steady but dripping with fear.

You know who this is...

Stan's light darted into every shadowed corner. "You sound like Claude, but that asshole's dead."

I am an echo of what once was...

"An echo of an asshole, then?" His last words were breathless, as though the air had suddenly chilled. Though I was nonphysical, the shift in atmosphere was palpable.

I'm here to claim what is due...

"Far as I can tell, you ain't due a damn thing."

Stan reached for his pistol—and alarm clanged through me. Instinctively, I pushed every ounce of will to stop what was coming.

Stan lifted the pistol in a firm grip, and he looked down at his arm rising, shocked by its movement.

"What the hell?" he asked as his arm continued to rise, obviously not under his control but manipulated by another.

Someone that wasn't him.

He dropped the flashlight, sending beams of flickering light wildly around the room. Stan grabbed his right hand with his left. Suddenly, both of his hands were lifting the gun toward his chin as his eyes grew wide.

No...

I projected the thought with all of my will, and for a moment, nothing happened. I locked my focus on Stan and reached out with my mind to stop what his hands were trying to do.

NO!

I repeated the thought, all my attention on Stan.

Stan dropped his hands, and the gun fell harmlessly to the floor.

Stan's eyes darted around the room as if trying to see what was in the shadows.

"Professor?" he gasped.

The good doctor. I wondered when you would show up…

Claude's cold taunts hammered inside me.

I gave as good as I got.

You're nothing, Claude. You're a bad memory, a nightmare someone is keeping alive…

Stan looked up to where I floated above him, though I was sure that he couldn't see me. "Len, is it really you?"

Claude didn't stop.

You cannot be everywhere. I will have my revenge…

I let out a bitter laugh into the void.

You don't get it. I have your mental spoor now. You go after anyone I know, and I will find you and stop you, just like I did tonight…

Silence.

I thought he fled—then words materialized, creeping like poison.

I know your weakness. It's always the women with you. That's how I will bring you down…

I reached out—only to find him gone.

No thunder crashed, no ghostly wail broke the night. Just emptiness where he'd been, drained and dispersed.

Stan bent to retrieve the flashlight and gun, his breath steadying, his eyes wary.

"Professor, are you still here?"

I projected my thoughts to him.

Fading, Stan. But I've got your back...

His breath was no longer coming out as a fog. "For any of the times I doubted you, I take it all back."

The room faded around me as a familiar voice brushed my mind.

Len, is that you...?

It sounded like Kate Yearling in my head.

Kate...?

I wanted to respond—but the draining effort of this manifestation left me spent. The scene unraveled. My body, heavy and empty, sank into the deep collapse of exhaustion.

Toward dawn, the nightmare returned with a sinister insistence, dragging me back to the cold stone floors of the church.

Once again, I stepped through the heavy, ancient doorway, heart pounding, breath shallow. The walls seemed to close in as I maneuvered past the robed figures, ignoring their silent, chilling presence. My eyes locked on the platform—the place where fate had revealed itself before. This time, I knew exactly who I was hunting.

The figure, cloaked in shadows, hooded, and motionless where the woman had been in my last nightmare, slowly and deliberately lifted its head.

Flipping the hood back, there he was: Claude himself. His eyes were black pits of malice, and his rasping voice cut through the heavy silence.

"I know your weakness," he croaked, drawing from beneath his robes a twisted, cruel knife that caught the faint light like a shard of darkness. He held it aloft—not threatening me directly; no, his focus was elsewhere.

My gaze flickered to the stone altar nearby. There, lying motionless, pale and vulnerable in nothing but a thin pair of thong panties, was April. Her chest rose and fell faintly, eyes closed—as if in a fragile, deadly sleep.

I tried to surge forward to close the distance faster, but something caught my legs, as if I were crawling through sludge.

April stirred, eyes still sealed shut, a smile curling at her lips.

Claude's hand rose, the knife poised like a viper's strike. It descended swiftly, cruelly, and pierced her heart.

Her eyes snapped open; a choke of air escaped her lips as she gasped, a wet, horrifying sound. She convulsed, arching her back, the implement stuck between her breasts. Then, her body collapsed with a sickening thud onto the unyielding stone.

"Noooo!" The cry tore from me like a desperate prayer as I jerked upright in my bed, gasping for air that refused to fill my lungs fast enough.

Heart hammering, I swung my legs over the side and limped to the bathroom, splashing cold water on my face to steady my racing mind. What had I just experienced?

This wasn't just a dream or a vision—it was a warning.

Claude knew about April.

He knew I was with her. How? I suspected Dan—either his whispered mental chatter or some loose word—had betrayed us.

Or perhaps Antoine Powell or his partner. Whatever the path, the truth was stark: April was in danger.

Every time I let someone in, someone I cared for, they became a target. Since returning to New Jersey, Wendy Wallace had died in flames. Then Jyanette Emery, haunted relentlessly by demons and madness until she broke free—by breaking us apart.

No wonder she left.

When April had drawn the Hermit tarot card during her reading—the card that mirrored my solitary existence—it suddenly made perfect sense: the only way to keep others safe was to stay alone.

I grabbed my phone; the glowing screen showed it was already well past 6:30 a.m.

Quickly, I sent April a text:

Call me when you wake.

Important.

My fingers hovered over the keys as I spotted an unread message from Anna, sent hours earlier.

It read:

It was you!

You stopped him.

I saw the entire thing.

Strange emojis followed this: a heroic-looking man, a medal, a ghost with a black eye. Symbols, it seemed. Great—were we really slipping into hieroglyphics now because words were "too hard"?

I replied with a simple thanks and told her I was glad she was watching my back. Then, I suggested we meet so I could start training her in basic mind control—an offer she accepted almost immediately, promising to talk to her father about scheduling.

Still reeling, I decided coffee was my best hope to clear the fog. Pajamas and robe barely in place, I shuffled to the kitchen when my phone rang.

"Hello?" I said.

"Really, can't you let a girl get her beauty rest?" April's teasing tone came through, soft and throaty.

"You don't need it. You're too beautiful as it is."

Her chuckle was like a balm. "Okay, I'll give you that one. Your message seemed urgent."

"Hence the word important," I reminded her.

"I was in the lab all night, about to crash. If you joined me, it would make it all worthwhile."

"I don't know where you live," I admitted, hoping she wouldn't talk herself out of the idea.

"My place is a dump," she groaned. "So, what's so important?"

"This case I'm working on—the knife that was stolen? I think someone is after you."

"Wait. What? The knife from that rich guy's house?"

"I believe a man took it and passed it to someone else."

"I still think that FBI woman took it."

"That's crazy."

"Is it? We removed the knife from the body at the scene to analyze the wound and angle. I was there taking photos. We secured it, placed it in the forensic van. But later, I saw your 'friend' there, and the knife was gone."

"That man I had an accident with? We think he stole it. I think he was watching both of us."

"Len, this all sounds ridiculous. Why would someone spy on us?"

"He worked for someone dangerous—someone who might target you."

"Why target me? I'm just a forensic scientist on probation."

"Because we're dating."

Her breath caught and silence stretched. Finally, she whispered, "Len, I don't know what you're talking about."

I pressed. "There was a man I stopped—a man named Claude Vandersteen. He used Brett Morgan's knife to kill a girl."

"Oh my God," she breathed.

"And now," I added, "he's after anyone connected to that case. Anyone involved with his death."

She was silent for a long moment. Then, incredulous: "The man who you think is after me... is dead?"

"It's complicated. He has an accomplice who escaped from prison."

"Len, you seem like a good guy—awkward, but a good kisser. But if you think some guy's coming back from the dead and sending an escaped convict after me, you're crazy."

"He ran a cult, like the Manson family," I said firmly. "Followers who might be just as dangerous. I'm worried about you—that's all."

"I can take care of myself. I'm going to bed."

"But April—"

"Good night, Leonard." She cut the call.

I stared at the screen, the urge to call her back clawing at me. She was right. To anyone else, a guy she'd barely dated warning of ghosts and cults would sound insane.

She had worked the lab the previous night, and I was holding on to the hope that I'd find her there again tonight.

The lab was a fortress, sterile and secure—a place where she might still be safe. But what if she wasn't?

How much had Dan revealed to the host? Did the host know her regular work locations? Did Claude know where she lived?

And in a world where a killer could reach into your mind, was anyone truly safe at all?

A few minutes later, I settled into my desk, clutching a steaming cup of coffee when my phone buzzed with a text from Anna Sokolov:

I can do an hour at 3:00 at the diner.

Is that okay?

I typed back a quick, reassuring agreement, and then told her I'd see her then.

I made a mental tally of the techniques I would teach her. The timing was ideal since I was driving to my parents' house tonight to light candles just as the early sunset draped the sky.

My parents, devoutly observant of the Jewish Sabbath, would soon gather to perform the Havdalah ceremony, marking the end of the full twenty-four hours of rest—a time when no one turned on lights or used devices.

Only after the closing rituals would we set up and ignite the candles on the Chanukah menorah.

Tonight's rites would stretch on, but I welcomed the pause. Beyond my brother and his girlfriend, my sister Rayna and her family would be there, too—equally observant, with their two boys, Ben and Judah, likely itching to dive back into their electronics once the Sabbath ended.

I remembered how, as a child, my brother Tom and I would impatiently await the moment we could resume video games after a full day cut off from screens.

With some time to kill, I reviewed the information Brett Morgan had compiled about my cane before his untimely death.

I first met Morgan soon after Vandersteen's allies had stolen his ritual knife. At that meeting, Brett had offered me ten thousand dollars for my old walking stick, no questions asked. But my mentor, Fritz Kohl, had gifted me the cane, so it was priceless to me—meaning my finances remained tight.

I scrolled through the documents on my phone; the research unfolding a remarkable lineage. My sword-cane was nearly two hundred years old, handcrafted around 1830 by the French company Klingenthal.

Brett had meticulously enlarged a tiny photo to confirm the company name, and the date etched faintly on the blade. Someone had replaced the original bamboo sheath around 1970.

According to Brett's notes, the sword-cane had once belonged to Jean Louis Michel, a Haitian-born man of mixed heritage. Michel was a legendary swordsman who served in Napoleon's army and received the Medaille de Saint Helene—an honor reserved for the most distinguished soldiers.

After retiring, he founded a renowned fencing school in Montpellier, France, living to the age of eighty, a rarity for his era.

There was an aged portrait of Michel later in life, his right hand resting on a cane topped with a cobra's head—eerily similar to mine. My gaze flickered from the portrait back to my cane, the resemblance striking.

The report traced the cane's path from Michel to one of his students and onward, jumping through various collectors before landing in the United States. There were gaps and uncertainties in the timeline, but the story was undeniably captivating.

Considering how painstakingly Brett researched his collection, this history seemed credible.

I ran my fingers over the snakehead grip, lifting the cane to meet the gaze of the serpent's cast eyes. Softly, I whispered, "Jean Louis, if you have any influence, please help me however you can."

Silence answered me. No surge of power, no faint vibration—nothing.

I'd owned the cane for two years now; the only energy coursing through it must be my own. But hope, desperate as it was, refused to die.

Just then, my phone rang. The caller ID flashed: Stan Frazier.

"Good morning, Stan," I said cautiously.

"Professor, can you explain what the hell went down last night?" His voice was low and tense because he seemed scared that someone might overhear.

"Are you alright? Nothing else happened to you?"

Stan exhaled heavily. "Nothing physical. But I was so damn scared, I couldn't sleep. I secured the gun in the lockbox, didn't dare touch it again. I finally dozed off around five in the morning."

Relief washed over me. "So, you're okay?"

"Yes," he blurted. "But who was that voice? And how on earth were you in my basement?"

"I was having an out-of-body experience. I was there to protect you."

"How did you know I needed help?"

"I'm tracking our enemy mentally. His focus on you helped me to be there."

Stan's breathing hitched. "The whole thing's nuts. That voice wasn't just any voice—it sounded like Claude Vandersteen."

I chuckled, trying to lighten the mood. "You told him off pretty well."

"Yeah... fun and games until my hand moved on its own, aiming the gun at me. You stopped it."

"I only distracted him. Controlling a person demands total focus. My presence yanked his attention from you, breaking his hold. That sort of mental projection burns through energy fast—I knew he couldn't keep it up."

"Well, I'm grateful, but also freaked out by what you can do."

"Please keep this quiet. I want as few people knowing as possible."

"Does McGee know?"

"Roughly," I admitted.

"How about Kate?"

"I've done this sort of thing with Kate."

"Is it frightening for you?"

"You have no idea."

Stan laughed—a sound of genuine relief. "Guess no one does. Thanks for the save, Professor."

"Any progress with June Steen?"

"Nothing from me. Kate said she might get a warrant, but Vanderbilt College is on winter recess or something like that—only a skeleton staff."

"Darren mentioned something about the NYC courts but didn't elaborate."

"The courts? What for?"

"I don't know. Can I ask—did you hear Kate's voice in your basement last night?"

A long pause. "Yes. Just before you faded away."

"So it wasn't only me?"

"No. And I'll be honest, Len, it's not the first time I've heard her in my head."

"What?" My voice caught. "Is Kate psychic?"

Stan sighed heavily. "She made me promise not to tell anyone."

"About what?"

"After the raid in September, Kate went through Vandersteen's notebooks. The FBI found pills of that Miracle stuff he'd been making. She wanted to replicate it."

"Good God." I swallowed hard. "Why?"

"She's been taking a reduced dose. She says it's helped her recovery. Honestly, it has. But she believes the mind thing is just a side effect."

16. HOLIDAY HINTS

The drive to Morris Plains was a blur. I struggled to keep my hands steady on the wheel, forcing myself to maintain the speed limit, but inside, my mind spun wildly.

Pieces of a tangled puzzle came crashing together—her warning the moment before the truck exploded, her words at Stan's house. It all made sickening sense. Had she truly been unaware of the dangers of that drug? Or was something darker at play?

What if the spirit of Claude Vandersteen had been puppeteering her mind, manipulating her into becoming his unwitting pawn, and she was the one helping Antoine Powell?

The thought chilled me to my core.

I finally spotted a parking spot and pulled in, hastily emerging from the car, limping as fast as my leg would allow.

Heart pounding with urgency and dread, I climbed the stairs as fast as I could. Passing through the first door, my eyes locked onto the FBI lab beyond the glass partition. How fully equipped was it? Did it have everything it took to manufacture the drug? Had she managed this alone, or did she have help? An icy knot formed in my stomach.

Without hesitation, I rounded the corner and shoved open the door to her office—no knock, no warning.

Kate looked up in surprise, her reading glasses perched on her nose, eyes sharp as she pivoted in her chair.

"Len?" she asked, cautious but calm.

I was breathing hard, fury and fear warring in my chest. "Stan told me."

Her hands rose in a calming gesture. "Len, it's not what you think—"

"Not what I think?" I almost shouted. "You've been taking *Miracle.*"

She stood, voice controlled but firm. "A watered-down version. Nothing like the doses Vandersteen used."

I couldn't keep the edge out of my voice. "Are you out of your mind? You're risking everything on a drug that drove him insane!"

"It's made from henbane and jimsonweed—herbs with a long history of positive brain effects," she said, spinning around to face me fully. "I took it to help me heal."

I clenched my fists. "If it's so miraculous, why not take it legally? Go through the right channels with the FBI's permission! You don't experiment on yourself."

Her eyes flared with anger. "If I'd waited for approval, it would be years before I saw results! I needed my miracle—now!"

I exhaled sharply. "How often did you take it?"

"Every night, before I sleep," she admitted, her voice dropping.

"Kate, don't you see? This drug suppresses your natural defenses—a dark entity—Claude—could use *you.*"

She frowned, disbelief clouding her features. "I'd know."

"Would you?" I pressed.

"Yes, I remember all of the—I don't know—you'd call them visions. That memory of Blackshale that you saw on your date. That accident you had with the red pickup, where you saved the guy, and I warned you. I saw what happened at Stan's, and I was asleep during all of those events. How could I be the one doing it and watch it at the same time?"

"You could have been a conduit. Claude or Powell using you to do those things to people, stealing your energy and your brain power to do it. Remember what you said? A strong masculine voice working with a submissive female."

"That's ridiculous."

"You have to stop taking it," I said firmly.

Her mouth tightened into a thin line. "I can't."

"Why?"

Looking down, her voice turned fragile. "What if without it... I become that... hag... again?" She stepped away from her desk, her hand covering her face, vulnerability suddenly raw and exposed.

I softened my tone. "You were never a hag."

"Don't lie to me," she snapped. "I saw my face every time I looked in the mirror, an ugly face looked back at me."

"You were sick, but you're getting better."

"But I need it," she whispered. "It helped me."

"Kate, *Miracle's* highly addictive and no one understands it. We've both studied psychiatry—we know addiction isn't just physical dependency; it's psychological. Like painkillers, you think you can control it, but it controls you."

She glared at me. "Like you and the alcohol?"

I froze, surprised.

"Didn't think I knew, did you? I followed you mentally the night of the accident. I knew you'd been drinking. The great Leonard Wise, preaching about addiction while he's back on the booze again."

I took a step back, feeling the sting of truth. "That's different."

"How?" she demanded, piercing me with those fierce eyes.

I met her gaze and had to admit she was right. I'd used losing Jyanette and sleepless nights as excuses to drink, but deep down, I just wanted it, felt that I needed it.

If I didn't quit, either the alcohol or the psychic fog it induced would end me—by accident or by my failure on a case.

Mrs. Higgins and Ashwan had been right. My path demanded clarity and control. I couldn't keep fooling myself.

I faced her, resolved. "Then let's both get clean."

"What?" she whispered.

I nodded. "You've been lying to yourself, just like me. You think the drug makes you better, but it's a shortcut that's not real."

She sank into her chair, the weight of the truth pressing down. "I don't know if I can."

I leaned over her desk, taking her hand gently. "We'll do it together. You and me."

Fear flickered in her eyes. "The thought of giving it up terrifies me."

I thought about the countless nights I'd used alcohol to drown out the psychic noise, craving that temporary peace.

"Me too," I admitted. "How much do you have left?"

She indicated her leather briefcase. "Just a few vials."

I opened it carefully; inside were several small glass tubes filled with blue liquid. "I thought he'd made pills."

"He did, but I diluted them. I told you, I used smaller doses."

I slipped the vials into my pocket. "My father knows people in pharmacological research. I'll get these into the right hands—people who can help others, not use it for personal gain."

Kate nodded wearily. "I copied Vandersteen's journal pages to my computer. Let me print them."

"Why don't you stay at my place through Christmas," I said firmly.

Surprise flashed across her face. "I can't—"

"I don't want you to be alone. Print those pages. I'll call Mrs. Higgins, then we go to your place and pack a bag."

Her gaze met mine—still frightened, fragile.

"Thank you, Len," she whispered.

The hours crawled by as I hauled Kate back to her apartment to pack.

I was shocked when I entered. Her once-pristine apartment had fallen into months of neglect.

We needed to toss aside piles of scattered magazines, half-empty coffee cups, and stray socks to unearth her battered suitcase beneath a stack of unopened mail. She apologized repeatedly, and I kept reassuring her.

Together we packed her clothes, toiletries, and whatever essentials she could gather in her frazzled state.

The air was thick with unspoken worries, but an undercurrent of relief waved gently as we locked the door behind us and started toward my house.

I'd called Mrs. Higgins, and it thrilled her to have a houseguest over the holidays. When Kate and I arrived, Mrs. Higgins transformed instantly into the perfect hostess. Her gracious smile and gentle hospitality could have soothed any storm.

Soon, we settled Kate into a guest bedroom upstairs.

But there was no time to linger. I had to meet Anna and then visit my parents.

Mrs. Higgins busied herself preparing tea, while Kate, drained from the emotional upheaval, admitted she craved a nap.

An hour later, I sat across from Anna in the dimly lit banquet room of Mindy's Diner. The back room did not experience the late afternoon noise of the main dining area, but there was tension between us.

I had taken her through her first training session, which was both mentally and emotionally grueling in equal measure.

"I still don't get it," Anna whined, her voice tight with frustration.

Anna had been pitching in at her father's diner all afternoon, bussing tables in a haze of exhaustion and resentment. Her youthful energy had shifted into the petulance of teenage rebellion, and the constant barrage of her unfiltered thoughts grated on my nerves.

"Anna," I said with a patience I was struggling to summon, "you're rushing it. You're not taking the time to set your intention... to calm your mind."

I wanted to shake some sense into her, but her stubbornness had been clear for the last forty-five minutes.

Still, a strong will was necessary for this kind of work.

Her mind spun wildly, projecting her muffled desires and half-formed fantasies, one of which caused her cheeks to flare bright red.

He's a pill. If he were a real man, he'd come over here and kiss me...

I snapped sharply, "Anna, you're not keeping your barriers up, and I have no intention of kissing you."

Her head dropped, her flush deepening. The sight almost amused me—after all the trouble she'd caused today, a little humility wasn't unwelcome.

I exhaled, tension ebbing slightly. "I think we're done for today."

"I didn't mean it," she said weakly. "I'm just so mad. And I hate working here."

"Everyone has to do chores they don't like," I replied. "But in your case, it's more than a chore—it's about control. You're a loose cannon, and if you don't master your emotions, you could draw something dangerous."

She gasped. "You mean like ghosts? Like the Echo Man?"

I nodded gravely. "It's possible. But the Echo Man—I believe he might have been using a friend of mine."

Her eyes widened in horror. "The lady who spoke just before you left that man's house last night?"

Caught off guard, I nodded. "Right... I forgot you saw the entire scene in your mind."

She frowned. "I don't think she was working with the Echo Man. She was too nice."

That warmed a small knot of hope inside me. "He probably used her without her knowing." I stood, signaling finality. "We're done for today, but don't slack on your practice. And next time, I expect you to be in a better mood."

"I'm sorry," she whimpered, her voice breaking. "It's all the visions, no sleep, and... I..."

Tears overflowed down her cheeks.

I fought the urge to scold or coddle her—that wouldn't do any good. Instead, I opted for blunt honesty.

"When my abilities first appeared, I drank myself to sleep every night just to drown out the noises in my head."

Her eyes widened. "Really? Alcohol?"

"Yes. For years. Until Dr. Kohl helped me find control. The first lesson is always self-control. If you can't give me your best, I can't help you."

Her gaze dropped again, heavy with shame. "Please... help me."

"Look at me," I said softly. She hesitated. "It's okay. I've got my barriers up."

She raised bloodshot eyes to meet mine. She blinked back tears and blew her nose with a napkin, wiping away the traces of frustration and despair.

"You can do this," I assured her. "And you can help people. Like I did last night—I saved that man."

She smiled faintly. "I'll try."

I grinned, channeling my best Yoda. "Do... or do not. There is no try."

She giggled—pure, sounding relief after an hour of grumbles and grimaces.

I stood resolute. "Tell your father you need an hour a day to practice. And tell him I said so."

Her face brightened. "If he hears that, he'll let me."

"Good. And call me immediately if you get any more visions."

She nodded eagerly, a spark rekindled. Why hadn't I lifted her spirits sooner? It would have saved us both a world of frustration.

It was becoming clear that teaching these mental disciplines was no simple matter—even for someone used to lecturing college students in parapsychology.

My mind spun as I left, the evening pressing on, the drive to Copeland stretching ahead. The Christmas weekend chaos was in full throttle. Highways choked with cars burdened with precarious spruce trees, bumper-to-bumper traffic, and desperation at every mall exit.

After an eternity, I left the nightmare of clogged freeways behind and slipped into tranquil small-town New Jersey. Cozy streets lined with quaint, two-story buildings gave way to neighborhoods where stately homes announced the wealth of doctors, lawyers, and trust-fund heirs.

Turning onto my parents' street, I eased my van into the final available spot in the winding driveway. Nearby was my sister's van, complete with stick-figure family decals on the rear windows, and next to it, my brother's flashy red convertible rental car, shining like a beacon against the muted winter landscape.

I leaned heavily on my cane as I climbed the three brick steps to the front porch and rang the bell.

The door swung open, revealing my father—a lanky man with silver hair slicked back and horn-rimmed glasses perched on his nose. He greeted me with a warm smile.

"You're the last one, son," he said.

"Sorry, Dad," I muttered, feeling the familiar pang of inadequacy. "Traffic."

He nodded understandingly. "Figured as much. Come in, say hello to everyone, and we'll get Havdalah started."

Inside the living room, my sister Rayna rose from her chair for a quick hug. Mark, her husband, who was significantly shorter, offered a firm handshake.

"Where are my nephews?" I asked.

Before she could answer, Mom's voice floated from the kitchen. "They're playing Legos with Tommy and Julia," she said, entering and wiping her hands with a dishtowel.

Small but energetic, her silver hair framed a warm, determined face. She wore a cozy dress with a sweater draped over her shoulders.

I limped the remaining few steps to her and kissed her cheek. "Hey, Mom."

"It's nice you came to one night of Chanukah, at least," she teased. "If you were truly dutiful, you'd come to two or three."

"I'm working on a case," I told her.

She threw up her hands. "For free! They should pay you!"

Suddenly, booming from down the hall came Thomas's voice. "Is that my intellectual brother?"

The noise of feet pounding, laughter, and shrieks announced my nephews, Ben—now six—and Judah, just four. They barreled toward me like a pair of wild elephants, their youthful energy threatening to topple me.

Thanks to Mark and Rayna's steady hands supporting my back, I avoided a full collapse as I bent to hug them.

"Let's get started," my father said firmly, breaking the heavy silence. We filed into the kitchen, which felt impossibly cramped with so many of us pressed shoulder-to-shoulder.

The air was thick and warm—the oven radiating heat, and several large crock pots brimming with food lined the counters, promising comfort and tradition.

"Where's your yarmulke?" my mother's voice cut through the steam and chatter.

Thomas didn't hesitate. "I'll get them." He slipped out toward the living room bookshelf, returning moments later clutching a decorative bowl filled with skullcaps—*kippot*, as they are called.

Only he and I weren't already wearing ours; the other men and boys had theirs settled firmly on their heads.

Dad had laid everything out precisely on the kitchen island: a shining silver cup, the Kiddish cup, next to a matching candleholder cradling the braided Havdalah candle, and a small silver spice holder shaped like a salt shaker.

He struck a match and lit the multiple wicks; the flame blossomed bright in the compact room. In rhythmic Hebrew, his voice carried the sacred words marking the boundary between the day of rest and the six days of labor.

He carefully placed the candle in its holder and raised the cup high, reciting blessings over the wine. He took a solemn sip and passed the cup around. I wasn't sure what to do—half out of respect, half out of hesitation—I lifted the wine to my lips but didn't drink; a single drop touched my mouth.

The boys received kosher grape juice instead. I should have asked for that.

Next, Dad lifted the spice holder and blessed the sweetness inside. We passed it from person to person, inhaling the sharp scents of dried orange peel, cloves, and cinnamon.

Rayna stooped to hold the *Besamim* close so even the smallest noses—Judah's and Ben's—could catch the fragrant spice.

Finally, Dad gave thanks for the glowing fire. We each stared at our fingernails—a centuries-old tradition. It had two purposes: to give the prayer meaning, so it wasn't a wasted blessing, and to check beneath our nails for dirt. No dirt meant we had rested properly, refrained from labor.

With a final blessing, we all sang *"Eliyahu Ha'Navie,"* voices rising together, filling the warm room with the haunting melody.

When the song ended, Dad poured the remaining wine onto the silver tray, extinguishing the candle by dipping it into the deep red liquid.

It had been almost a year since I had last shared these rituals with my family. Sabbath traditions hadn't been part of my life lately, and as I looked around, I wrestled with a quiet question: had I been cheating myself by ignoring this heritage so completely?

"Should we eat first and light candles later?" Dad asked Rayna, a playful glint in his eye.

"No!" Judah and Ben wailed in perfect harmony.

"Not unless you want a riot on your hands," Rayna said with a calm smile, her wisdom defusing the boys' protest.

Together, we moved to the living room where the *Chanukiah* —a nine-branched menorah—waited, its polished silver gleaming beneath the soft lights.

"Nice to see you, Lenny," Julia Tannenbaum said, smiling as we walked by.

"Sorry you guys couldn't make Thanksgiving this year," I replied.

"Can we focus on the blessings, please?" Dad reminded us gently.

He lit the *Shamash*, the helper candle, and we chanted together. The second blessing followed, then the song *"Ma'oz Tzur"* known as *Rock of Ages,* filled the room as the candles crackled and burned steadily.

"Presents?" Judah asked hopefully, evoking laughter from the adults.

"Yes, presents," Mom assured him. "Now dinner's going to be buffet style tonight, so I need to set up a few more things."

"I'll help, Momma," Rayna said eagerly.

"Me too," Julia chimed in as she followed Rayna toward the kitchen.

Thomas and I exchanged a look, and he shrugged.

The pile of presents was generous—teddy bears and toys for Ben and Judah, electronic gadgets they were eager to unwrap and play with.

In our tradition, no mysterious stranger delivered gifts. The boys knew to thank Mom, Dad, and their grandparents firsthand.

The adults exchanged gifts too—wallets, coats, jewelry—and each received warm praise and smiles. I felt awkward showing up empty-handed, but nobody seemed to mind.

Then, my father stepped over to me and handed me an envelope. "A very special present for you, Lenny."

I nodded with a small smile and tore it open. Inside was a simple card, but the message was astonishing:

This entitles the bearer to
One total knee replacement
From Doctor Irving Hirschfeld

My eyes widened. "Are you serious? I was told that fusing my leg was the only option."

"What's that?" Rayna asked curiously as I handed it to her.

Dad just gave me a knowingly pleased smile. "My friend Hirschy looked at your old X-rays and believes he can do it. Imagine, Lenny—you'll be able to bend that leg again, walk normally."

"You'll be a real, live boy!" Thomas joked, grinning.

"Dad," I said, my voice steadier than I felt inside, "you know I have a medical degree. The quadriceps damage on that leg... I've lost muscle strength and mass."

"Hirschy says he can use synthetic mesh to support your leg. You might still need a cane, but you'll have movement again."

Everyone nodded encouragingly while I sat, stunned, staring at my frozen leg.

"It's a gift, son," Dad confided quietly. "Hirschy owes me a favor and wants to do this. I want him to."

Tears clawed at my throat. "Thanks, Dad. Really."

"Before Lenny gets all watery-eyed," Tom interrupted, standing up abruptly, "I have a very important gift for Julia."

Without hesitation, Tom extended his hand to Julia. She took it, eyebrow raised in bemused curiosity. Then—kneeling down— he pulled a velvet box from his pocket.

"What's he doing?" Judah whispered to his mother.

"Shh!" Rayna hissed.

"Julia Tannenbaum," Tom began, his voice serious, "every day with you has been the best I've ever known, and I want to say words I thought I'd never say."

He opened the box to reveal a sparkling engagement ring. Julia's hand flew to her mouth, eyes wide and shimmering with tears.

"Julia, will you marry me?"

She looked around the room at all of us before nodding through her tears. "Oh yes!"

"Mazel tov!" Mark shouted.

Mom ran over to hug Julia. "I'm getting a Jewish daughter-in-law! Hashem truly hears my prayers."

Tom stood, slipping the ring onto her finger with a mixture of pride and joy.

"The food's ready!" Mom called from the kitchen. "Come, let's eat. We have so much to celebrate."

I pushed myself up and caught Dad's arm as he passed. "Thanks, Dad. I truly mean it."

He placed a hand on my shoulder. "I know you do. Now come on, eat something. You don't want Mom complaining that you're too skinny, do you?"

I smiled. "No, definitely not."

We lined up to choose from the delicious spreads laid out before us—brisket, various cholents, vegetable kugel, and the freshly baked challah Mom made on Friday. Rayna corralled the younger boys to get their plates first.

Carrying my plate back to the living room, I caught sight of Tom sitting close to Julia. I felt a warmth toward him—she was a remarkable woman, and if she could anchor my brother's wandering spirit, that was something amazing.

I finished my plate and was about to get seconds when my phone buzzed. The display said it was April.

Stepping quietly into the hall, I answered. "Hi April."

"Len?" Her voice trembled, tears breaking through.

Alarm coursed through me instantly. "April, are you okay?"

"No," she sobbed. "There was a man... a black man and a woman... in my house..."

My heart pounded. "Did you call the police?"

"No, Len. She sprayed something on me... something sweet. I think I blacked out..."

"Where are you? I'll come to you."

"I don't know." Her voice grew weaker. "Len... I'm tied up."

An icy dread squeezed my chest so fiercely it was hard to breathe.

"Can you see anything? Anything at all?"

"Y-yes. There's a sculpture... or a painting... I don't know. The naked lady sculpture I saw when we kissed. Do you remember?"

I did. The image of Astarte from the basement of the church where Claude had practiced his dark rituals.

"That's where I am. I can see it... on the wall."

I shook my head wildly. They tore down that church.

"Are you sure?"

"It's right here, Len," she cried. "You were right. I don't know what to do. I'm cold…"

"I'm coming, April."

But then the line went dead.

My cell showed the call ended.

Powell. It had to be him. He had been Claude's host the entire time. But who was the woman helping him? June Steen?

The one thing I knew was that Fresco existed only in one place: the basement of the church where I'd fought Vandersteen.

Although the church was gone, its underground chambers did remain.

Whoever held Vandersteen's power was down there—with April, a prisoner.

Claude's warning echoed in my mind: "The women are your weakness," as the memory of that knife plunging into April's heart flashed sharply.

I stepped back into the living room. All eyes turned to me.

"Len?" Tom frowned. "You look like you've seen a ghost."

"I think I have," I whispered. Then louder I said, "Everyone, I'm sorry, but I have to go. I just had a breakthrough in the case I'm working on." I stopped and turned to my father. "Dad, can I talk to you?"

He followed me into the hall, brow knit.

I pulled out the small vials filled with blue liquid and offered them.

"What's this?"

"An experimental drug that could save many lives," I explained, unfolding papers Kate had printed for me showing the formula. "Do you still know people at Roxygen?"

"The pharmaceutical company? Yeah, I know the CEO."

"Take these to him. It's a new psychotherapeutic that activates parts of the brain."

He hesitated but nodded and took the vials and the papers. "Okay, I'll do it."

"Thanks, Dad. For everything. I really mean it."

He replied with a slow nod, still confused by my sudden urgency.

Just as I turned toward the door, Mom beat me to it.

"You be careful out there, Lenny. I love you."

"I love you, too, Mom. But if I don't stop this, someone's going to die."

"Be safe," she whispered, pulling the door open.

I stepped into the cold night as the first snowflakes fell—silent, soft, eerie—just like the night I had faced Claude Vandersteen before, walking toward that same dark place.

With nothing but sheer determination, I moved down the driveway and climbed into my van.

My parents stood in the doorway, ghostlike silhouettes watching as I drove away into shadow and snow.

17. DOUBLE DANGER

T he falling snow thickened, turning the Staten Island Expressway into a slick, treacherous artery choked with sluggish traffic.

It wasn't the quantity of snow that was the problem—barely a dusting—but the relentless freeze that helped the flakes cling stubbornly to the ground. And suddenly, every driver around me seemed to forget how to navigate a winter storm.

Cars hesitated, tires spun, brakes screeched. The crawl to Staten Island became a nightmare of stop-and-go frustration.

Being a New Jersey native, I'd weathered my share of brutal winters; this was nothing compared to some blizzards I remembered from my youth.

Still, the creeping panic inside me clawed at my chest, fueled not by the weather, but by what haunted my thoughts: the nightmare of Claude—that ritual knife driving mercilessly into April's chest. Over and over, the gruesome vision replayed, refusing to let me go.

I needed backup, desperately. I'd barely survived my first encounter with Claude—only thanks to the FBI tracking my phone that night. I couldn't face Antoine Powell and his accomplice alone.

No wonder the voices people heard sounded like two voices. It had been two people the entire time.

I took out my phone and dialed Darren Ward. He answered on the first ring.

"Darren, it's Len. I need your help."

His voice was immediately sharp with concern. "What is it? Another attempt on Erica?"

"No. Worse. They've kidnapped the woman I'm dating."

There was a long pause. "What? How?"

"Dan Cressley—the guy who nearly ran me over—found out about her and tipped off Antoine Powell. He took her."

"What can I do to help?"

"I think Powell and a woman are holding her in the catacombs under that church where I confronted Vandersteen."

"Len, I told you—they tore that church down months ago."

"Not the basement. Someone must have dug it up. I'm telling you, that place still holds secrets. Can you come meet me there?"

"I'm not close. I'm in Mountainview."

"What?" I tried to steady my voice.

"I'm at Tylissa's place. We had a date tonight."

I let out a tight breath. "Right, a date in New Jersey, and now it's snowing like hell."

"Tylissa and I will figure something out, Len."

"No, I'll call Stan and McGee. They're as far away as you are, but there is a three-state APB on Powell. McGee can get the NYPD. I think June Steen is working with him."

"Len, I got a photo of June Steen—from her student ID."

"What can you tell me about her?" I said.

"A friend at Vanderbilt College said June was a troublemaker when she was a student. Also dug up a court case—she changed her name."

"To what?"

"Not clear, it was over a year ago. She likely took 'Steen' to honor Vandersteen. She was dating him."

"There's the connection," I said.

"Yeah. Also, I looked at her class schedule. It was nuts—she took so many classes she barely had time to breathe, let alone sleep."

I frowned, absorbing the details. "Can you text me the photo?"

"As soon as I hang up. And I think I might know someone who can help you."

"I really need backup."

"I'm on it. Talk later."

"Thanks, Darren."

The call ended as my van crawled forward, snow whirling in thick puffs against the windshield. If I'd had any sense, I would've called Darren the moment I left my parents' house—but panic had muddled my judgment.

April's words echoed in my mind: "a woman" sprayed something on her—something that made her black out. It had to be June Steen.

Then another possibility ran through my mind.

What if it were Kate, under Claude's control?

No, April met Kate; why call her 'a woman' then?

I dialed Mrs. Higgins. The line rang endlessly. No answer. She could be out to dinner—and old-fashioned Mrs. Higgins didn't have a cell phone.

I cursed under my breath. No time to waste.

Next, I called McGee.

"Hey, Len, what's up?"

"Powell and a woman kidnapped the woman I'm dating."

"Whoa, slow down! What?"

"April said a woman sprayed her with something in her apartment. Chloroform, I think."

"How did you find out?"

"They tied her up but left her phone within reach."

"Why would someone do that?"

The question struck me hard. Why? My mind spun in search of an answer.

"I think to force me to get involved. Claude came to me in a vision—said he knew my weakness was women."

"What do you need from me?"

"First, go to my place and check on Kate Yearling. Make sure she's still there."

A pause. "Why is Kate at your house?"

"She's staying in a guest room upstairs. Bill, she was taking *Miracle*."

"What? How?"

"Never mind that. But she's involved."

"I'm on my way."

"Also, call the Staten Island Precinct—the 120—and get them to go to Vanderbilt College. Powell is holding April in the catacombs beneath the remains of an old church, off College Road. Tell them my van will be outside so they know exactly where."

"Len, the weather's turning bad out there."

The snow was heavier now, drifting fast and thick beyond the windshield. "Get NYPD, Bill. Anything."

"Don't go in alone. That's just stupid."

I ended the call. Bill knew me better than to expect caution. Stupid had been my trademark—the reason people had shot, beaten me, and nearly blown me up. Why change now?

My phone beeped with a text. But the road demanded all my focus.

I pulled off the highway, starting slowly up the steep hill outside the college. It was slippery. With the college on hiatus, no cars had passed on this side street in hours.

The van slid once, a heart-stopping slide around the last curve, but I caught it. Made it up, breathing hard.

Why did anyone build a college on a frigging hill?

On College Road, the snow stretched unbroken—save for my tire tracks. Across the street, the empty lot lay beneath a soft white blanket. Fortunately, tall sodium lamps still burned, casting eerie yellow pools over the snow even without headlights.

I eased the van off the road just above what was once the entrance to Saint Albertus Magnus School for Boys. Two old wooden posts marked the way—chained and locked tight, blocking the road to the church ruins.

Darkness swallowed the path beyond as snowflakes danced quicker, heavier, smothering everything in icy silence. My pulse throbbed in my ears.

Tonight, beneath the snow and shadows, the nightmare wasn't over. It was just beginning.

It was almost exactly the same as when I'd confronted Claude the previous March: the biting cold; the snow pressing down like a silent witness.

But this time, something gnawed at me deeper. Had the drug, *Miracle*, imbued the host with the eerie ability to summon snowy weather? It deserved to be coincidence—had to be.

At least, that's what I wanted to believe.

I slipped my leather gloves out of the pocket of my heavy coat, the familiar creak of the worn leather surprisingly comforting. From the car, I grabbed the flashlight I always kept beside me. Last time Claude had practically guided me straight to the church's doorstep, but now it was a minefield of rubble, buried beneath an unsettling layer of snow. Navigating it would take caution—and extra light.

My fingers trembled slightly as I pulled out my phone to check the message Darren had sent earlier. The name "June Steen" stared back at me from a separate text, accompanied by the photo of the woman we'd been looking for since all this madness began.

Shock hit me like a thunderclap. I peeled off a glove to zoom in, scrutinizing every detail of her face. The pieces suddenly clicked into place like jagged fragments forming a clearer, terrifying picture.

I silenced the phone, then slipped it back into my coat. I planted my cane firmly in my right hand, flashlight in my left, and took a deep breath.

The snow crunched beneath my shoes as I stepped onto the hill, heart thundering in my ears. The beam stretched beyond the car toward what had once been a driveway but was now nothing but a vast, white expanse.

Step by cautious step, I moved down the snowy lane, leaving footprints that might as well have been beacons in the white void. My rubber-soled shoes gripped the ground just enough, but the cold soaked through the cloth, biting into my feet. Just like last time.

Familiar yet unwelcome.

I kept the flashlight trained on the uneven ground. No sense in hiding; if my adversaries used *Miracle*, then they already expected me.

Around me, the barren trees, once budding green the last time I'd walked here, now stood stripped and lifeless, like silent sentinels watching my every move.

Ahead, two rounded stone pillars emerged dimly beneath the snow, near the limp, diagonal school sign that swung mournfully in the biting wind. I cautiously raised the flashlight, my eyes searching for the remains of the church.

Workmen reduced the church to rubble months ago; and now, only a chaotic pile of stones and shattered foundations remained, covered by wind-sculpted drifts. It stretched before me, a sea of untouched snow without a single footprint or tire track.

Then, in the center of the debris, I noticed it—a strange light. Dim, but insistent, glowing upward from beneath the snow, making the falling flakes shimmer like spectral lanterns in the cold air.

Moving cautiously, my muscles tense as alarm bells rang in my mind. I sharpened my senses, ready for whatever twisted trap might lurk in the shadows.

Reaching the rubble, I felt my heart constrict with sorrow. Claude had desecrated something beautiful, and though the ruin sat covered in snow, the corruption beneath was still alive and waiting.

I edged past jagged chunks of stone and unstable ground, each step sending sharp pains through the soles of my shoes. My breath came out in shallow fog as cold air stung my lungs.

The glow emanated from a dark opening nestled among the stones: a spiral staircase cutting down into the earth, its worn stone steps curling tightly below.

Nearby, a sheet of plywood lay half-buried in snow—the crude covering for this hidden entrance.

I hesitated only a moment before switching off my flashlight and stepping into that quiet, underground void.

Descending was disconcerting. The spiral staircase, narrow and steep, twisted sharply without a handrail, forcing me to cling tightly to the icy wall. Stone steps beneath my feet were ice-chilled even through my shoes, my body heat leaking away with every cautious step. The air grew heavy with a suffocating sweetness—a putrid mix of damp earth and coppery iron, the unmistakable tang of old blood.

This was the place where Claude had kept Erica Marconi a prisoner—a grim cellar beneath the monks' old quarters, walls adorned with his deranged attempts at devotion to his dark goddess.

At last, I reached the main chamber, stretching beneath what had once been the church's sanctuary. A harsh bulb on a tripod cast light over the room, powered by a battery base that anchored the setup.

Two frescoes dominated the walls. One was the naked woman with bird-like claws I'd seen haunting my visions—the embodiment of something unnatural and cruel.

Across from her, a red-skinned demon with curling horns and piercing yellow eyes leered back at me, muscles rippling under flawed paint.

The same demon that had appeared outside my car the night Cathy died.

Beneath that monstrous figure, scrawled words stabbed the air: "And walks among us." Nearby, in crude marker, were the chilling words, "Sacrifices must be made."

And then my gaze landed on April.

She sat on a folding chair, her wrists and ankles bound tight with zip ties, duct tape over her mouth, silencing her. Despite the gag, her glasses caught my light, and fear flashed painfully in her eyes.

To my left, dark doorways yawned—old monk's cells swallowed in shadows where someone could easily wait, holding Brett Morgan's gleaming knife.

I lingered, my cane at the ready, muscles coiled for defense. Every instinct screamed at me to be patient, to wait for the perfect moment to draw the hidden sword in my cane—or risk everything.

Slowly, I stepped up to April and yanked the tape from her mouth. The tearing sound echoed off the cold stone. I stepped back, my back to a wall with no doorway.

"They're crazy," April whispered, her lips raw. "Get me out of here."

I straightened and called out into the dark, my voice firm and steady. "Come out, June. I know you're here."

"Untie me," April spat fiercely. "We have to get out of here—now."

I looked down at her, my eyes narrowing. "Which one of you was I dating?"

Confusion flickered across April's face. "What are you talking about?"

"Twins," I said, my voice low but sharp as I stepped further away. "You told me on one of our dates. My mistake was thinking only one of you worked with Claude. It was both of you."

"That's... crazy," April stammered, disbelief coloring her voice.

I held up the phone, the grainy photo staring back. "A private investigator sent me June's student photo. I've figured out the entire scam."

"Untie me," she hissed, desperation flashing in her eyes. "We don't have time."

I stayed where I was, studying her face. "And since you don't have the scar under your chin, I'm pretty sure you're June." My gaze returned to the photo. "You went on the first date. After that —you were the one that night at my place."

A voice cut through the tension, chilling and cold: "He's figured it out, June."

From the shadows of one cell, a woman stepped forward—dressed entirely in black, her warm coat barely a shield against the cold. She slipped into the harsh light, revealing a face nearly identical to April's, except for a faint, almost invisible scar on her chin.

The real April.

In one fluid motion, she raised a delicate pistol, the barrel aimed straight at me.

"Hands up, and move toward my sister," she warned, her voice icy.

For a split second, I considered throwing myself behind April's chair, using her as a shield, but the truth hit me: it would be useless. April wouldn't hesitate. She'd just walk over and pull the trigger.

The weight of the moment pressed down like the very snow above—they had drawn the line, and I had nowhere to run.

"I think getting close to her would be a mistake," I said, as I raised my cane carefully, gripping it about halfway up the shaft as I limped further away from June, who still sat defiantly in the chair. I held up my hands at shoulder height—an unspoken signal of peace, or maybe just surrender.

The cramped space worked against me; my cane nearly grazed the low ceiling, clattering softly as I moved.

June stirred, pulling her hands free with a swift, practiced motion. The restraints around her wrists were loose at the bottom, intentionally designed to allow release—she could have freed herself anytime she wished. And now, she did.

Her gaze darted to the side of her chair. With a gleam in her eye, she lifted the Morgan's twisted blade from its hiding place.

Meanwhile, April's cold eyes never wavered, the gun she held locked firmly on me.

My voice cut through the tension. "So you kept Powell here, which is why the police couldn't find him."

"It seemed logical," said April with a smile, still holding the gun.

"I thought he'd be here, helping you."

June stood playing with the knife and smiled in a way that chilled me more than the wintry weather.

"He's right in there," she said, pointing to a monk's cell behind me. "Go ahead, have a look."

I glanced at April and the gun.

"Don't worry," June assured. "We won't shoot you in the back. Unless we have to. Go ahead, look. You can even use that flashlight."

I slowly lowered one hand and extracted the flashlight, watching the gun the entire time. Then, with my hands raised, I stepped back into the small room and clicked on the light.

I gasped at what I saw.

Antoine Powell stood cruelly pinned against the cold, jagged stone wall, massive iron nails ruthlessly driven deep through his shredded wrists and tightly crossed ankles.

His body hung stretched and contorted in a grotesque mockery of the crucifixion. Thick, congealed blood oozed from the puncture wounds, seeping down the wall in three gruesome, dark streams that clotted along the coarse surface and pooled on the floor.

His head lolled forward, neck limp and slack, a macabre marionette's puppet with no life left to command it. Yet, when my gaze locked with his, those hollow, lifeless orbs seemed to stare straight at me—cold, empty, and merciless—a void where humanity had long since suffocated.

No warmth, no cry for mercy, just an abyss of death's cruel embrace.

In that moment, the brutal truth slammed into me: this was where Antoine had been since his escape from prison. Here, in this forsaken chamber, pinned and broken—dead for days.

A suffocating knot of dread clenched my stomach and sent waves of icy terror crawling beneath my skin. The air seemed heavier, thicker, infused with a sinister silence that pressed down like a shroud.

I could almost hear the sounds of his final, desperate struggles echo faintly in the darkness, a grim reminder that death hadn't just visited Antoine… it had claimed him utterly.

"We didn't find him useful," June said.

"Now, now, he was an excellent diversion for the police," April agreed. "That's why we couldn't have him wandering around."

I turned to face the pair of them. I now knew the totality of their cruelty. What did they have in store for me?

I needed to keep them distracted, to keep them talking.

"You stole the knife," I said flatly, glancing from April to June. "Whichever one of you it was."

June grinned cruelly, raising the knife high, so it caught reflections from the stark light of the tripod LEDs.

"That's all me," she taunted. "So generous of that FBI bitch to show up—gave me someone to blame." Her grin twisted with satisfaction.

"Had you planned to meet me there?" I asked, struggling to keep my voice steady.

April's tone snapped like a whip. "No. The plan was just to grab the knife." She kept the gun trained steadily on me. "But horny little June here saw an opportunity—to follow you *and* have some twisted fun."

June chuckled softly. "We both know women are your biggest weakness."

April laughed darkly. "Yeah, he can't resist the damsel in distress."

I shifted my position, and she tightened her grip on the gun, her voice sharp and threatening. "One wrong move, and I'm pulling this trigger."

June stood, knife glinting in her hand like a predator preparing to strike. "Claude prefers we use the knife."

I took a slow, cautious step into the room, hands raised, getting closer to the light's tripod. "Which one of you has been taking the drug?"

"Both of us, asshole," June said evenly, moving just enough not to block April's line of fire.

The realization hit me like ice. "So that's how you did it," I breathed out. "Both of you on the drug—working together. That gave you the mental edge to control your victims, to push them into killing themselves."

April aimed the gun squarely at my head. "Well, look at you— finally piecing it all together. While June was out on that sushi date with you, I used the drug to make Cressley almost side-swipe you with his truck."

"You were the one sending me that mental message—'I'm coming for you'—in Claude's voice?" I pressed.

June added smoothly, "And I used the drug to manipulate Cressley into crashing into you after your date with April."

"Why?" My voice was a rough whisper.

"To mess with you—wreck your van, scare you," June said nonchalantly.

April snorted derisively. "Of course he missed. What a screw-up. I was the one who went to the hospital and fed him the message to tell you. Just flashed my CSI badge and got right in."

June chuckled darkly. "Then, on our date—the one with the Thai food—I took the drug and sent the image of this place to you."

"Plans changed when June got called into work," April continued, nodding. "She had the knife stashed in the trunk."

I stared at June, the weight of the truth sinking in. "You were going to stab me while I slept?"

June's face twisted into a wicked grin. "After I got you drunk enough so your 'abilities' wouldn't save you." She shrugged casually. "At least you'd have gotten laid."

"She was going to make it look like you did it to yourself," April added gleefully.

The smile on June's face turned so chilling it felt like ice sliding down my spine. "My starring moment—the desperately heartbroken girlfriend forced to witness her new boyfriend commit suicide."

A bitter laugh slipped from April. "Then lay the blame on you for the stolen knife."

"Nice touch," I said, trying to keep a resentful tone out of my voice.

"Yes," June agreed. "But plans kept shifting."

"And we kept you guessing," April snarled with relish. "Like the little present June left in your bedroom—to keep your sleep disturbed."

I frowned. "You left something?" My mind spun at the fragments of their plot, but I needed to keep them talking. "June, you changed your name—from Simpson to Steen—because you dated Claude?"

Her gaze snapped up, the knife still poised. "We both dated him."

"What?"

"I changed my name because Claude told me to. Said it was necessary," June snapped.

April picked up the thread eagerly. "Had to pretend there was only one of us out there. We had to plan our days not to overlap. So no one realized there were two of us."

I faltered, struggling to grasp the full meaning. "Why?"

Suddenly, their laughter exploded—a mad, cackling sound like something escaped from the depths of an asylum.

"Because he saw the future," April said, her voice eerily calm as the gun stayed trained on me. "Saw what we would become."

"And you took Claude from us," June screamed, lunging toward me with the knife gleaming.

I jumped back, swinging the cane in one swift arc at the tripod light. I hit it, and the LED fixture fell to the ground, shattering the lights, and plunging the entire room into utter darkness as the tripod clattered to the floor.

Instinct took hold—I darted toward the frescoed wall, moving as silently as possible. I could hear their snarls and shouts of frustration rippling through the darkness.

"Where is he?" one voice demanded.

"Doesn't matter," the other replied calmly. "The drug is taking hold—I can feel it."

"Me, too." The eagerness underlying their words made cold steel seize my heart.

They'd dosed themselves with *Miracle* before I arrived.

The room was pitch-black. I felt my way along the wall, careful to be as quiet as a ghost.

Something was happening—a storm swirling not in the air but in their minds. A mental tempest pounded eagerly against the walls of my consciousness, threatening to break through. The assault was overwhelming, a hurricane of thoughts and dark desires.

I slipped into one of the monks' cells and forced my breathing to slow, raising my cane as a fragile shield to block the doorway.

Mrs. Higgins' story flickered through my mind—about the possessed rat, driven mad by the spirit inside it until it destroyed itself. That's what had happened here. Claude Vandersteen's drug, and whatever darkness had come with it, had driven these women insane.

But knowing that offered no comfort.

I will have you…

The thought slammed into me like a fist, reeking with vile hunger for my destruction.

NO!

I fought to shove it away, but it was like holding back a tornado with bare hands.

Then, a shattering realization struck me.

The voice I'd heard—off, twisted—not from a single mind, but two.

June and April had combined their enhanced mental powers, working together as a terrifying collective.

Why had I missed it before? There was always the elusive presence of more than one mind in those attacks—I'd assumed one was Claude.

Twins. They'd grown up together, sharing a secret language only they could understand. I'd known that instinctively from my childhood with Thomas—my best friend, sometimes tormentor—but when we united, with a shared purpose, no obstacle was too great.

June was the dominant personality—the ruthless leader.

April, who relished the sting of pain, was more submissive.

Kate was right. This wasn't just one killer—it was two, paired and unstoppable.

A deadly team.

The room, already steeped in bone-chilling cold, seemed to grow colder still, the air frigid and suffocating around me like an invisible shroud.

My left hand twitched, then moved on its own, utterly beyond my control. It was the most terrifying and surreal experience—completely conscious, fully aware, yet not in control of its motions.

I could feel my free right hand reaching for my cane, fingers brushing the polished shaft in a trembling, mechanical movement. My left hand grasped the cane's shaft, its grip cold and ironclad, then found and triggered the hidden latch.

My right hand slid the slender, deadly twenty-four-inch sword free from its sheath.

I fought with every ounce of willpower to shove the blade back into its enclosure. For a heartbeat, the sword hesitated—as if resisting my command—then continued sliding free in slow, inevitable release.

A chilling voice boomed in my head.

I don't need to see you to kill you…

It was Claude's voice—at first. But a sickening realization grew inside me. That voice wasn't Claude's at all. It was June and April, the two women with minds fused into a terrifying, invasive consciousness.

They projected the echo of Claude's voice, a cruel mimicry that had fooled my psychic senses. Now, stripped of all pretense and artifice, their true nature pressed down upon me—a pair of malevolent, enhanced minds commandeering my body, forcing me toward self-destruction.

Their beauty had been a trap, a deadly snare that had kept me blind. April had done a background check on me, but I had never done one on her. I never dug into her dark past while they scrutinized mine with cold precision.

My right hand twisted slowly, against my deepest desires, lifting the honed steel blade toward my trembling throat. The sharp edge promised swift, silent death—just the faintest gesture and it would slice through my jugular like paper.

NO!

A desperate voice erupted inside my skull—but it wasn't my own. My hand jerked to a halt and lowered the blade, breaking free from the unholy command, as my own indomitable will surged back into control.

Don't do it. You can't do that… the voice whispered in my mind.

I reached out, clinging to any lifeline.

Anna…?

Len, it's not you. Put the sword away…

Anna's calm, clear voice replied inside my mind.

But Claude's voice shattered through the mental fog.

Who is that…?

The echo warped, splintering into the softer, more feminine tones I'd heard when dining with them; the bifurcated thoughts clashed and doubled, making the mental assault a symphony of confusion and menace.

With trembling limbs but my mind my own again, I still gripped the cane's shaft. Slowly, carefully, I slid the blade back into its sheath, though my heart pounded like a war drum.

Anna, I'm fine...

You're in danger. I see it...

Outside, the pit brightened suddenly as a shaft of light pierced the underground gloom, reflecting from the snows above. Shadows writhed like malevolent spirits, twisting and swirling, mimicking oncoming headlights.

I pressed myself flat behind the crumbling stone wall of the monk's cell, desperate to remain unseen.

April, vigilant as a predator, must have glimpsed me—because a pistol shot echoed through the chamber, deafening in its intensity.

I slammed my back harder against the cold stone, desperate to put the wall between myself and the bullets that would follow. They wouldn't just stab me here and let me bleed out. No, April would use the gun—the efficient instrument of death — to end me quickly and without mercy.

Then the ground trembled violently above us—a brutal shudder that rippled through the very air, shaking loose dust and debris.

A vehicle screeched to an abrupt, jarring halt nearby, its tires shrieking like wounded beasts.

The light outside blazed, cold and unforgiving, getting brighter, reflecting down into the catacombs.

For a tense heartbeat, a suffocating silence swallowed the pit, every breath lodged thickly in my throat, each second stretching impossibly long.

The women melted into the shadows as though swallowed whole, working with deadly intent—silent vipers poised, muscles tense, waiting for when the silence would shatter and chaos would erupt.

Suddenly, a new sound sliced through the oppressive stillness: a sharp, metallic ping followed by the muffled thunk of something heavy dropping into the pit. My heart pounded in recognition before my mind could even grasp it—I knew exactly what it was.

Without warning, I dropped to the ground, squeezing my eyes tight, arms cradled over my face and head.

The darkness exploded into an unbearable blizzard of blinding white light and bone-rattling noise that slammed into the chamber like a tidal wave. The world shattered into shards of sound and fury, searing into my senses with merciless intensity.

It was a stun grenade—a "flash bang," as the police called them —an incendiary device meant not to kill, but to cripple through sensory assault.

Piercing screams tore through the chaos—high, terrified cries of the girls swallowed up in the explosion. And beneath the screaming, the rapid staccato of gunshots cracked sharp and deadly, echoing in the pit like thunder.

Risking everything, I forced my eyelids open—just in time to watch a silhouette step swiftly down the spiral stairs, wielding a flashlight like a weapon of justice.

He was a giant of a man who charged toward April, still trembling and blinking—the gun still in her grip.

Without hesitation, the man smashed the flashlight into her temple and she crumpled to the ground.

He bent over, seizing the pistol and slipping it silently into his pocket.

June staggered to her feet, clutching her blade, unsteady and wild-eyed. She lunged at him; he parried with brutal efficiency, then smashed a fist into her face. Blood erupted from her nose as she crashed down.

I tried to roll over, to sit up—to fight—but my limbs betrayed me.

The sword cane was still in my grip, but my body felt like weighted lead, my dexterity gone. Suddenly, a crushing fist slammed squarely across my face, sending stars exploding behind my eyes. As I fell back, helpless and dazed, a massive foot crushed my left hand to the dirt floor, pinning it.

He leaned in close. The glare from behind him highlighted the grim smile on his face—it was Pete, Marconi's bodyguard. The shadow of dread tightened around me.

Apparently, Darren had called him for this "rescue." The taste of bitterness rose in my throat.

"This is for Louie," Pete snarled, grinding his boot into my hand. An unbearable scream tore from my throat as something inside the limb snapped. Darkness pulled me under.

Then, mercifully, he hauled me up the spiral steps, all but carried me out into the icy embrace of the snow-drenched night. My cane still clutched in my right hand, but my left felt numb, broken, agony burning through every nerve.

A large, rugged four-by-four idled nearby—a beast built for backwoods and foul weather survival.

Pete released me abruptly, and I collapsed into the snow as a pickup truck approached, tires chained against the ice. Doors yawned open, and Darren Ward and Tylissa Booker stepped out.

"My God, what did you do to him?" Darren's voice thundered with disbelief.

"I saved him. Flash bang did its job. If not, he'd be dead," Pete said flatly, as if his brutal methods were beyond question.

"NYPD is on its way," Tylissa called out above the howling engines.

"Then I can't be here," Pete growled.

He pulled the twisted blade and April's pistol from his pocket, wiped each down with a handkerchief, and dropped them into the snow. He stalked toward his vehicle, a grim sentinel leaving the battlefield.

"Two girls are still in the pit. They'll need medical attention," he warned.

Darren and Tylissa helped me to my feet.

"Cold," I muttered through cracked lips. The searing pain in my hand blurred its edges with the cold bite of the winter night as they carried me toward the pickup's passenger side.

"Help is coming, Len. You'll be fine," Darren reassured me, but the shadows behind his eyes betrayed the urgency none would voice.

Tylissa said something else, but my mind was already succumbing, drifting into the welcoming abyss of unconsciousness.

18. TUNNEL EFFECT

I woke up in the same place where I had regained
consciousness too many times before—a hospital room. The
persistent ringing in my ears blurred into the fog of
painkillers, dragging me somewhere between pain and sleep.

My left hand throbbed, encased in a cast that felt heavier than
it should. Pete had indeed broken at least one of my fingers—
probably more—but as petty revenge went, it was modest.

Then again, he had saved my life, and somehow that twisted
everything into a messy balance.

Gangsters have a peculiar way of setting things right.

I squinted around the unfamiliar room. The fluorescent lights
hummed softly overhead, and closed Venetian blinds shielded the
window, making thin lines of sunlight slice through the gloom.

It looked like Staten Island University Hospital—the same
dim, clinical space where I'd visited Erica Marconi recently.

Just great. Another hefty copayment on the horizon. I'd
probably burned through more GSU health insurance benefits
than any other professor.

Before I could sink deeper into my swirling thoughts, the door opened with a confident thud. Anthony Marconi strode in, his presence larger than life, casting a long shadow that brought both relief and unease.

Pete lingered behind him, eyes dark but unreadable.

I wanted to bolt—fight or flight screaming in my veins—but the beeping machines, the IV drip tethered to my arm, held me firmly in place.

"Doc, I heard you were up. How're you feeling?" Marconi's voice boomed, a mix of authority and something softer beneath it.

I croaked, "I've been worse."

He locked eyes with mine. "Those two broads—the one with the knife, the other with the gun. Were they the ones who hurt my niece?"

I nodded, voice strained but steady. "I think so, but they're no threat to her now. From what I can tell, they used a drug—a kind of mind enhancer—to manipulate Erica. Without it, they're harmless."

Marconi's gaze narrowed, skeptical. "You sure about that?"

"Absolutely." I met his stare evenly. "Even if the authorities can't pin the suicide murders on them, they'll charge them for Antoine Powell's death, stealing that knife, and assaulting me."

He glanced down at my cast. "Are they the ones who broke your hand?"

Without hesitation, I met his gaze directly. "Yes. They caught me off guard."

He nodded slowly. "And this drug—how critical is it to their operation?"

"It's everything. They need a high-end lab to produce it. Prison's no place for that."

Marconi exhaled, then said quietly, "So, you're sure they can't hurt my Erica?"

I lifted my head; it felt like it weighed a ton. "Positive. Mr. Marconi, I mean no disrespect, but I'm familiar with your ways. There's been enough killing."

He managed a small grin. "Who said I want more bloodshed? You'll notice I kept my word after what Powell did—drugging Erica, kidnapping her. I didn't touch him 'cause you asked me not to. But what those women did to him—well, I ain't gonna weep over it."

I sighed, "You're a man of your word."

He nodded once, sharply. "That's why I like you, Doc. And don't forget, you saved Erica twice. That doesn't go unnoticed, *capisce?*"

"Thank you, Mr. Marconi," I murmured.

He shrugged and turned. Pete glanced at me, a flicker of something unspoken passing between us. I inclined my head in return—the closest thing to a truce we could manage.

The two men left, and exhaustion crept over me like a heavy cloak. I closed my eyes, craving silence.

But peace was fleeting. A firm shake startled me awake. Blinking through the haze, I saw Kate Yearling standing over me, her fiery wig catching what little sunlight spilled into the room.

"Christ, you're a mess," she said with a wry grin, collapsing into the chair Marconi had vacated.

"What are you doing here?" I rasped.

"I hitched a ride with McGee," she said easily.

"Right. I sent him to check on you."

Kate's eyes glittered with challenge. "Imagine my surprise when I heard you thought I'd kidnapped your girlfriend."

I felt a flicker of defensiveness. "Well, you two never exactly got along."

She leaned forward, mock-serious. "I was right about her, wasn't I?"

I groaned softly. "Please don't start—"

"Anyway, I dragged Bill into the interrogation room to give a profiler's take on the two perps." She grabbed my chart from the end of the bed, her fingers flipping through it.

"Hey—that's confidential."

She shook her head. "Broken hand, multiple contusions... You really need to stop dating the jealous types, Len."

"I didn't know they were jealous... I mean, if I was aware they'd been pining for Claude Vandersteen, I would've steered clear."

Kate frowned, eyes sharp. "I saw those two lunatics this morning. They said you were dating both of them?"

I blinked. "I thought I was only dating one."

"Which one?"

"I'm not even sure. One of them told me she had a twin, but I thought little of it."

Her expression darkened. "The interrogations were surprisingly easy. They both confessed—to everything."

"Everything?"

"They bragged about the murders, stealing the knife, attacking you, even killing Powell. They're both proud as hell. How did you get convinced to go out to that godforsaken hole in the ground?"

I sighed heavily. "June—one of them—called me. She said Powell had kidnapped her."

Kate shook her head, a mix of disbelief and frustration. "And you fell for it. Len, a pretty woman smiles at you, and you lose your damn mind."

"I tried to get backup. I called Darren."

"Yes, and it's a good thing you did. Otherwise, that hole in the ground might've been your grave." She studied me. "But why did they want you there? What was the significance?"

"I think they meant to offer me as a sacrifice to Claude. I think that's what they did with Powell."

"Wait, you saw Antoine Powell in that pit?"

"Yes, my guess is that June and April were waiting for him with a car, and took him there. Now, he'll never leave."

"What did they do to him?"

"Crucified him," I reported as Kate gasped.

I shook my head. "The problem with the whole case was that I was wrong. I operated under the mistaken belief it was a spirit attachment."

Kate scoffed, then surprised me by reaching out to brush my hair from my eyes. "You? Admitting you're wrong? Hell must've frozen over."

The tenderness of the gesture surprised me. "Thanks."

Before either of us could respond, a booming voice interrupted.

"Is this a private party, or can anyone join?" Bill McGee's silhouette filled the doorway.

"I was telling Len about the interview with the princesses this morning," Kate began, her voice low but eager.

Bill, already pulling a chair over, sank into it with a grin. "I rarely come to Staten Island on a Sunday, but hearing that? It was worth it." He glanced at Kate. "Has this guy told you what happened?"

Kate smiled, a glimmer of satisfaction in her eyes. "He actually admitted he was wrong."

Bill quirked an eyebrow. "Did you record it? Because I want that on an endless loop—to listen to it over and over." He winked. "So... what, exactly, were you wrong about?"

"The spirit attachment," I confessed, leaning forward. "I thought it was Claude using some kind of host. Totally wrong. Turns out, it was the twins—the two of them—creating a voice that sounded like Claude to trick the victims. It was them, and only them."

Kate chimed in, smirking. "Len was dating both of them."

Bill's smirk widened as he glanced at me. "Wait... what? You sly dog!"

I raised my hands, feigning innocence. "As I told Kate, I didn't know it at the time. But there were odd things..."

Kate's brow lifted. "Odd things?"

Bill leaned in, intrigued. "When exactly did you put it together? Was it when they had you stuck in that hole in the ground, weapons aimed at you?"

"No," I answered quietly, the memory still sharp. "It was right before I went in. Darren Ward found a photo of June from her student ID, and when I saw it was the same girl I knew as April, it clicked."

Kate's eyes narrowed. "In what way?"

"Inconsistencies," I explained. "Things I told her on one date that seemed like surprises the next time. The scar on her chin—sometimes there, sometimes not. Even her preferences—what she liked—changed—"

Bill raised his eyebrows. "Are we really going there?"

Kate laughed. "Of course we want to know."

I grinned, shaking my head. "Honestly, they both kissed differently. I thought it was weird, but I didn't figure it out until I saw the picture. After that, I put two and two together and why they wanted me to come out and go into that hole."

Bill cleared his throat. "I talked to Doug Millbank when this blew up. He said he never had a woman named April Simpson working for him. When I described her, Millbank said her name was—"

"June Simpson," I cut in. "Also known as June Steen."

"That was the woman you were looking for, right?" McGee said.

"Right. When Claude was alive, he was involved with both of them, instructing them to act as a single person. Plus, the attacks didn't start sooner because they had to use *Miracle* for an extended time to boost their minds first, learn to combine their powers. They practiced on Dan Cressley."

Kate murmured, "That's terrifying."

I nodded. "Exactly. When I kissed one of them, I got psychic flashes—memories blending. The first time, it was a nightmare Kate had that April and I shared."

Kate shot Bill a pointed look. "Not my fault! I was having a nightmare."

"The second time, I think they planned it," I said. "One took the drug and projected that fresco in the basement into my mind. The other probably reached out to share the vision."

Kate's voice dropped, tense. "You think they coordinated everything—the attacks, when they happened... even making people believe Claude's voice was there?"

"Yes. That's exactly it."

Bill considered this for a moment. "Were they addicted to the drug, like Claude?"

"I don't know for sure," I admitted. "They only took it at night, so it didn't affect them during the day. I think that's why

June got the forensic lab job—to access the equipment needed to synthesize the drug."

Kate frowned. "How did they know how to make it?"

"They must have learned from Claude himself," I said. "They both dated him for two years and were skilled chemists."

Bill looked puzzled. "So how did June Simpson become June Steen?"

"Darren Ward explained June had legally changed her name through the NYC courts. She admitted it in the pit—it was to honor Claude."

Kate shook her head slowly. "Their devotion to their master was truly great. I don't even need to change the profile I worked up; it's exactly what I suspected: the subservient women living out the fantasies of a dominant male."

"Even after he was dead?" I wondered.

Kate nodded grimly. "They kept serving his wishes, supporting each other all the way."

I added, "June stepped up as the dominant one—the planner behind everything."

"They confessed," Bill said firmly. "They'll stand trial in New York for murdering Powell; we have them cold on that. New Jersey is also charging them for first-degree grand theft. That knife is worth over two hundred and fifty thousand."

I laughed aloud, shocked. "Wait… that knife was worth that much?"

Kate confirmed. "Oh yes."

Bill's voice darkened. "They committed murder during the theft. That's going to put them behind bars for a long time."

I swallowed, a bit self-conscious. "What about my assault?"

Bill shook his head. "It's serious, but only major if they'd shot you, Len."

I sighed bitterly. "Next time, I should let the bad guy shoot me."

Kate cast a glance at Bill. "Maybe we don't tell him the good news until his attitude improves."

Bill grinned. "We could tell him now."

I raised my injured hand, brandishing my cast. "Wait—what good news?"

They exchanged an irritatingly pleased smile as I tried to stay patient.

"The Brett Morgan estate has offered a reward for the Kris knife," Bill said.

"So?" I blinked.

Kate grinned wider. "Want me to tell him?"

"Yes, please," Bill urged.

Kate looked straight at me. "Ten thousand dollars, and it's all yours."

Suddenly, the pain in my hand felt a little more bearable.

"Wow," I whispered, staring at my cast again. "Hopefully, it won't all vanish into medical bills."

Bill chuckled. "Relax, Len. Someone already paid those."

I frowned. "Who?"

Bill shrugged. "No idea. They told me so when they gave me your release papers."

For a moment, I considered possibilities—and a name flickered in my mind: Anthony Marconi.

"I guess today really is a joyous holiday for me after all."

The drive home was deceptively calm, the quiet hum of the engine a stark contrast to the storm of thoughts swirling in my mind. The painkillers dulled most of the soreness, muting the sharp edges of my injury and lending a surreal softness to the world outside the window.

Bill spoke softly, breaking the silence as he told me Darren had driven my van back to my house the night before. They'd found me just as the snow stopped falling, the storm retreating as quickly as it had begun.

The roads gleamed under the streetlights, completely clear yet thrumming with the rush of holiday traffic. Christmas was only days away, and the world was alive with that peculiar blend of urgency and warmth.

A fresh coat of snow still covered the landscape, making everything magical and turning even the darkest corners festive.

As we pulled up to the house, Mrs. Higgins was already waiting, her compact frame lit under the porch light. She practically appeared out of the shadows, rushing to the car with a worried frown etched deep into her face.

She fretted, reaching over to gently touch my injured hand, saying, "You've come home looking much worse. Yer poor hand —it's no' right."

Kate and I both stepped out of McGee's car, waving to him as he drove away.

Inside, the warmth of the house wrapped around me like a blanket. Kate and Mrs. Higgins led me to the kitchen, where a pot of steaming coffee and a plate of scones awaited on the table. The familiar smells grounded me, offering a semblance of peace.

Kate offered a small, reassuring smile as she settled into the seat beside me. "At least it's your left hand," she said lightly. "Means you can still drive."

I managed a nod, the movement awkward but true. My right hand handled the van's controls without hesitation, a minor comfort in the chaos.

"It'll mess up my typing for a few weeks," I muttered.

Mrs. Higgins sighed, lifting her teacup with a practiced grace. "Ye'll be ready for when classes start again, no doubt," she said, her voice firm but kind.

"I'm probably going back to bed soon," I admitted, rubbing my covered hand. "Hopefully, I can sleep without nightmares."

Kate's smile faltered. "You've been having nightmares, too?" she asked softly.

Before I could answer, Mrs. Higgins set down her teacup deliberately, rising from her seat with an air of quiet determination. Her hand slipped into the pocket of her dress as she fixed me with a steady gaze.

"I hope ye dinna mind," she began, "but I went to yer bedroom and looked around."

Surprise flickered through me. "No problem, Mrs. Higgins. But why?"

She drew a slow breath, eyes narrowing slightly. "Well, once I knew it was that woman who caused all this,"—her voice hardened—"I started thinkin'. Your nightmares began right after she visited, did they not?"

Kate's expression twisted into a mix of amusement and disgust as she glanced between us.

"It's nothing," I muttered quickly. "We had dinner, and then she went to change."

Mrs. Higgins' fingers emerged from her dress pocket, clutching something small and dark. She set the object on the table—a tiny rectangular enamel pin.

"I found this, slipped under the corner of your mattress," she said quietly. "Figured it might be what's stirring up yer trouble."

I picked it up hesitantly, feeling an odd tingling at my fingertips. The pin bore an intricate design, a careful reproduction of a tarot card. At the top, the Roman numeral "IX" marked it, dominated by a scattering of swords across the upper half.

The image was haunting: a figure sitting upright in bed, hands covering their face in torment.

Kate leaned in, curiosity winning out. "What is that?"

I shrugged, struggling to explain. "It's a tarot card... June was into that sort of thing. Seems like a... a 'gift' she thought to leave me. Something to mess with my head, maybe. I don't know what it actually means."

Mrs. Higgins smiled faintly, a self-satisfied gleam lighting her eyes. "The Nine of Swords," she announced proudly. "I looked it up on the internets."

I met her gaze, waiting for her verdict. "And?"

"It's a fear card, speaks of nightmares and torment. That evil woman turned it into a charm—darker than any charm should be —to disturb your sleep. Did ye look at the back?"

Turning the pin over, I noticed a faint brown circle staining the metal.

Kate's brows furrowed sharply. "Is that dried blood?"

I set the pin down gingerly, an uneasy chill creeping down my spine. "I think it is."

Mrs. Higgins' voice was low and serious. "Then the question is: whose blood?"

I swallowed hard, the room suddenly feeling too small, too charged. "Probably Claude's."

Kate's frown deepened. "Then the real question is—how did she get it?"

EPILOGUE

"Very good," I praised gently. "You're doing much better."

Anna opened her eyes slowly and flashed me a shy smile. Seeing her happy like this warmed me. It was clear she had been practicing the techniques I'd shown her, and that gave me hope.

We sat together in the living room of my house, the soft glow of the lamp casting warm light over us. Her gaze drifted to the large evergreen standing proudly in the corner, its branches heavy and ready for decoration.

It had been a long, exhausting day. I'd started early at the morning AA meeting led by Bill McGee. Bill beamed when he saw me; his joy was palpable.

After the meeting, he pulled me aside and said, "Your commitment to sobriety—being here today—is the best gift I could ask for."

That meant more to me than I could say.

Later, I picked up a fresh Christmas tree from a street vendor. With Kate's help, the two of us spent the entire morning anchoring it into its stand, fluffing the branches, and prepping it for the ornaments that would come later. The scent of pine filled the house, peaceful and grounding.

Anna's soft voice broke through my thoughts. "I'm still amazed Mrs. Higgins waits to decorate the tree until Christmas Eve. Poppa put ours up weeks ago. But of course, it's fake. He says he doesn't have the patience for a real one."

I glanced at her. "Everyone has their traditions. Was your father upset I wanted to work with you on Christmas Eve?"

"No, not at all. He's just relieved I'm happier. Not hearing everyone's thoughts all the time—it makes things a lot less stressful, especially at the diner," she admitted with a small sigh. "I was also glad to get out of there for an hour."

I smiled at her. "We'll practice again on the 26th. Does that work for you?"

"Sure," she said, swinging her backpack over one shoulder and slipping on her coat. "It's nice… not waking up in the middle of the night anymore."

"I agree," I admitted, standing and pulling on my heavy coat. Together we made our way to the door.

As we climbed into the van, she suddenly looked at me with a faraway expression. "Why did I get those visions of those people? And how was I able to see what was happening to you?"

I put the vehicle into gear, the tires crunching softly on the gravel as I considered her questions. "I think it's because of the connection between us—the bond from when I rescued you months ago. I was their target from the very beginning."

"Really?" Her voice was barely above a whisper, her eyes wide with disbelief.

"That's what I believe. With everything the sisters did, and because you and I already shared a psychic link, your mind traced what was happening. I don't fully understand it myself, but you saved me when it counted."

She straightened up with newfound confidence. "I did, didn't I?"

I smiled, curious. "I have a question for you—do you think parapsychology might be your field?"

Anna considered me carefully. "I have a guidance counselor who's pushing me toward computer sciences. They say I have a real aptitude for it."

"Well, if you decide to go to GSU, I think I could get you a scholarship," I offered.

Her face lit up instantly. "Really?" Her excitement made her nearly bounce in her seat.

"Anna, calm down," I chuckled, amused by her enthusiasm.

"Sorry! It's just… that would save Poppa so much money," she gushed. "And I would study with you, right?"

I grinned. "I'm willing to sweeten the offer. My teaching assistant is leaving after this year. You could take over as my TA— and it's a paid position."

She practically sang with joy. "Wow! What a Christmas present!"

"Don't thank me just yet," I said, reining her excitement in. "Positions like TAs usually go to juniors or seniors, not freshmen."

"I can do it," she declared firmly.

"There's more," I warned. "It would mean no summer vacation for you—you'd have to get up to speed with Teddy Santos. You'd still have your own classes and work, plus extra work for me."

We pulled into the diner parking lot, and I slid the van into a space.

"It would be tough. But your gifts would be invaluable for the work I do. What do you think?"

She bit her lip thoughtfully. "I think I should talk to Poppa about it."

I grinned and nodded in approval. "Good answer."

"It all sounds wonderful," she breathed, eyes sparkling.

Anna unbuckled her seat belt and leapt over to hug me tightly.

I am so in love with you...

"Anna," I said softly, "you're leaking thoughts again."

She jumped back, flushed crimson as if I'd shocked her. "Sorry."

I smiled, warmth flooding my chest. "Merry Christmas, Anna. I'll see you on the 26th."

She returned the smile, then bounced out of the van, practically dancing toward the diner. I watched her go—she was going to be a handful and a mind full. But if I could teach her to focus those amazing talents, she would be nothing short of magnificent.

I headed home, the heavy, tense rush of Christmas Eve traffic making the hectic weeks leading up to today seem easy in comparison. Everyone was in a mad dash, jockeying for time and space before the holiday.

I was looking forward to the evening with Kate and Mrs. Higgins. Kate had blossomed in the past few days, growing calmer and more focused since she'd given up the drug.

Turning on the radio, I let Christmas music wash over me, and soon enough, I quietly sang along with the familiar tunes as I inched through the restless holiday traffic.

Later that night, Mrs. Higgins, Kate, and I gathered in the dim glow of the firelight, our eyes fixed on the tree standing proudly in the corner.

The decorations were finally complete—glass balls shimmering and catching the flickering colored lights, casting prismatic reflections across the room.

Kate and I settled onto the couch, while Mrs. Higgins reclined comfortably in her favorite chair. The only sources of light were the fire's dancing flames, the glowing tree, and a white electric Chanukah menorah in the window, festooned with five steady orange bulbs that added a warm, steady glow to the scene.

Mrs. Higgins had outdone herself, preparing a lavish feast, and now the three of us were comfortably full. The two women sipped quietly from glasses of port, the tension of the day melting into a shared serenity. A cozy silence wrapped the room, punctuated only by the crackle of burning logs.

"Peace on earth," Kate sighed softly, a dreamy smile touching her lips. "I have to admit, this quiet feels almost unreal."

I nodded, feeling the moment's fragile calm settle over me.

However, Mrs. Higgins turned toward me and looked thoughtful, breaking the silence. "When are ye planning to have the surgery, Doctor?"

I exhaled slowly. "Late January. With all the tests and preparatory work, it's going to take that long. After that… I'll be a wheelchair user until the muscles in my leg are strong enough to bear my weight again."

"Your father did a good thing for ye," Mrs. Higgins remarked, her voice soft but certain.

I forced a small smile but confessed, "I just hope there's still enough muscle left in that leg to make it work."

Kate's gaze was steady as she stood. "You'll make it work," she said firmly. Then, with a casual grace, she added, "Well, I'm heading upstairs. Good night, both of you."

We wished Kate good night and a Merry Christmas as she sauntered toward the stairs. Once she was out of earshot, Mrs. Higgins let out a pleased sigh. "So good to see her up and about."

I nodded. "I agree."

Her sharp eyes studied me. "Ye know, ye could do a lot worse than that lady."

I blinked, caught off guard. "What?"

"Oh, as if ye don't see she has a liking for ye."

I chuckled, brushing it off. "Mrs. Higgins, Kate and I are friends, colleagues—nothing more."

She narrowed her eyes, unconvinced. "So ye say, but I see what I see." She rose slowly. "Well, I'm off to bed. Merry Christmas, Doctor."

"Merry Christmas, Mrs. Higgins," I replied, standing as well.

After she left, I moved toward my part of the house. In my sitting room lay several wrapped boxes—gifts I'd purchased with the check from the reward and my publisher's payment.

Among them was a top-of-the-line Apple phone for Mrs. Higgins, far beyond what I could normally afford but vital to ensure I could reach her whenever I needed.

There were also earrings for Kate, similar to the ones I'd gotten for Trisha Heywood.

I undressed, slipped into pajamas, and got between the sheets, desperately hoping tonight would be free of nightmares.

But just as I was drifting off, I heard a soft tap at my door.

I rose and opened it. Kate stood there, a delicate silhouette in a diaphanous nightgown composed of multiple layers of thin, silky fabric that seemed to float around her.

"I couldn't sleep," she admitted quietly.

"Come in," I said, stepping aside.

She slipped into the room, and I closed the door behind her. Moving closer, I asked, "Do you want to talk?"

"No," she breathed. Then, almost without warning, she got up on tiptoes and pressed her lips to mine.

The kiss was slow, sensual—each moment stretched out, consuming the room until it felt like time had frozen.

When I pulled back, breathless, I hesitated before asking, "Are you sure you want to do this?"

Her eyes half-lidded, her cheeks flushed with desire, she reached out to touch my face. "Yes. But don't read too much into it—I want you…but only as a friend."

I smiled and kissed her trembling palm. "That's perfectly fine."

"Then stop talking," she said with playful insistence, pressing her lips to mine again.

Our kiss deepened, tongues exploring, hands gliding beneath the thin layers of fabric until I finally pulled back, gasping for air.

"Take off the wig," I whispered.

"What?" she gasped, startled. "Why?"

"I want to see the real you."

She hesitated, eyes avoiding mine. "It's not pretty, Len."

I shook my head gently. "Neither is my leg. But you're going to see that."

Her expression grew serious, weighing my words. After a long moment, she nodded slowly, taking my hand with quiet resolve, and guided me into the bedroom.

Mrs. Higgins' candle sat on the dresser, a lighter sitting conveniently beside it. I lit the candle as Kate turned away, carefully removing the wig and setting it gently on a bookshelf.

Underneath lay a scalp marked by a patchwork of skin grafts and scars—different shades and textures telling stories of pain and resilience. I could see the discomfort in her eyes, the vulnerability as she refused to meet my gaze.

"I'm ugly," she whispered.

I stepped close, softly turning her to face me.

"No," I said firmly. "You're beautiful."

I pressed a kiss to the crown of her head and traced my fingers over the varied scars. A shiver ran through her body as I held her close, the warmth of her against me steady and real.

She pushed me back with a whisper. "Show me your leg."

I nodded and slipped out of my pajamas, tossing them aside. She saw how aroused I was, but it didn't deter her. Slowly, her fingers traced over the twisted flesh of my leg as if committing it to memory.

"I get it," she said finally, meeting my eyes. "Our scars…they're part of who we are. What we've endured."

With a slow, deliberate grace, she peeled the nightgown off over her head and stood before me—proud, bald, and completely naked in the candlelight.

Together, we sank onto the bed, merging into each other's arms, finding in our shared brokenness an unspoken understanding that neither words nor wounds could erase.

INFECTION IN THE MIND

DOCTOR WISE BOOK 10

ARJAY LEWIS

MIND
BENDER
PRESS

INFECTION IN THE MIND

Ziya was an artist.

Not just a scientist, and far more than merely a chemist, he was a man who took living cells and sculpted masterpieces of doomsday.

He was surrounded by the tools of his art: microscopes, bunsen burners, culture dishes, dissection pans, and sealed cages where infected test rats lurked.

He checked the seals on several canisters, giving them a final wipe with disinfectant.

He carefully removed the hood and detached the breathing unit from his hazmat suit. The exhaust fan in his lab had been running for hours so the air smelled fresh with the aroma of strong cleaners. He'd spent hours cleaning every surface in preparation for his guests.

He pulled on a new pair of nitrile gloves just as there was a knock at the door.

"Come in," he yelled with his thick Romanian accent.

A thin man with a crew cut peeked in. "Is it safe?" he asked with a Southern drawl.

"Yes, yes, I have been cleaning for hours. I knew you were coming," Ziya gushed.

Today he would get his money and leave. His lab had been the center of his life for many long weeks, and it was time to move on.

The door flew open and four men and two women entered, all fit, each wearing camouflage military outfits and heavy gloves.

A bearded man nodded at the four large canisters. "Will it work?"

Ziya fought a wave of revulsion. *Beards*, he shuddered. Collectors of dead skin cells and oil from the skin. Breeding grounds for bacteria, yeast, and every other microorganism imaginable. Ziya shaved every part of his body, even his head and eyebrows. To have a beard, all that *filth* right under your mouth, was abhorrent.

"Will it *work*?" Ziya repeated with his thick accent. "It was tricky, I had to suspend the virus in tanks of liquid nitrogen. When released into the air, when the virus becomes warm, it will do its work. You are not getting a weapon, you are getting a portrait of death."

One of the other men spoke to the bearded leader. "Y'all sure gas masks will protect us?"

Ziya nodded and opened a trunk to reveal six gas masks. "I modified them. They will work, even with direct exposure."

The bearded man smiled. "Good."

Ziya frowned. "You do understand how the canisters function?"

"Yeah, we ain't stupid," the blond man said.

The others chuckled.

The bearded man raised a hand and the group quieted. "Yeah, I knew we had to get atomizers that could release it slowly. It'll discharge in small bursts so the frozen liquid won't clog up the spray."

"On a timer?" Ziya asked.

"Just like you told me."

"I am sorry I could not have the atomizers for you today."

"We got that handled," the bearded man assured him. "Check your account, you'll find the money is there. Let's move it out, men."

The three other men and the women collected their masks, one at a time.

One of the women spoke, and Ziya noticed there was something odd about her eyes, but he couldn't tell what it was from where he stood. She ordered the others to collect the canisters. A tall man with a scar on his head picked up one canister and easily flipped it up onto his shoulder.

The two men carried one canister and the women left with another held between them. Only the bearded leader remained with the final canister.

Ziya checked his phone and smiled broadly.

"You got your money?"

"Yes, this is good, very good," he said and turned to face his buyer. "I believe you Americans say, 'it was pleasure doing business with you'."

The bearded man didn't offer to shake hands. "What are you going to do when we set these off?"

"Do?" Ziya smiled. "I will be gone, the lab closed. You told me you are detonating them here in New Jersey. I will be back in Romania."

"And you're okay with the fact that *you* will be the cause of a pandemic?" the man asked with raised eyebrows.

"You don't understand. I have spent my life learning about poisons, viruses and creating new forms of them. You wish to bring your god's wrath on people who do not believe the way you do. I take god's creations and help them become the weapons of such wrath."

The man nodded. "There will be a purging, my friend. This country will be better because of it. The survivors will build a new America. I just have to clean up any loose ends."

He turned and headed for the door.

"By the way… *you* are one of those loose ends."

Ziya turned to face the bearded man across the room. The man wore his gas mask and stood next to the canister, a gun pointed in Ziya's direction.

There was a loud "thwack" and Ziya fell into his chair, pain overwhelming him. He fought for breath as he looked down to see a red stain blossoming on his chest.

As Ziya watched, too stunned to move, the blond man returned with a glass jar filled with amber liquid and a rag protruding from the top. He passed it to the leader and grabbed the final canister.

Removing his mask and reaching into his pocket, the bearded man extracted a lighter.

"I will see that they glorify your name, Ziya Stanislaw, that I promise you."

He lit the rag and threw the flaming jar in as he shut the door.

Fire bloomed over the concrete floor, and Ziya thought how beautiful it looked as brushstrokes of flames splattered against him.

He was an artist. Death was, indeed, his masterpiece.

TO BE CONTINUED IN

INFECTION IN THE MIND

DOCTOR WISE BOOK 10

AUTHOR'S NOTE

Hello, scholar of the odd.

Echoes In the Mind goes back to one of the repeating Leonard Wise themes, that of the past confronting you in the present. In the Satanic Verses, Salman Rushdie wrote, "Now I know what a ghost is. Unfinished business, that's what."

It makes sense that a man who deals with ghosts and hauntings becomes haunted with the past and the choices both he and his adversaries made. I liked this book because even though my editor, Libby Broadbent, figured out the villain early on, the fact that it was twins fooled her completely.

I also got to explore the concept of the drug Miracle some more, and the effects it can have both for good and ill. Like any drug, it can help a condition, but overused it can become addictive and destructive. Believe me, you have not heard the last of it in the series.

I enjoyed that Anna is coming into her own, and growing as a character and a person. Her role becomes clearer in future books.

I thought the ending was both touching and very real. Two broken people finding a bit of happiness together on Christmas Eve. I couldn't think of a better ending.

In case you think Jyanette is completely out of the picture, I ask you to get yourself ready for the next book, *Infection In The Mind*.

—Arjay Lewis

ABOUT THE AUTHOR

Known as the "Wizard Of Odd", Arjay Lewis is an actor, magician, and multi-award-winning author.

I write tales of the strange and the horrifying.

I have spent my life as an entertainer, amusing people as a street-performer in the 1970s; a Broadway and casino artist in the 1980s; a party performer in the 1990s and 2000s; a cruise ship performer in the 2010s.

Stories have always been in my mind, and I have been writing since the 1990s. My reason to write is simple: to entertain. I write the type of books that I like to read: murder mysteries, strange tales of unnatural gifts, odd happenings and horror.

Please visit my web site and sign up for my mailing list to be "in the know" for upcoming books. Visit me on Facebook, Twitter, or my Amazon Author page.

And thank you for reading. You are the reason I write.

www.arjaylewis.com
www.facebook.com/arjaylewis
www.twitter.com/arjaylewiswrite
www.amazon.com/Arjay-Lewis

ALSO BY ARJAY LEWIS

Paranormal Mystery
Fire In The Mind
Seduction i In The Mind
Reunion In The Mind
Haunted In The Mind
Devotion In The Mind
Asylum In The Mind
Specter In The Mind
Vengeance In The Mind
Echoes In The Mind
Infection In The Mind
Justice In The Mind
Ritual In The Mind
Vanished In The Mind

Horror
The Muse
Kept In The Dark
The Vanishing
Digger
Ghost Writer

Romantic Suspense
(with Debra Snow)
A Study In Murder

NYPD Wizard Detective
The Wizards Of Central Park West
The Vampires Of Greenwich Village
The Werewolves Of Washington Square

FREE NOVELLA

VOWS

AND OTHER TALES OF THE MACABRE

A collection of short stories that have been published in *Weird Tales, The Ultimate Halloween*, and *Sherlock Holmes Mystery Magazine*. If you tried to get them from their original sources this collection would cost over $20.00. But you get them for FREE by going to Arjay's site!

Enjoy this collection of scary stories from the Scaremeister himself:

VOWS: A story of devotion that extends beyond death itself.

SIREN: A Sci-Fi fantasy of a condemned prisoner lost in space.

DREAMCATCHER: A walk in the woods...but you are not alone.

THE TRAVELER: What do you do if your flight is delayed...forever?

INTO THE ABYSS: A makeup artist gets the dream job...at a cost.